OUT OF MANY

Multiplicity And Divisions In America Today

Edited by
Camille Goodison
Racquel Goodison
City University of New York

Out of Many: Multiplicity And Divisions In America Today
© 2018 by Cat In The Sun Books
ISBN: 1-946606-05-7
Joe Weil, *Publisher*
Emily Vogel, *Editor*
Cover art, design and layout by Angela Mark

CAT IN THE SUN BOOKS, *Part of the Redux Consortium*
www.pubredux.com

TABLE OF CONTENTS

Out of Many: Multiplicity and Divisions in America Today began, in part, as a means for the both of us to promote work by accomplished new writers. These were writers who we felt were doing laudable things with style and form, and, also content. They were progressive, refreshing, idiosyncratic, inventive, uncompromising, and delightful new voices. These were men and women we encountered at literary conferences and at open mics across the country, as well as through a call for fiction and nonfiction: "emerging writers for an emerging generation."

Our other equally powerful intention was to create a quality anthology of short fiction and creative nonfiction for use in college classrooms nationwide. We felt an anthology providing a showcase for a new generation of writers worthy of a greater audience, in other words, a book worth reading on its own, would also make the perfect textbook.

Together, we have taught at public high schools, community colleges, and universities throughout New York State for over twenty years. We have taught English composition and literature at the City University of New York for a decade: Racquel at the Borough of Manhattan Community College; Camille, at the New York City College of Technology. Our combined teaching experience informed our final selections.

Our classrooms are filled with students coming from all corners of the globe, from all walks of life, and consequently filled with a wealth of perspectives. Realizing that this variegated cultural landscape is our present American reality, whether one is located in a rural or urban area, whether in the North, South, East or West, we wanted a text that recognized this new truth, not only in terms of the usual forms of identity (race, class, gender), but also in terms of perspective and aesthetics. We wanted a text with personality, a text as unique and distinctive as our students.

Our students demand texts with depth and heart; stories and essays which override whatever expectations they have already built up around the idea of "literature," and which speak directly to their desire for greater understanding of this increasingly complex and confounding world they find themselves in.

We believe *Out of Many* would serve everyone, students included, who prefer reading that which is more challenging than the usual fare; stories and essays that acknowledge a world nearly as complex as the one they're coming from, and the one they are now creating. Even anthologies that tout diversity, or otherwise recognize the present multicultural landscape of youth, can stay close to a simple idea of what coming of age in a pluralistic society such as ours means. We wanted whatever we present to be meaningful, surprising (in a good way), thought provoking and fresh.

Our contributors include Nigerian American and winner of The Caine Prize, Tope Folarin, with "Miracles," a story of faith-filled ambition; Cuban American and Callaloo Creative Writing Fellow, Gina Rodriguez, with "Burial and Diaspora," a tale of family and exile; "Notable" essayist (Best American Essays) Alexandra Marzano-Lesnevich with the artful "Step One"; Nita Jalivay's story of love across borders; Astraea grant winner and Fine Arts Works Center scholar, Racquel Goodison; widely celebrated, multifaceted poet and veteran of the Iraq and Afghanistan wars, Maurice Decaul; lead musician of world renown bhangra band Red Baraat, Sonny Singh; the subtle, penetrating and insightful memoirist, Aisha Sabatini Sloan, among many other wonderfully talented and brilliant writers.

We hope these stories and essays will delight and charm you, as well as illuminate all those aspects of humanity that continue to mystify us and keep us in its thrall. We hope you will enjoy these selections as much as we did, and derive all the benefits from careful reading (listening) with an open heart.

If we had any suggestions to offer our readers it would be, read for pure enjoyment. There are countless ways a person could approach this book for use in the classroom. *Out of Many* can be used as a supplement or complement to existing classroom texts in creative writing, composition or literature. We view this collection as a convenient means for including additional contemporary voices one may not otherwise hear.

There are any number of ways to do that, whether orienting classroom discussion around plotlines or connecting to current events or social histories or cultural narratives as may be relevant; reading like an artist through observing form and structure; crafting creative exercises or personal narratives in response to a reading (ex. travel writing, a how-to…); comparing and contrasting themes; working out alternative ways of telling (ex. different time, place, ending, character…). The possibilities are infinite. Please engage freely, and use as wish.

Honoring the many ways of being an American today is necessary for building loving communities, and loving community is needed more than ever.

Dr. Camille Goodison, Ph.D.
Dr. Racquel Goodison, Ph.D.

FICTION

"Boys" by Maria Alejandra Barrios

Maria Alejandra Barrios is a writer born in Barranquilla, Colombia.
She has lived in Bogotá and Manchester where she completed
a Masters degree in Creative Writing from The University of
Manchester. Her story "Luna" was shortlisted in 2017's Bare Fiction
competition in London. She was a writer in residence at the Vermont
Studio Center thanks to a fellowship awarded by the center. Her
fiction appears in *Reservoir Journal, Hobart Pulp* and elsewhere.

My mom says that I'm a *loca*. If I had a dad he would say that I have
to learn how to keep my legs closed. My best friend, Adalina, says
that I'm lucky: pretty, smart, all the works! I tell her that she had such
a hard life I look like a princess next to her. She laughs. The truth is
that it wasn't always like this, I wasn't always the bad kid. I was the
queen of the *barrio*, the latin-Oprah of school, bringing misfits and
popular kids together, I was the girl all the boys wanted and couldn't
get. Now I'm the black sheep who's at least had enough sense not to
get pregnant, but hasn't had enough sense not to try everything else:
perico, men, running away from home, coming back after running
away from home, you name it, I've done it. I'll try everything once
and twice, maybe three times, because like *mami* says, I don't learn.

2017 marks my last year of high school, Trump is president and
my mom tells me to always look who's behind me on the train: "be
careful with those *locos blancos*," she says. Angry white men. *Mami*
believes some of them are mad at us, that they're even more mad at us
because we're not poor and we have a corner store. She says that they
might even be mad at me because I'm beautiful. And I am, I barely
have to do anything for people to tell me I am pretty. My hair is long
and straight, my complexion is light-brown but sun-kissed, even in the
winter I am tan and I have dimples and little wrinkles on the sides of
my eyes that make me look like I'm always smiling. Men love that.

I met Marco at the corner store one Saturday morning, my mom
didn't like leaving me alone in the store anymore after a customer

had grabbed me and kissed me because he knew I was alone. He had kissed me like I was something else that he could open, consume and pay for at the end. When he saw that home girl could scream, he left, so quickly you would think he hadn't meant it in the first place. My lips still wet with his saliva.

But Marco wasn't like that; he was tall, and dark with thick hair and moles on his arms. He had green eyes, and when I told him how much his cigarettes was, he smiled and looked at me, never looking down, always keeping his chin up. Marco wasn't hiding and I liked that. I wrote my number quickly on a piece of paper and I put it in his hands, I put my index fingers on my lips: "Shhh," I said. He laughed and put the paper in his pocket.

Marco texted me as soon as he left the store. His texts were eloquent, he wrote without abbreviations, and used punctuation. That's when I knew he was over 25. He could spell and he knew it made him different from the boys I was dating. Marco knew that I liked that he was grown.

We texted all day and I had learned that his family was Italian. Marco was in grad school studying political science and he lived alone in East Harlem because it was difficult to find roommates when you had a Labrador retriever.

"I bet all your ex-girlfriends are white," I texted.

Marco admitted that he didn't know a lot of brown girls growing up or in school, so yeah, they were. I texted back with the beds on my fingers on fire: "I knew it."

"How old are you?" he texted. "I'm 28. FYI."

"I'm 18." My heart was racing.

"Oh, I'm a bit older than you," he texted back. My heart sank. "But we look about the same age, right?"

Our first date was at an Italian restaurant on the Upper West Side, I tried to curl my hair but after 10 minutes the curls fell out. I painted my lips red and I wore one of my mom's black dresses. Short, but not so tight that everyone would look at me in the restaurant and think that I was more out of place than I already was. "Wow," he said when he saw me. "You look incredible."

"Thanks," I said, looking at his jeans and T-shirt.

He paid for everything that night. Appetizers, cokes, entrees and dessert. I had never eaten anything that was over 35 dollars before. For birthdays, my mom, Adalina, and I went to the Cheesecake Factory and ordered 20-dollar pasta plates. If we had had a good week at the store, my mom would even let us order tea and dessert.

We didn't kiss that night, nor on our date at the movies after that. On our third date, I asked him if I smelled.

"Do I have bad breath or something?"

"Listen…" he said. My heart skipped a beat and I got ready to never see him again. "I really like you. You're wonderful."

"Quit the crap," I said, speaking loudly to stop my voice from breaking. "What's up? You have a girlfriend?"

"No, it's just you're too young. I like you but I don't think we should date."

"So you just take me out for dates and pay for shit and expect *nada*? Nothing," I said, correcting myself, angry words in Spanish wanting to come out.

"I… I do like you."

"So what are you waiting for?"

He kissed me. His kiss wasn't quick and wet like the ones the guys my age gave me; it wasn't desperate and aggressive. In a way all the kisses before Marco didn't matter, it was like those sorry-ass-losers never existed, his lips were washing all the other boys away.

We kept dating. I began staying at his house and he kept going to the store to buy bread and orange juice. When my mom wasn't looking, he would slip notes over the counter. *You look gorgeous today. I miss you. I can't stop thinking about you.* The first night that I went to his house and before taking our kissing to the bed, he asked: "Is this your first time?"

"Baby, please," I laughed, pulling him closer. Rex, the dog, started barking at us.

"Mariela," he said, "You always do whatever the fuck you want, right?"

"I don't even listen to my mama." I kissed him, feeling his warm breath against my lips. "Shhhh," I whispered in the dark to Rex. "I think you need to take your dog for a walk."

"Do you want to come with us?" he asked, standing up and looking for his t-shirt on the floor.

"Nah, I'll wait for you here," I said, taking off my bra and getting under the covers. His bed smelled like sweat and peppermint shampoo. I heard his phone vibrating and saw a text light up the screen.

"r u up." A girl called Marissa texted him. My face felt warm; my ears rang with all the things that my mom had ever told me about waiting until marriage and waiting for the one. About how I had to be smart about men because they don't just love anyone, they love the right girl. The good girl. The pure one. How could I have been so stupid? I thought about throwing the phone down the toilet or on the sink and letting the water drown it until all you could see was a sad face on the screen. But I sat still and waited for him, shivering like a scared child getting soaked in the rain. When he finally arrived, I said: "Who's Marissa?" I handled his phone in my hand like a grenade. "My sister," Marco said calmly, entering the apartment with Rex and closing the door behind him. I stood up, my hands now shaking with anger, and I knew that in that moment my life was in his hands. My head was spinning faster and faster with thoughts of either kissing him or pushing him to the ground. I closed my fists, and I got closer to him, letting my body decide for me.

He pulled me into a hug; I could feel the warmness of his body and the musky smell of his cologne combined with that lingering smell of the cigarette he always smoked before meeting me. Marco kissed my cheek softly and said: "I know it was only like 10 minutes but I missed you."

I gave him his phone. I wanted to ask again who Marissa was but I felt like I couldn't speak. I was suddenly in a play where I had forgotten all the lines, my role was to sit quietly in a corner and see everything go by. I swallowed hard and I felt like I was swallowing my old self. He looked at his phone and his face lit up like mine did whenever I received a text from him or he visited me at the corner store.

"Who's that, really?" I asked, my cheeks getting warm and my mouth getting dry as if someone had stuffed a stocking down my throat. My stomach clenched and I stood there afraid that he would respond with the truth.

"My sister," Marco answered, still smiling, still texting.

"At 1 am?"

"Uhm… she doesn't sleep very well. She's just checking on me." He put his phone down and grabbed my hand.

Marco wasn't my first or second time, but I did feel like something was shifting. I felt the thing all my friends talked about when they were chasing after boys who didn't call or who left them crying after an unanswered text. Sometimes I grabbed my phone and waited for it to ring like I was trapped in a 1950s movie. I waited for his texts like someone waiting for electricity to return after a blackout. I waited a lot those days. And it wasn't like Marco wasn't there: he called, he texted, he was affectionate but he had obligations alright. He had school, a dog, work. He had phone calls to make to his family. He had a life that didn't revolve around me and I had a life where I pretty much only wanted to make space for us.

"Have you ever thought what you want to do after school?"

"Yes," I said, "I want to take a sabbatical. I really don't know what to study or where to apply. My mom says sabbaticals are for *ricas*, but you know, she could use more help around the store."

"But you really don't want that, right?" he said, sitting up in the bed.

"Why not? Adalina is not going anywhere either. It will be fun."

"But what about your dreams, aspirations, all that, don't you want to leave?" He was speaking quicker now, his tone suddenly more agitated. In his voice, I could hear a hint of you're not doing enough combined with "is the barrio enough for you?" It didn't hurt coming from the white counselors at school, but it hurt coming from him. For Marco, I was just another *morenita* who couldn't leave the *barrio*.

"Marco, I have dreams. I just don't go around telling the first person who asks. Don't you know that telling people about your dreams and caring a lot just makes it harder when things don't go your way? It's not like I see a lot of Broadway girls or scientist girls in the *barrio*. I know I have to keep my stuff for me so five years later people don't look at me and think, 'Oh yeah, didn't this one wanted to be the next J-Lo? Look at where she is now. Still a loser."

"So you want to be a singer?"

"No, Marco. I don't want to be anything that will lead me to disappointment. I want to suffer as little as possible."

"But you are a good student," he said, his tone softening.

"I'm also good at fucking and you don't see me wanting to become a prostitute, right?"

Marco lowered his eyes and went silent for a second. He looked like he had realized just now that he was fucking someone way younger than him.

"I'm just saying… I'm here if you want to talk about this stuff."

"Ujum." I got ready to get on top of him and kiss him so he would shut up.

That night we tried *perico*. Marco had some cocaine left over from a party last week and he wanted to do a line.

"Have you done it before?" Marco asked while petting Rex.

I considered lying for a second. "Not really," I said, "But I want to try."

Marc took a framed picture of his parents that was on his nightstand to break down the coke with his black American Express. He did the first line quickly, as if he was scared it was going to fly away like snow on a windy day.

"You don't have to do it if you don't want to."

"I want to," I said, kneeling down to snort. I felt a burning sensation in my nose. A couple of seconds later the tip of my tongue started to feel numb. After 10 minutes the euphoria come in waves. A warmth that makes you feel that everything is going to be okay. Like *mami* saying, you're god's favorite child, you've got this. "Do you like it?" Marco asked when he saw me smiling. "I love it," I said, throwing myself on the bed. "It makes me feel like anything is possible."

"I love you," he said, grabbing a little bit more coke and brushing it on his gums. "I know it's been three weeks but it feels like I've known you forever."

I was touched that he remembered how long ago we had met. I couldn't help but smile at the thought that Marco really cared about me and that we weren't just fucking.

"You're just high," I said, kissing him on the lips and vaguely tasting mint.

"I'm glad you're enjoying yourself, baby," he said, kissing me on the cheek.

The truth was that I was enjoying everything with him: the coke, the sex, the fancy dinners and the Netflix. In those days there wasn't a tomorrow: I didn't care if I hadn't sent my applications to schools; I didn't care about my grades nor about the excuses I was giving my mom for going out on school nights; I didn't care about the shifts at the corner store or about the fact that Marco hadn't introduced me to anyone; I didn't care about that bitch, Marissa. In that moment, high on the feeling that everything was okay, I let myself think that if I didn't care it didn't matter. I had never wanted Marco more than at that moment. I looked at him from across the bed and said: "You're beautiful."

His wavy hair fell in his face like he had spent the whole day rolling in bed. He smiled and I climbed on top of him.

"I want to study literature," I said. "I think I could go to college and then apply to Columbia or one of those Ivy League universities. My mom wouldn't approve, she would say I would probably make more money running the corner store."

"Bullshit. You, Mariela, can do anything you want with that beautiful face of yours," he said pointing at my chest.

"Do you really think so?"

"You could rule the world, Mari. You just have to send those applications on time. I'll help."

"Do you promise? I've been working on them for a long time, I just need someone to look at them."

"For you, anything," Marco said, grabbing me and getting on top of me. I felt the familiar weight of his body and instead of feeling comfortable, I felt as if he was crushing me. I felt a knot in my stomach; like I wanted to suddenly ask all the questions about us I had been too afraid to ask but, my mouth was too numb to speak.

"You okay, baby?" he asked and caressed my cheek.

"I'm fine, yeah," I said, pushing him to the side and standing up. I ran to the bathroom to puke. Marco caressed my back, pulled back my hair and waited patiently for me to stop. When I finally was done, I lifted my head from the toilet, so weak I was afraid I was going to fall into the water.

"Don't freak out."

"What, what?" I said, touching my face and feeling the warm liquid coming down my nose and getting to my lips. I tasted the saltiness of the blood.

"Do you have any tampons? Your head! Back!" Marco stood up.

"I don't have any tampons," I said, putting my head back. Rex came to see what was happening, sniffed my hair and lay on the floor with me. We both waited for Marco to solve the problem.

"I think I might have some that my ex left here." He ran to his bedroom and brought back a pink box. Marco grabbed one of the tampons and he put it in the nostril that was bleeding. "Better?"

"Sure," I said, "Much better." I looked down and I saw the drops of fresh blood on my shirt.

The smell of puke and salt woke me up. I was on Marco's bathroom floor and my hair was a mess of knots of puke and dust. I felt a piercing pain in my right eye. Rex had slept beside me. I opened the door and prayed that it was the middle of the night but there was light out and Marco was still asleep. What was I going to tell my mom? I shook him until he was awake. He covered his eyes with his hands to block the light coming from the windows.

"Yo, you left me on your bathroom floor."

"You okay?" he asked, wrinkling his eyes and not moving from his bed.

"You left me."

"I'm sorry, I was pretty fucked up." Marco finally sat on his bed. "Last night was crazy. Maybe too crazy…." he said, unable to look at me.

"Is this the part where you say you're too old and crazy for me?"

"I mean," he paused. "Yeah."

"Save it, monster." I picked up my purse from the floor. "Who wants a weak-ass-man who can't even carry a girl who's high to his bed?" I picked up my coat from the floor and left the room.

"Mariela?" He called from his bed, "Be careful the dog doesn't go out with you when you open the door." I closed the door behind me.

"Mariela? That was crappy of me to say. Come back. Chill for a second."

Once outside the door, in the hallway, I buttoned my coat all the way up so my mom wouldn't see the bloodstains. I waited until I was out of the building to cry. I was sobbing and it made my migraine worse. I could feel his eyes on me, like he was looking at me from his window. I looked up to meet his eyes but, no one was there; you could only see the wind moving his white curtains and the darkness of his room.

I walked another block and took out my phone. Thirty-six missed calls from mom. She texted several times: Where are you?

12:00 am You're grounded for life!

1:00 am Did you run away again?

1:15 am I'm worried sick about you!

1:30 am Adalina says you're hanging out with this new white boy. Is not the guy who kissed you at the store, right?

2:00 am Hija?

2:30 am Are you pregnant ? Is that why you're running away?

3:00 am Just come back.

Adalina texted saying that she was sorry.

3:00 am I didn't meant to tell your mom about Marco. We're both so worried. So worried.

3:30 are U mad at me?

I wasn't far from home, I could walk if I wanted to but I splurged on a taxi. I sat in the back seat and cried, thanking god I was in New York and the driver wasn't going to ask what was wrong. I paid for the taxi and entered the corner store. I saw my mom holding a rosary. She looked at me like she hadn't seen me in 10 years. My mom held tight the rosary and exclaimed, looking up: *Gracias Dios Mio!*

I looked down and cried harder. "*Mami*," I sobbed, "*Mami,* I'm sorry, I'm so sorry."

"Shhh… you're home, *nena.* You're home," Mami said, pulling me into a hug. "You're home."

I didn't go to school or the corner store for days. I locked myself in my room and didn't open until I knew mom was at work. I fed my-self toast and drank lots of water so my eyes wouldn't go dry. Marco didn't text and mom didn't stop asking what was wrong.

"Nena, you know that you can tell me what happened." Mom would stand outside my room, her ear against the door.

"No one raped me mom. If that's what you're worried about. I went to a party and did too much coke."

"Hija!" she would scream, calming herself down after. "You're not like that. I know that's not it. A mom knows…" she said softly.

"No, mom, you don't. Go away," I screamed through my locked bedroom door.

I never told *mami* what happened that night. I didn't tell Adalina either in case she would tell *mami* if I ever disappeared again. I returned to school but went home immediately after. I only talked when it was absolutely necessary. I read and began smoking.

"Your teeth are going to turn the shade of American cheese," My mom said when she saw me smoking outside our building.

I shrugged, put out the cigarette with my boot, and lit another one as soon as she went inside.

I thought of Marco every day. Not because I wanted him to call or to look for me but because I felt he owed me something. I had told him my dreams and in return he had left me with puke in my hair, lying on his bathroom floor.

Most days, after the third cigarette I would stare at our text conversation and imagine he was texting me an apology. I would look at my phone for several minutes, sometimes even an hour, and I would write the text that I would never send: "So the problem is not that you have only had white girlfriends, is that you can only have white girlfriends? Gotcha."

Was it the age? It didn't feel like it was. It felt as if everything changed when I told him I wanted to take a year to help out at the store. He had finally seen then how different we were. His boys probably could accept a girl ten years younger than him if she were blonde, going to college and living on the Upper West Side but, a brown girl ten years younger living above a bodega? Forget it. Now I worried my dream would come true since I said it out loud. I never told anyone about my school applications, and I wondered on those days, applications in my hands and deadlines close, if brown girls ever left their *barrios*, if people ever expected better of us, the ones who tick the mixed-other box on forms. On worse days, I wondered if I was even real, if I only came into existence by white request. And on days that I couldn't even get out of bed, I imagined all the applications that I sent out coming back with notes in red saying: "We only accept white girls."

That spring, I saw Marco walking down the streets of my neighborhood. He was alone and he was wearing a black coat that looked like he hadn't washed it in years. His hair was tangled and I noticed some wrinkles when he smiled that I had never noticed before. My hair was in a dirty ponytail and I was wearing a pink sweatshirt from The Gap.

"I got my first acceptance letter today for college," I said after Marco said hello.

"Wow, that's amazing," he said, in an exaggerated voice, as if I was five and he was congratulating me for going to the bathroom alone.

"You don't have to say that," I said, "People get accepted into college every day."

"I know. It's just…"

"I need to leave," I said. "Good luck."

"Mariela!" I heard him call me from the other side of the street but my feet were already walking forward. As I was moving farther and farther away from him, I wondered if what *mami* said about me never learning was true. I was curious. Did Marco intend to apologize when I left? Then say he wasn't surprised? That it was obvious that I was going to be accepted into college? That he really thought a brown girl like me could rule the world? But as I made it closer to home and got ready to tell the news to my mom about college, I smiled at the thought that next year I would be miles away from East Harlem and the bodega. I would be one of those brown girls who left the *barrio*. I would be one of those brown girls who proved white boys wrong.

"Like Water on Stone" by Zeeva Bukai

Zeeva Bukai was born in Israel and raised in New York City. Her stories have appeared in *Mcsweeney's, December Magazine, Flash Fiction Magazine, Women Arts Quarterly Journal, Calyx, Lilith, Heeb, The Jewish Quarterly* and elsewhere. Her story "The Abandoning," featured in December (2017) won the Curt Johnson Prize and was nominated for a Pushcart Prize. Her stories have received honorable mention in *Glimmer Train* and won the fiction award in *Lilith Magazine* and the *Irwin Shaw Award*. She was a New York Center for Fiction fellow and holds an MFA from Brooklyn College. She teaches at SUNY Empire State College in NYC. "Like Water on Stone" first appeared in *Image Journal*.

Salim peers through the peephole in the men's room in Temple Bnai Moshe and sees two girls standing side by side at the row of sinks in the ladies bathroom. One is tall and slim with golden hair that cups her scalp like a swim cap. The other is several inches shorter with a belly that lolls over her skirt like a tongue. Her hair is stringy, her shoulders beefy. The golden girl rolls her sleeves up past the elbow and soaps her hands while her lips move in prayer. Her movements are fluid. They make him think of water, of currents skipping downstream and sunlight flickering through a canopy of leaves. The other girl reminds him of his mother whose face is a desert of lines, deep and parched, a patchwork of disappointments. He closes his eyes and when he opens them the girls are gone.

He is seventeen. The same age as the students who attend Bnos Rivkah, an all girl yeshiva that rents rooms on the second floor of the temple. He has never known girls like these. Their skin is like milk. They wear their hair in ponytails. Their ears glitter with diamond studs. They smell of weekly allowances and strawberry lip balm. He isn't allowed near them. He isn't allowed to look at them. He sweeps the floor, replaces burnt bulbs and damaged ceiling tiles; he cleans the bathrooms.

Ruchie, did you hear? Faygie's engaged. Yocheved, are you coming for Shabbos? Their conversations wash over him like rain. He's worked in the building for three months. Sometimes when he's in the hall, he imagines they're sending him a signal with a toss of a head, a swing of a hip, a pursing of lips; he hasn't yet been able to decipher their secret code.

The door creaks and he jumps off the toilet seat and grabs hold of the floor mop. His father walks in slapping his hands together.

"Salim, you've got to work faster. Don't make me fire your ass." He flashes his teeth. They cost $1,700, implanted by a distant relative from Syria who set up shop in a fifth floor walkup on McDonald Avenue, flush against the elevated tracks. Last month his father took him to the same dentist, a rough-looking forty year old with a Valentino mustache, a photograph of his wife and five kids on the wall, all of them glistening as if they'd been greased for the occasion. When he used the drill, Salim felt like the D train had barreled through his head.

He clenches his jaw. "I'll be done soon, dad man."

"What is this dad man business? You gotta talk English."

His father jabs a knuckle hard into Salim's forehead then ruffles his hair. The man is full of vicious affection. Salim tries not to grimace at the pain. His father preens in the mirror. He's unable, Salim thinks, to see things as they really are: the ravaged face, the tarnished whites of his eyes. Once he was well-groomed, hair polished to a brill cream shine, aftershave steaming off his neck, pinky nails sharpened to a point (a leftover from his boyhood days when he ran with a gang in the streets of Haret el Yahud, the Jewish quarter in Damascus). He was someone to fear then, someone to watch your back.

Salim remembers how his mother's sisters gave his father the eye. They came to the house wearing floral skirts and gold bangles, kissed Salim's cheek, pinched his ass, gave his balls a quick pat, "He's growing up, God bless him." His father sent them a knowing look and made sure to squeeze past them down the narrow hall between the kitchen and living room. They squawked like hens when he crushed them against the wallpaper. His cheerful brutality was alarming, but they never complained. His mother watched quietly in that way Salim hated, like she was sinking into a well and it was no use calling out or sending down a rope. Her retreat into silence left Salim panicked and ashamed.

There are oil stains on his father's shirt – a struggle with the boiler. His belly jiggles over the cheap belt bought on East 2nd from the Mitzrahi, the Egyptian – another Jew with an embarrassing trace of Africa in his veins. When his father bends down to clean his shoes, Salim sees the crack of his ass. Bastard, he recalls how his father danced the dubkah at a neighbor's wedding – shaking his butt, jerking his shoulders, beckoning all to look. They looked and remembered whose grandson he was, whose hand their grandfathers kissed, the great Baba Salim, chief rabbi of Damascus. No one in his family remarks on the short distance between honor and disgrace. They're glad they made it to Brooklyn alive.

"Pick up your pants." Salim has the urge to spit.

His father laughs. "Drop a quarter in my slot, see what pops out."

Pig, Salim thinks, keeping his expression blank.

His father splashes water on his face, blows his nose into his hands. He puts on a clean shirt, brushes the dust off his trousers with a moist paper towel. Salim feels a headache coming on.

"Where you going now?" He asks.

"Out." His father says.

"Where?"

"Since when are you the Baba?" His father cuffs him across the jaw, not hard, but with enough force to let him know who's boss.

Salim stuffs his hands into his pockets, tempted to shove his father's smiling face into the mirror.

"Tell your mother I'll be home later."

"You tell her."

"Don't start," his father blisters him with a look. "Finish the fucking job," he says.

Salim grips hold of the mop.

At the end of the day, girls billow out of the classrooms. They drug him with their musk. He imagines a film of Talmudic text on their hair and skin. Given the chance he would read them like commentaries. Their chatter is loud, raucous like his aunts'. He stands in the hall with his broom, white knuckled. A girl knocks into him, mutters sorry, and speeds away. It's the golden-haired girl from the bathroom. His skin grows clammy.

He regards them all from beneath his lashes. He smells the sharpness of his own flesh and can almost hear their nostrils flare in disgust as they pass by him, careful not to touch him. He wishes he smelled more like them. He wishes he wasn't so dark – not so much an Arabische Yid, an "Arab" Jew.

They exit and the building is smaller. He sifts through the clothes they leave behind: sweaters, hoodies, sniffs their sneakers, lifts the sleeve of a cardigan to his cheek. He picks up a prayer book and bows right and left. He takes his time going from room to room. All of them are in shambles, as if the act of learning has been riotous. Chairs are overturned, books are on the floor, balls of paper are strewn near the garbage bin. He picks up candy wrappers, protractors, empty cans of baby corn, bags of salad and kosher Italian dressing. There's a coffee spill on a desk. He lifts a copy of Huck Finn: You don't know me..., he recites and puts it in a cubby. He finds loose change and pockets it, notes on the French Revolution, polynomials, and symbioses. He works methodically, goes from desk to desk. He finds a tube of moisturizing cream and takes it for his sister, Amira, who is thirteen and reads books like Anne of Green Gables. She sits on the good chair in the salon with her legs tucked under her; her kneecaps gleam like river stones.

In the last room there are shelves with books on Navi and Chumash. He's read these texts on the prophets, on the exodus, on Moses the deliverer. Salim kisses the binding of one, the jacket cover of another and pictures himself in the synagogue in Damascus with its stucco walls, wooden pews and holy ark carved of wood and mother-of-pearl inlay. His great-grandfather is beside him dressed in a white Sabbath robe and fez, rheumy-eyed, fingers grasping a Torah pointer. He reads the weekly parsha; the temple is quiet as the congregation strains to hear the Baba Salim. Later he blesses them and after Havdalah when the braided candle is lit and the spices are sniffed and they wish each other a good week, they form a line outside his house at the end of a cul-de-sac where an almond tree perfumes the yard. Night descends and for a moment they forget the incendiary streets outside the Jewish quarter. Women ask the Baba to cure them of infertility. Men ask for business advice and dispensations. Students question the knotty arguments in the Gemara. They want to know what Rashi said and what Maimonides had to say about redemption and retribution.

Salim sweeps the garbage into a pile. He thinks of the upcoming Sabbath and the synagogue on Ocean Parkway, the one his father insists on attending so that he can be seen in the company of rich men. The columns at the entrance make Salim feel small. He listens to his father talk to the men who were with them on the last convoy out of Damascus in '92. They had gotten off the plane in their checkered shirts and polyester slacks, their round-faced children and tired wives tumbling after them, blinking at the cold New York sun. They sit in the last rows of the temple, prayer books open on their laps, watching the backs of the millionaires in the front pews. They talk business between the Amidah and Kaddish prayers and in tones that sound like the shuffling of crisp hundred dollar bills they say, I'll get you a good deal. His father tells them about his company, Damascus Maintenance, how the contracts are rolling in. They look at the pilling on his suit and return to their prayers. Salim grits his teeth and wonders since when have he and his broom become a corporation.

On the blackboard he writes, The Adventures of Huckleberry Finn. Someday he wants to go back to school, though his father says that a man needs only a good strong arm and the ability to count to do business, unless he is going to be a rabbi or a doctor. To his father, all rabbis and doctors are crooks, even the Baba Salim who collected donations and pocketed a percentage. Everyone is out to screw everyone else. Salim's heart sinks when his father talks to him about the nature of men. His mother, who rarely looks him in the eye, promises this job will last only a short while, but he's been working with his father for two years already. Until the debts are cleared she says, until they get their green cards for which they have to pay a lawyer, a shamie, a Damascus Jew, whose family emigrated before '48, before all hell broke loose over there and the arrests began. His father hates the shamie though he would hate him more if he were a halabi, from Aleppo. Lawyers, he says, are the worst crooks.

Salim erases the blackboard. Sometimes he thinks he'd like to be a teacher, stand in front of the yeshiva girls and talk to them about Huck Finn, which he's read twice. He'd tell them that he is like Jim, snatched from his home, lost and running. Sunlight would fall on the girls and their cheeks would glow the way morning sparkles off bits of glass in the asphalt. Identity is a stone, he'd say. They'd write these words in their notebooks, pens hissing like insects scuttling across paper. America is a river that wears it away. The girl with the golden hair would raise her hand, her sleeve pooling below her elbow. "So the loss of identity is a geological phenomenon?"

"Yes."

"Aren't we all stones?" she'd ask.

"No. The lucky few are water." He'd decide right then to marry her.

At night he'd tell her what was in his mind: the one sided conversations, bits of music, strains of the oud floating through deserted alleys, the driving beat of the tarabuka drum like the pounding of a stick on the ground, the rancid smoke of burning tires, the sound of doors closing, glass shattering, the shouting voices of his parents, the way his mother withdraws behind a fortress of silence he cannot scale, the way his father leers at women, at the yeshiva girls when he believes no one is looking. She'd get it – all that destruction imaginary and real living like a twin inside him.

A shoe scrapes against the linoleum; his broom crashes to the floor. He turns in fear as a girl enters the classroom. She's startled to see him, but quickly composes herself, brushing the hair off her forehead.

"Are they all gone?" she releases the barrette at her nape. Her mousy hair is lifeless around her shoulders.

It takes him a moment to understand what she's saying, to realize that she's not part of his inner landscape, not the girl with the cap of golden hair. She is the other girl, the short, chubby one.

"Do you speak English?" she looks him over starting at the sneakers he found in a bin at a discount store, one shoe a size larger than the other, and ends her exploration at his brow. He rubs his palms on the back of his jeans.

"Yeah," he says, disappointed. "What are you doing here?"

"It's a secret," she says.

She isn't beautiful. Her eyes are grey. There are pimples on her chin and her face is long. She is almost fat and her skin is greasy. He feels a stirring of rage. For months all he's thought about is approaching one of the yeshiva girls. He's practiced talking to them, showing off the Hebrew he knows and the English he's taught himself. He could read to them from the Torah or from any one of the texts they pour over. He could recite a few psalms by heart and wear the yarmulka the Baba Salim wore on weekdays. He takes the yarmulka out of his back pocket and puts it on. He wants to show her that he is more than just the boy with the broom. She pulls a bag out from the bottom of the large armoire against the back wall.

"Is that a kippah?" Her voice is muffled as she takes off her running shoes and puts on a pair of high heels.

"Yes."

She rolls the waistband of her long skirt until the hem reaches above her knees.

"Are you from around here?" she asks.

"Not far."

She smears on lip gloss. Her mouth looks wet.

"Where are you from?" he asks.

She looks at him with suspicion. "Why?"

"It's what you asked me."

She shrugs, "So?"

His shoulders feel tight. He can't help staring at her.

"What? Not pretty enough for you?"

When he doesn't answer she says, "Doesn't matter. Some boys think I'm pretty."

"What boys?" he asks.

"Just boys." She turns away.

He thinks maybe she's lying and feels rotten about his earlier thoughts. She isn't so bad. "I don't think anything, except that you're here after school, putting on makeup. You meeting a boy now?"

"None of your business what I do."

"Okay." He lifts his broom and sweeps, moving the pile of dirt closer to the bin.

"Are you going to tell anyone you saw me?" She puffs up with fright. "They wouldn't believe you."

He imagines slapping her hard across the mouth and grips the broom until his palms burn. He shakes his head.

She exhales. "You're the cleaning boy?"

He nods.

Even in high heels she barely reaches his shoulders. Her skin is a buttery yellow under the light. She looks like a baby chick he once saw running loose in the souk.

"I thought yeshiva girls weren't allowed to talk to boys?" His hands are shaking.

"So?"

"Why are you talking to me?" he asks.

"I'm not talking to you. You're talking to me." She combs her hair.

Salim laughs, a shrill sound. She ignores him, stuffs her books into a cubby, picks the dirt from under her nails, then blots the oily spots around her nose and chin with her sleeve. When she's done she looks about helplessly, then opens the doors of the armoire and sits inside it, leaning against the rabbis' coats. Her legs stick out in front of her; they're surprisingly slender for a chubby girl.

"What are you doing in there?" he asks, hesitant, afraid she'll get angry and leave.

She looks up at him. "Can you keep a secret?"

"Sure." He leans forward, everything in him alert.

"I don't want to go home yet."

"Why? Don't you have enough of this place?"

She doesn't answer and takes her time pulling a cigarette out of her bag. She lights up. Her eyes squint against the smoke. He tells himself there's no need to feel anxious, but he worries nonetheless, afraid he'll be the one accused of stinking up the books and coats and losing his father this contract. The thought makes him feel sick.

"I've seen you around," she says, waving the hand with the cigarette. "We all have. Just so you know, no one thinks you're handsome. But you're the only boy around, so we look."

He kicks a hair clip across the floor.

"Wanna cigarette?" She picks a piece of tobacco off her lip.

"You're not allowed to do that in here." He winces, knowing he sounds like an idiot, but he's flooded with images of the rabbis complaining to his father that the room with the holiest texts smells of cigarettes. He's reminded of his father's punishments – painful, object lessons that use whatever object is in the room.

"Who's going to tell? You?" She peels open a pack of gum and sticks two pieces into her mouth. She takes a drag without inhaling and blows smoke into a bubble. When it pops a puff bursts into the air. She laughs. "I've been practicing that for weeks."

He gives her a weak smile, gazes at her legs, then looks away.

"I have good legs," she says.

"Yes."

"Sit down already." She points to the spot beside her, "You're making me nervous standing over me like that."

They sit in silence. The smoke irritates his eyes, but he doesn't move. He barely breathes.

"I'm getting married in two months. Right after school ends."

He turns to her surprised, thinking this is her secret. She stares straight ahead. Her hair touches his shoulder. He wonders if he should move it, afraid she'll think he's being forward.

"To who?"

"A boy." She takes a deep drag and coughs.

"Have you met him?"

"No. Our grandmothers knew each other in some screwy village in Romania. Their husbands were butchers together."

"That's our way too." He focuses on the books on the shelf. "My parents grew up next door to each other." The gold leaf letters waver before assembling into titles.

"He's coming over tonight. My fi-an-cee. Him and his parents. For a formal introduction and a Le'chaim," she says.

"Is that why you don't want to go home?" When she doesn't answer he asks, "Don't you want to meet him?"

She shrugs and then turns to Salim. "Are you engaged?"

"No. I'm not even a citizen," he says.

"How come you're so dark? You're Jewish, right? Or did you steal that kippah?"

"I don't steal. I'm the same as my great-grandfather. He was a great Rabbi, the Baba Salim, better than any butcher." He says this through his teeth.

She crushes the cigarette butt under her heel. "Calm down. So you're an Arab Jew. Do you know there are Jews blacker than you are?" She seems impressed by the incongruity, then leans back further into the coats until only her legs are visible. She takes a mirror out of her handbag and looks at herself solemnly. "Does it bother you being so dark?"

He shrugs.

"I like it." Her voice is soft.

"Sure," he says, but something in him begins to race.

"I do. It's different. Look at my skin."

"Like buttermilk," he blurts, then squeezes his eyes shut at her laughter, feeling like he's being pried open.

He slides further into the closet and draws his knees up, and then closes one of the doors. She pivots toward him and pulls her knees up too, resting her chin on her hands. They face each other; the noses of their shoes touch. The coats flatten against the back wall of the armoire. His eyes fall on the white strip of her panties. His gaze is riveted there.

"Have you ever seen this boy, your fiance?" He wishes she would close the other door.

"Only in a picture."

"What does he look like?"

"Tall, blonde. My mother says he has blue eyes and good teeth. He looks like a nice boy."

Salim feels an ache in his chest. "You like him?"

"I don't know him."

"You like me? Don't answer. Don't answer." He ducks his head. There is something sly and earnest in her gaze, a coyness he doesn't understand. "I disappoint you."

"No." He stretches his arm toward her, then snaps it back.

"When I first walked in I did."

He flicks his hand, telling her without words that what happened earlier means nothing now.

"It's so dark I can hardly see you," she says.

"Better this way."

"Why?"

"Easier. We're more alike in the dark." After a moment he asks, "Why don't you want to go home? Why don't you want to meet him?"

She doesn't answer.

"Tell me." His hand slides along the floor until it reaches her ankle.

She freezes at his touch, then in a small voice says, "What if he doen't like me?"

"He will."

"How do you know?"

While Salim searches for an answer she continues, "I get so angry. Especially when I'm home."

"Why?"

"I don't know. Soon as I walk in I'm ready to explode. You ever feel that?"

"Sure," he says.

"My house is so crowded. There's more room in here."

He laughs.

"Don't," she says. "I got six brothers and sisters. Sometimes it's fun. Mostly it's just loud. My mom's always tired. Dad comes home to eat, then goes out again to study until late at night. I hardly ever see him. She's left there with the laundry piling up, dishes piling up, children piling up. I feel buried under her mountain. She wants me married. She can't wait; it's all she talks about. One less pile."

His eyes strain to see the strip of her panties. "My mom's a magician. She makes herself invisible, specially when my dad's around."

"How does she do that?"

He tugs on a shoelace. "She gets real quiet and then sorta disappears." He leans forward. "You pray?"

"Every morning. So what?" She picks at a loose thread on her skirt. "It isn't going to help. Just the way things are."

"You want to pray? I know how," he says.

"Now? Are you kidding?"

"Please."

"Why?" she asks.

"So I can show you."

She smiles. "All right," and begins to recite a psalm he doesn't know.

"Not that one." He can feel her eyes on him.

Inside the armoire the smell of moth balls seeps out of the wool coats like a gas. He wants to be with her in a place with no light, where it doesn't matter if their eyes are open or closed. He stretches his right arm toward the open door beside her and pulls it shut.

She cries out.

"Sshh, it's okay," he says and recites the psalm, "by the rivers of Babylon we sat and wept." He runs his left hand along her leg; the heat of it against his fingertips. He imagines himself dressed in an embroidered silk robe and fez. His voice fills the armoire the way the Baba Salim's voice filled the temple. He places his other hand on her thigh. His eyes are shut. Her skin is velvet. He wonders if she's fallen asleep. She is so quiet. He recites the prayer for sleep and the prayer for travel, edging nearer; their knees bump. He's jumbled the words, but she doesn't correct him. She listens to his voice lift and drop in a cadence that is nothing like her ground down t's that have been turned into s' and her o's that have been crushed into oy's. His is the language closest to god's. She says something he doesn't quite catch. He wants to tell her that he's a better man than his father, as good as the Baba Salim.

"I'm going to study Torah for you," he says and moves to sit beside her, the coats draped around them.

One side of his body presses against hers. His mouth brushes her ear.

She mumbles something about opening the door, that it's getting hard to breathe.

"It's okay," he says. "When it's this dark you feel like you're floating in water."

"Please, I have to go." She reaches for the door panel. "My mother will worry. I told her I was at a friend's house. She's probably called there looking for me."

He snakes an arm around her waist. "Close your eyes."

"I'm scared of the dark. Please open the door," she says.

His heart swells. "I'll take care of you. I promise. Like the Baba Salim. Don't worry," he tells her in Arabic, forgetting himself for a moment. "This is the best place. This is where I want to be. With you." He nuzzles her neck, smelling her scent, like the musk of a small animal.

"I think you better let me out." Her voice is tremulous.

"Ana behibak, I love you," he says.

There are tears in her eyes. No one has ever cried for him, not even his mother. He draws her face toward his and kisses her mouth. His hands curve along the tender flesh of her cheeks. She jerks against him, whimpering and tries to push him away. She cries out. He wonders if maybe she is a tease, the kind of girl his father warns him about. His hands tighten, holding her head steady.

He kisses her eyelids, tastes her tears. He will make her love him more than the boy she's engaged to. "You have to stop," he tells her.

"Let me out," she screams.

He pulls her onto his lap and recites a prayer to calm her. She tries to kick him. He grabs hold of her legs. Her cries fill the armoire. He buries his head in the rabbinic coats. "Shut up, shut up," and clasps his free hand over her mouth. All of her flush against him, making him sweat. He can almost hear his father chuckling, look at her squirm like a sharmuta.

"Stop acting like that." The palm of his hand is wet from her breath and saliva. "If someone finds us," he hisses into her ear, "you'll get a bad reputation." His hand bears down firmly over her mouth. Her eyes flash in the bar of light coming through the bottom of the closet door. "You think I can't take care of you? You'll see, when my father comes I'll tell him we're getting married. Let him try to separate us. I'll kill him."

He rocks her back and forth, clutching her hard, eyes closed and pictures her dull hair dripping over one shoulder, the long white face, her grey eyes blinking shut. She slumps against him quiet now, no more struggle. They are so close he feels like he could slip through the border of her skin. Her breath is soft in slumber, the weight of her against him a comfort. How could he have questioned the rightness of her? She is everything he's ever wanted. When she wakes, he'll tell her that one day soon they will go to Damascus, to the synagogue, to the house he once lived in. She will know him through the winding streets that smell of smoke and almonds.

"Tomorrow, we'll tell your mother you love me," he brushes the hair off her brow, "and when she asks, who are you? I'll say, You don't know me, but I'm the great-grandson of the Baba Salim."

"Transfer to the Blue Line" by Jeanie Chung

Jeanie Chung's fiction, essays, and author interviews have appeared in *Fifth Wednesday Journal, Numero Cinq, Writers Chronicle,* and elsewhere. She lives in Chicago.

Christmastime is the best time of the year for him, no question. Holiday cheer, lights everywhere, smell of popcorn in the Loop, maybe a nice clean dusting of snow if he's lucky. Sets the mood. The tourists, the grandparents, the suburbanites, they all come into the city to go shopping, take pictures of the big tree at Field's, maybe see a show, and in that kind of mood they tend to think of Charlie as a delightful part of the urban experience, not a con man.

Still, the city cracks down more than they used to back in the eighties. Now and again he can slip past their vigilant patrols, run a few games in the Loop, in front of a store on State Street or something, but usually they'll chase him underground, down the steps to the El, where he can work the platform or, more likely, get on the Red Line, ride it all the way to Howard and back down to 95th, running four or five games each way, especially now that there are no conductors on the cars.

It doesn't seem to him like it's been so many years. That first day he took out a small board, a pea-sized chunk of asphalt and three bottlecaps: one Pepsi, one Mountain Dew, one Coke. His cousin learned to shill, worked with him for years until the diabetes got so bad he couldn't put shoes on. He has other people working with him now. Never hard to find someone who wants to learn from the master.

"Ladies and gentlemen, I have a special opportunity for you today. In front of me I have three bottle caps and one pea. I'm going to move them around. All you need to do is tell me which bottlecap the pea is under, and you can win some money, buy that pretty lady some flowers." He winked at a power-suited couple. "One, two, three, simple as can be. Here we go now. Come on, who wants to play?"

"I do, I do," his cousin would say, elbowing his way from the back of the train.

"Think your eyes are faster than my hands?"

"Sure."

"One dollar to play. Here we go then: one, two, three, let's see if you're better than me. Round and round, keep watching, keep your eye on the pea. Hup! See that? Keep going now, OK, now we stop. Where is it?"

His cousin pointed to the cap on the left. With great dramatic flourish, he lifted it, revealing the pea.

"Aaah. Lucky first-time winner. Try again, double or nothing."

His cousin grinned, nodded.

"Ready? Here we go. One, two, three, keep your eyes on that pea. OK, where is it?"

His cousin pointed left again, and sure enough, there it was.

"Ladies and gentlemen, it may be that I need to retire. This young man's eyes are too quick for me. Who wants to be the next one to win some money?"

The key is to hold the board steady as the train bumps and grinds along. It's too easy for the player to claim that a spill is cheating somehow, even though the spill has nothing to do with it. Usually.

He always tries to have at least two other shills on hand, but sometimes it's too little money to divide among too many people. On days like that, he and his cousin would play a few more games, with his cousin losing, but always winning it back. Until some stranger stepped up and said, "I'll play." He's pretty sure they don't care about the money. They just want the show.

He has a good memory for faces. Has to. First thing he'll do when he gets on a car is look at the crowd, make sure there's no one on the train he's played before. You never know when someone might call the police, or decide to start hassling you, vigilante-style. Over the years he's gotten good at spotting trouble. Then there was that one guy, in the leather jacket that winter. He was sure he'd recognized him, had played him in the warmer weather, when he had on a Sox jersey and shorts. Still, the guy stepped up to play and, just as he went into the patter, winked at him. He let him win that one, and sure enough, another guy in a heavy wool overcoat, the kind that cost more than a year's worth of rent, stepped up to play, trying to impress the woman on his arm, who looked young enough to be his daughter but wasn't holding on to his arm the way a blood relative would. Ended up playing him for twenty.

He scans the crowd and his eyes stop on a face. Thinks, I've seen this young man before. But not exactly him—no, of course not. He would've been just a little kid at the time. It was Christmas Time then, too. Ten years ago, maybe more.

Why that particular boy on that particular day stuck with him, Charlie doesn't know. It was one of the days he was able to get a game going in front of Field's, take advantage of the Christmas season. He looked up and there they were: a tall, fine woman, could've almost been a model, in jeans and a wool coat, holding the red-mittened hand of a boy, looked like he was around eight. Maybe they just stood out as two of the few brown faces in the white holiday-shopping crowd at that moment. But it wasn't just that. The boy's eyes had locked onto his hands, and he was smiling.

"Mama. Look what that man can do. Look how fast." The kid started to jump up and down, until his mother jerked his hand to still him.

"Roosevelt. Baby, people like that, they might as well just be begging for money. Come on. We gotta go."

The fine woman dragged her son away from the makeshift table Charlie had set up with the board and a milk crate.

Sure, he remembered faces month-to-month or even year-to-year out of necessity, but he'd never had much need to think about what an eight-year-old would look like more than ten years later. This kid, his face is thinner, stubbly, which of course it should be, now that he's a man. But it's the same kid. Has to be. After all this time. It was the eyes that gave him away. Those eyes that locked on, taking in everything they saw and storing it away somewhere, for someday his hands might need it.

This kid–this young man, really–rides the Red Line by himself in an aisle seat, from Howard downtown. Long legs, big feet jutting out into the aisle. Headphones on. Hoodie and jeans. Staring out the window. Charlie forgets to even run a game, he's so absorbed watching this kid. He can't figure out why, until the kid, probably without thinking about it, rests a long arm on the windowsill and starts to drum his fingers. His own fingers are shorter, wrinkled too, but he recognizes it: that same dexterity, that same sinuous economy of movement. This kid can make magic with his hands–his feet too, probably.

Charlie looks up to those eyes, still staring into space, staring at nothing. Behind them, though, he can see that mind working, churning, chugging and rolling along like the wheels on the train. Can't tell from his face whether the thoughts are good or bad. Bag under his other arm, something square in it. Has to be Christmas presents. Going home to Mama, Grandma, probably.

Spending as much time as he does underground, somehow Charlie had stopped noticing the passage of time. Not like things don't change on the el. He saw the appearance and then the disappearance of high-top fades, the crowds swelling coming downtown during the Bulls championship years, then diminishing. Saw the crowds swelling coming downtown in general, really. Only thing that hasn't changed is the mayor's name on every sign every time there's construction anywhere.

He doesn't talk to strangers when he's not working, and as a result he's shocked when the kid gets up, steps right in front of him as the train approaches the Loop.

"I remember you," the kid says. "Did you used to do a shell game outside Field's?"

"Still do. Did you ever play?" He asks, even though he knows the answer.

The kid shakes his head, smiles. "I didn't need you taking my money. But you know, I coulda watched you all day. I saw you one time, around Christmas, and then I never saw you again. I didn't come downtown that much, but I tried. I would've looked for you on the trains if I knew you were on here."

"Usually work the Blue and Red, sometimes the Brown."

"I take the Green most of the time."

"No money on the Green, son."

The kid laughs, looks at him sideways, like he's trying to read something written in code on his face. "You, you watch basketball?"

"Little bit. Back when Michael and Scottie played."

"Not," the kid pauses, looks down. "High school? College?"

"Nah."

The kid reaches into his bag, pulls out a *Sentinel* sports page. He flips to the middle, showing the centerspread: "Hillside Heroes: The best players in tournament history." Below the headline is a picture of the kid, younger, wearing a Coolidge High School uniform, a basketball arcing off the tips of his fingers. Toward the basket, Charlie assumes.

No, he hasn't seen him in the newspapers or on TV. He almost never reads the paper, and when he has the opportunity to watch TV, he'd rather watch a movie or a game show. If he were going to watch basketball, he'd watch the NBA. He doesn't even like college basketball. If you're watching, watch the best, he'd say.

"Well, look at that."

"Yeah."

"That's real nice, son."

"I guess."

The train's stuck between stops, which is so routine that no one on the car notices.

"Your mama must be real proud of you."

"Thank you. Yeah, she is. My dad, too."

The doors open as people get on and off at Lake Street. The kid doesn't move, doesn't say anything else.

"Son? Can I ask–I mean, you seem like a nice young man, and I'm happy for your success. But can I ask why you're showing me this?"

The kid's mouth chuckles, but his eyes don't. "I don't know. It's funny, running into you like this, after all these years. I mean, I still remember that day. You probably don't. I mean, why would you?" He speaks quickly, avoids Charlie's eyes, like he's embarrassed.

"Actually, son, I do. I was just trying to place where I knew you when you came over and introduced yourself."

"Really? Not because you, like, saw me before? Well, whatever. I mean, like, so the reason I wanted to show you was, once I was sure I had the right person, I know it sounds kind of weird, but you really inspired me. You *worked* that crowd. It wasn't like I wanted to run a shell game–not that I could if I wanted to–but something about you, I don't know, I never forgot it."

"Get out. Really? Well, looks like you gonna outdo me by a ways. Surprised people on this train don't recognize you."

The young man shrugs.

"Some people do. They say hi, get an autograph or whatever. A lot of them, I think they might know who I am, but they don't say nothing. I can see them looking at me, though. Thinking."

"What do suppose they're thinking?" Charlie really wants to know. The kid starts to say something, but before he can, the train lurches back into motion.

Finally, he speaks. "I mean, it's not like I know, exactly," the young man continues. "Probably something like, 'Who does he think he is?' People, as soon as you're, like, some people have heard of you, everybody gets this attitude like you think you're too good for them. Or else, maybe they think, 'Wow, I bet his life's easy. He ain't got no problems.'"

"Everybody got problems," Charlie says. "But what about yours, son?"

Before the young man can continue, the loudspeaker announces, "Doors open on the right at Jackson. Transfer to the Blue Line."

A minute later, the kid says, almost as if he were apologizing, "This is my stop." The doors open at Jackson, and he steps out with the rest of the crowd.

What a polite young man, Charlie thinks to himself. Finally, someone who appreciates my craft. Then he thinks: that boy should be on top of the world, winning awards, all that stuff. Why on earth does he look so sad? What are his problems? They can't be about basketball. No, he's never seen the kid play, but he can tell just from looking at him. Those hands, those feet, the way he stepped off the train, even. He's a kid who sees three, four plays ahead of the moment. Who can make that ball do whatever he wants. A virtuoso knows a fellow traveler. Whatever is giving him trouble, it's not basketball. It's gotta be something else. After all, basketball players have families and girlfriends and haters and complications in their lives like anybody else does.

The kid won't have money problems, not if he's smart. That way he's got Charlie beat. But what's the good of money, or the promise of money, if it's got you walking around looking like that, having to tell your problems, or at least start to tell them, to strangers?

When people ask Charlie why he does what he does, he talks about how hard it is to get a job—no high school education, and now, especially, who'd hire an old man like him, can barely read? The truth is, he'd do it for free. He has raised the shell game to a fine art.

Shit, if they gave awards for this stuff, short cons? He'd be the MVP, the Oscar winner, the World Champion. He'd be the Nobel Laureate of the Pea. Who has quicker fingers, moves that pea, those bottlecaps easy as waving a hand through the air? Nobody. Who else delivers that kind of personal service, making each mark feel special even after he's taken the money? Nobody. Who else gives the bystanders a little entertainment, probably just wishing they could give him their money? Nobody.

He takes pride in his craft the way so few people do today, and you better believe he's worked hard at it. Ask anybody, they'll tell you it's a pleasure giving him their money, and they never expect it back if they're going to get a show. Cheap at twice the price. When he was a boy, sure, he wouldn't have chosen this vocation, living on the thready edge of life, not much to hang onto. Somebody turns up tomorrow, asks him if he wants to work in a fancy office, wear a suit, have a nice house in the suburbs, he won't say no. But that, as they say, ain't happening. So, if he has to be poor doing something, he's glad to be having this much fun at it. Making this many people happy. Being this good. He's able to survive by being smart, tough and inventive, which is more than a lot of people wearing thousand-dollar suits in steel-and-glass skyscrapers can say.

"Ladies and gentlemen, I have a special opportunity for you today. In front of me I have three bottle caps and one pea. I'm going to move them around. All you need to do is tell me which bottlecap the pea is under, and you can win some money. Not gonna buy a new car, but maybe you can get you one of those nice fancy cappuccinos. One, two, three, money for free. Here we go now. Come on, who wants to play?"

"Accomplices to a Tradition" by Jeff Fearnside

Jeff Fearnside lived and worked in Central Asia for four years. His short-story collection *Making Love While Levitating Three Feet in the Air*, a finalist for the New Rivers Press MVP Award and for the Permafrost Book Prize in Fiction, was published by the Stephen F. Austin State University Press. His individual stories have appeared in many literary journals and anthologies, including *The Pinch, Fourteen Hills, Crab Orchard Review, Everywhere Stories: Short Fiction from a Small Planet (Press 53)*, and–most recently–*Story, Pacific Review, Valparaiso Fiction Review,* and *North Dakota Quarterly.* He teaches at Oregon State University and is at work on a second collection of stories and a novel.

I'd almost made it home to my microregion when I was flagged down. I stopped, grabbed my registration papers from the glove compartment–and some money from the ashtray in case I needed to pay a bribe–but before I could get out of the car, the policeman was already standing at my door.

"I need a ride," he said.

I'd seen him at this corner many times before. If I refused him now, he would likely make my life difficult later. So even though my wife was waiting for me, I motioned for him to get in. I was guessing he wanted to buy some vodka and then have me take him home.

Go to the next street and turn right," he said from the back seat. I did, but as we were passing the store that sold liquor, he didn't say anything more.

"Here?" I asked.

"Farther. I'll tell you when to stop."

He asked for a cigarette, and we both lit up. He was a strong-looking ethnic Kazakh, though not as strong as me, about my age. I was twenty-five then, newly married, and though it was a beautiful summer evening, I wanted to get home to my wife. But we just drove along in silence, him pointing directions, until we were nearly out of town. Now I began getting worried. Was he taking me somewhere out of the way so that he could shake me down for a really big bribe? Then why did he stop me, just another young guy in an old Lada? I'd only just started working as a guard at one of the tourist hotels in town, and my wife and I were still living with my parents.

"There," he said finally, pointing to three people standing by the last bus stop at the end of town, where the steppe began. "I need to pick up my friends."

I stopped, and they all got in, a young man with a bag and a girl holding roses joining the policeman in back, another girl sitting up front with me. They all looked like ethnic Kazakhs, the new guy also about twenty-five, the girls about eighteen.

"Do you know the lake?" the policeman asked. I nodded. "Good. That's where we're going."

I looked at my gas gauge. The policeman must have been looking over my shoulder, because he said, "You have enough." He then said something to his friends in Kazakh, and they all laughed.

I was beginning to wish he had just asked me for a bribe and let me go. This was going to end up costing me a lot, I figured, but I didn't know what else to do. So I just started driving and tried to enjoy myself, lighting up another cigarette. It was hot out on the steppe, but still very beautiful. I would have enjoyed it more if I hadn't been driving but drinking a little vodka instead. The guy with the bag must have been thinking the same, because after about five minutes he pulled out a bottle. They passed it around to everyone and then offered it to me. Though I wanted some, I said that I had a long way to go. The policeman seemed to think this was funny.

"Good, good! You shouldn't drink while you drive. It's against the law."

When talking directly to me like that, they spoke in Russian, but with each other they spoke in Kazakh. I've lived in Kazakhstan all my life, but I was never able to learn any more Kazakh than what I picked up from friends at school, mostly slang. I could actually swear pretty good whenever I needed it in a fight. But I only understood a word here, a phrase there, of the conversation now going on in my car. It seems the men were close friends who'd known each other for years. The girls were, too, though they'd only known the men for a short time. Something about mutual acquaintances, a family connection. There was talk of "a party" and "swimming." Since it was Friday, I guessed they were planning on spending the weekend at the lake. They all seemed comfortable with each other, and they quickly finished off the bottle.

By now I knew all of their names. Arman was the policeman, Nurken his friend. The woman sitting between them was Saparkul. She had the long, thick ponytail that many Kazakh girls wear before getting married, a dark mole on her cheek matching her dark eyes. I kept staring at her in the rearview mirror, though she never looked at me. Perizat was sitting up front. Both women were smartly dressed, short skirts, high heels, very modern. I could see that they had swimsuits on underneath their clothes.

"Brother, do you want to join us at the lake?" Arman asked.

"No, no, I can't. My wife's waiting for me at home."

"Who's in charge?" he cried, slapping me on the shoulder. "You or your wife?"

In the rearview mirror I saw Nurken smirking, but Perizat turned around and said, "The man may be the head, but the woman is the neck." Everyone howled at this, and Arman started arguing with her, comparing the intelligence of men and women. He thought he was winning, but while she'd probably only just finished her first year at one of the local universities, she was clearly better educated, from a good family, not a village girl. She and Saparkul both seemed this way. They didn't smoke, and they drank modestly, leaving most of the vodka for Arman and Nurken. The men held their alcohol well, hardly seemed drunk at all. I was actually beginning to like them, but they didn't seem the best match for these girls. I guessed they were all just looking for a little fun. I'm not sure exactly what the girls had been told, but whatever it was, they didn't seem to mind.

Nurken pulled out another bottle, and we continued driving through the evening. My wife wasn't going to be happy, but what could she do? Being taken for a ride by the police wasn't that uncommon. I wouldn't even have to lie this time.

As we approached the turnoff for the lake, Arman leaned over me and said quietly, "Turn left."

"But–" I began, but he squeezed my shoulder with one hand and pointed with the other. He was even stronger than I'd thought.

"You made a wrong turn," Saparkul said to me. When no one else said anything, including Perizat, I began to get a bad feeling.

"The lake is that way," she repeated. Still no one said a word.

Suddenly she began screaming. I didn't understand everything, but I understood enough.

"Stop the car! Stop the car!"

Now I knew why Arman had flagged me down. Saparkul was being "stolen." It was an old Kazakh tradition. It was also against the law. I thought of slamming on the brakes, but then what would I do? Arman was a policeman. He could accuse me of doing anything, and no judge would rule otherwise. I could've fought both of them if I had to–I'd fought more before–but they were strong and had been drinking, and we were in the middle of the devil's land. If I lost they'd just throw me to the side of the road, and who knows when I'd be found? I'd be helping no one then.

Saparkul tried to crawl over Arman and open the door, but he grabbed her around the waist and pulled her back. She then began beating him on the head and neck, so he took hold of her arms. I was having a hard time staying on the road, turning to see what was happening and wondering if I should interfere.

"Keep driving," Arman said calmly. "To the village."

Saparkul began pleading with me in Russian.

"Please stop the car, please. You have to help me. I don't want to get married. I want to finish my education. I have a boyfriend in town. Please help me."

I almost slowed the car.

"You're hurting her," I said.

"He's not hurting her," Nurken said. "Everything is fine."

"She says she doesn't want to go."

"I said everything is fine. This is our *tradition.*"

It was true. Often it was done with the girl's approval, a way for her poor young fiancé to avoid paying the bride price. Often it was done without the girl's approval or even her knowing it was going to happen. Saparkul was clearly in this second group. It was hard to say why Arman wanted her. Perhaps he truly loved her. Perhaps he just found her beautiful. But once the kerchief was tied around her head by his grandmother, the girl had no choice but to accept her fate; otherwise she'd bring shame to her family.

The village came into view through the shimmering heat rising from the steppe, like something from an ancient caravan scene. Why didn't I stop the car, or better yet, turn it around? All I know is that I was confused. Though bride stealing was against the law, it was tolerated then just as it is today. The only time a case could be formed against anyone was when the girl really caused a scene. Suppose Saparkul got this chance. What would happen to me? I was an accomplice to all this. After all, it was my car she was being stolen in. Arman would say I'd known about it from the beginning, maybe even helped plan it.

"This isn't right," I said.

Perizat moved for the first time since the turn.

"You don't understand," she said. "This is our tradition."

Saparkul began screaming at her friend in Kazakh. I knew the curse words. The men told me to mind my own business. They'd known lots of women who'd been stolen and learned to love their husbands. Arman's grandmother was one, he said. Perizat nodded in agreement, and without turning around, though she raised her voice, she said that Saparkul would get used to her new life and be happy.

We had arrived at the village. I felt like I was in a dream as Arman directed me down one narrow dirt lane and then another. I didn't need him to tell me which house to stop at. I saw the old grandmother standing in the doorway in her brightly colored housecoat, the kerchief in both hands. Several men stood in the yard, empty shot glasses between their fingers. Another man was butchering a sheep hung from a tree, while children played around the entrails. Arman and Nurken had to drag Saparkul from the car, prying her fingers from the doorframe. She began screaming again, her ponytail, now pulled loose, wild over her face and shoulders. My only thought was of whether she would keep that beautiful hair. Arman closed the door and leaned in through the open window.

"Thank you," he said.

I turned the car around and drove very slowly back to town.

"Miracle" by Tope Folarin

Tope Folarin won the Caine Prize for African Writing in 2013, and was shortlisted once again in 2016. He was also recently named to the Africa39 list of the most promising African writers under 40. He was educated at Morehouse College and the University of Oxford, where he earned two Masters degrees as a Rhodes Scholar. He is the author of *The Proximity of Distance* (Simon & Schuster). "Miracle" first appeared in *Transition Magazine.*

Our heads move simultaneously, and we smile at the tall, svelte man who strides purposefully down the aisle to the pulpit. Once there, he raises both of his hands then lowers them slightly. He raises his chin and says *let us pray.*

"Dear Father, we come to you today, on the occasion of this revival, and we ask that you bless us abundantly, we who have made it to America, because we know we are here for a reason. We ask for your blessings because we are not here alone. Each of us represents dozens, sometimes hundreds of people back home. So many lives depend on us Lord, and the burden on our shoulders is great. Jesus, bless this service, and bless us. We ask that we will not be the same people at the end of the service as we were at the beginning. All this we ask of you, our dear savior, Amen."

The pastor sits, and someone bolts from the front row to the piano and begins to play. The music we hear is familiar and at the same time new; the bandleader punches up a pre-programmed beat on the cheap electronic piano and plays a few Nigerian gospel songs to get us in the mood for revival. We sing along, though we have to wait a few moments at the beginning of each song to figure out what he's playing. We sing joyful songs to the Lord, then songs of redemption, and then we sing songs of hope, hope that tomorrow will be better than today, hope that, one day soon, our lives will begin to resemble the dreams that brought us to America.

The tinny Nigerian gospel music ends when the pastor stands, and he prays over us again. He prays so long and so hard that we feel the weight of his words pressing down on us. His prayer is so insistent, so sincere, that his words emerge from the dark chrysalis of his mouth as bright, fluttering prophecies. In our hearts we stop asking *if* and begin wondering *when* our deeply held wishes will come true. After his sweating and shaking and cajoling he shouts another *Amen*, a word that now seems defiant, not pleading. We echo his defiance as loudly as we can, and when we open our eyes we see him pointing to the back of the church.

Our eyes follow the line of his finger, and we see the short old man hunched over in the back, two men on either side of him. Many of us have seen him before, in this very space; we've seen the old man perform miracles that were previously only possible in the pages of our Bibles. We've seen him command the infirm to be well, the crippled to walk, the poor to become wealthy. Even those of us who are new, who know nothing of him, can sense the power emanating from him.

We have come from all over North Texas to see him. Some of us have come from Oklahoma, some of us from Arkansas, a few of us from Louisiana and a couple from New Mexico. We own his books, his tapes, his holy water, his anointing oil. We know that he is an instrument of God's will, and we have come because we need miracles.

We need jobs. We need good grades. We need green cards. We need American passports. We need our parents to understand that we are Americans. We need our children to understand that they are Nigerians. We need new kidneys, new lungs, new limbs, new hearts. We need to forget the harsh rigidity of our lives, to remember why we believe, to be beloved, and to hope.

We need miracles.

We murmur as the two men help him to the front, and in this charged atmosphere everything about him makes sense, even the irony of his blindness, his inability to see the wonders that God performs through his hand. His blindness is a confirmation of his power. It's the burden he bears on our behalf; his residence in a space of perpetual darkness has only sharpened his spiritual vision over the years. He can see more than we will ever see.

When the old man reaches the pulpit his attendants turn him around so he's facing us. He's nearly bald—a few white hairs cling precariously to the sides of his shining head—and he's wearing a large pair of black sunglasses. A bulky white robe falls from his neck to the floor. Beneath, he's wearing a flowing white *agbada*.

He remains quiet for a few moments—we can feel the anticipation building, breath by breath, in the air. He smiles. Then he begins to hum. A haunting, discordant melody. The bandleader tries to find the tune among the keys of his piano, but the old man slaps the air and the bandleader allows the searching music to die.

He continues to hum and we listen to his music. Suddenly he turns to our left and points to a space somewhere on the ceiling:

"I DEMAND YOU TO LEAVE THIS PLACE!" he screams, and we know there is something malevolent in our midst. We search the area his sightless eyes are probing, somewhere in the open space above our heads. We can't see anything, but we raise our voices in response to the prophet's call. Soon our voices are a cacophonous stew of Yoruba and English, shouting and singing, spitting and humming, and the prophet from Nigeria speaks once more:

"We must continue to pray ladies and gentlemen! There are forces here that do not wish for this to be a successful service. If we are successful in our prayers that means they have failed! They do not wish to fail! So we cannot expect that our prayers will simply come true; we must fight!"

We make our stew thicker; we throw in more screams and prayers until we can no longer distinguish one voice from another. Finally, after several long minutes, the prophet raises his hands:

"We are finished. It is done."

And we begin to celebrate, but our celebration lacks conviction—
we haven't yet received what we came here for.

The prophet sways to the beat of our tepid praise. The man on
his left stands and dabs his forehead. The prophet clears his throat
and reaches forward with his right hand until he finds the microphone. He grabs it, leans into it.

"I have been in the U.S. for two months now…" he begins, rhyth-
mically moving his head left and right, "I have been to New York, to
Delaware, to Philadelphia, to Washington, to Florida, to Atlanta, to
Minnesota, to Kansas, to Oklahoma, and now, finally, I have arrived
here."

We cheer loudly.

"I will visit Houston and San Antonio before I leave here, and
then I will go to Nevada, and then California. I will travel all over this
country for the next month, visiting Nigerians across this great land,
but I feel in my spirit that the most powerful blessings will happen
here."

We holler and whoop and hug each other, for his words are confirmation of the feelings we've been carrying within ourselves since
the beginning of the service.

"The reason I am saying that the most powerful blessings will
happen here is because God has told me that you have been the most
faithful of his flock in the U.S. You haven't forgotten your people back
home. You haven't forgotten your parents and siblings who sent you
here, who pray for you every day. You have remained disciplined and
industrious in this place, the land of temptation. And for all your hard
work, for your faithfulness, God is going to reward you today."

Some of us raise our hands and praise the Father. A few of us
bow our heads, a few of us begin to weep with happiness.

"But in order for your blessings to be complete, you will have to
pray today like you have never prayed before. You will have to believe
today like you have never believed before. The only barrier to your

blessing is the threshold of your belief. Today the only thing I will be talking about is belief. If I have learned anything during my visits to this country, it is that belief is only possible for those who have dollars. I am here to tell you that belief comes before dollars. If you have belief, then the dollars will follow."

Silence again. We search our hearts for the seedlings of doubt that reside there. Many of us have to cut through thickets of doubt before we can find our own hearts again. We use the silence to uproot our doubt and we pray that our hearts will remain pure for the remainder of the service.

"Let me tell you, great miracles will be performed here today. People will be talking about this day for years and years to come. And the only thing that will prevent you from receiving your share is your unbelief…"

At this moment he begins to cough violently, and the man on his right rushes forward with a handkerchief. He places the handkerchief in the prophet's hand, and the prophet coughs into it for a few seconds, and then he wipes his mouth. We wait anxiously for him to recover.

He laughs. "I am an old man now. You will have to excuse me. Just pray for me!"

"We will pray for you Prophet!" we yell in response.

"Yes, just pray for me, and I will continue to pray for you."

"Thank you Prophet! Amen! Amen!"

"And because you have been faithful, God will continue to bless you, he will anoint you, he will appoint you!"

"Amen!"

"Now God is telling me that there is someone here who is struggling with something big, a handicap that has lasted for many, many years."

We fall quiet because we know he is talking about us.

"He's telling me that you have been suffering in silence with this problem, and that you have come to accept the problem as part of yourself."

We nod in agreement. How many indignities have we accepted as a natural part of our lives?

"The purpose of my presence in your midst is to let you know that you should no longer accept the bad things that have become normal in your lives. America is trying to teach you to accept your failures, your setbacks. Now is the time to reject them! To claim the success that is rightfully yours!"

His sunglasses fall from his face, and we see the brilliant white orbs quivering frantically in their sockets, two full moons that have forgotten their roles in the drama of the universe. His attendants lunge to the floor to recover them, and together they place the glasses back on his ancient face. The prophet continues as if nothing happened.

"I do not perform these miracles because I wish to be celebrated. I perform these miracles because God works through me, and he has given me the grace to show all of you what is possible in your physical and spiritual lives. And now God is telling me; you, come up here."

We remain standing because we don't know to whom he is referring.

"YOU! You! You! YOU! Come up here!"

We begin to walk forward, shyly, slowly. I turn around suddenly, and I realize I'm no longer a part of the whole. I notice, then, that the lights are too bright, and the muggy air in the room settles, fog-like, on my face. Now I am in the aisle, and I see the blind old man pointing at me.

"You, young man. Come here. Come up here for your miracle!"

I just stand there, and I feel something red and frightening bubbling within me. I stand there as the prophet points at me, and I feel hands pushing me, forcing me to the front. I don't have enough time to wrap up my unbelief and tuck it away.

Then I'm standing on the stage, next to the prophet.

The prophet moves closer to me and places a hand on top of my head. He presses down until I'm kneeling before him. He rocks my head back and forth.

"Young man, you have great things ahead of you, but I can sense that something is ailing you. There is some disease, some disorder that has colonized your body, and it is threatening to colonize your soul. Tell me, are you having problems breathing?"

I find myself surprised at his indirect reference to my asthma. But now the doubts are bombarding me from every direction. Maybe he can hear my wheezing? It's always harder for me to breathe when I'm nervous, and I'm certainly nervous now.

"Yes sir," I reply.

"Ah, you do not need to confirm. I now have a fix on your soul, and the Holy Spirit is telling me about the healings you need." He brushes his fingers down my face, and my glasses fall to the ground. Everything becomes dim.

"How long have you been wearing glasses my son?"

"Since I was five, sir."

"And tell me, how bad is you vision?"

Really bad. I have the thickest lenses in school, the kind that make my eyes seem like two giant fish floating in blurry, separate ponds.

"It's bad sir."

The prophet removes his hand from my head and I can feel him thrashing about, as if he's swimming in air, until an attendant thrusts a microphone into his groping hand.

"As you guys can see, I know a little about eye problems," he booms, and although it sounds like he's attempting a joke, no one laughs, and his words crash against the back wall and wash over us a second time, and then a third.

"And no one this young should be wearing glasses that are so thick!" The congregation cheers in approval. I hear a whispered *yes prophet.*

54

"I can already tell that you have become too comfortable with you handicap," he roars, "and that is one of the main problems in this country. Handicaps have become *normal* here." I see the many heads nodding in response. "People accept that they are damaged in some fashion, and instead of asking God to intervene, they accept the fact that they are broken!"

More head nodding, more *Amens*.

"Let me tell you something," he continues. He's sweating profusely; some of it dribbles onto my head. My scalp is burning. "God gives us these ailments so that we are humbled, so that we are forced to build a relationship with him. That is why all of us, in some way or another, are damaged. And the reason they have come to accept handicaps in this country is because these Americans do not want to build a relationship with God. They want to remain forever disconnected from His grace, and you can already see what is happening to this country."

The *Amens* explode from many mouths; some louder, some softer, some gruff, some pleading.

"So the first step to getting closer to God, to demonstrating that you are a serious Christian, is declaring to God all of your problems and ailments, and asking him to heal you."

A few *Amens* from the back overwhelm everything. I squint to see if I can connect the praise to the faces, but I can only see the featureless faces swathed in fog.

"So now I'm going to ask God to heal this young man who has become accustomed to his deformity. But before I touch you, before I ask the Holy Spirit to do its work, I must ask you, before everyone here—are you ready for your miracle?"

I stare at the congregation. I see some nodding. I've never thought of a life without glasses, but now my head is filled with visions of perfect clarity. I can see myself playing basketball without the nerdy, annoying straps that I always attach to my glasses so they won't fall off my face. I imagine evenings without headaches, headaches that come after hours spent peering through lenses that give me sight while rejecting my eyes.

"Are you ready?" he asks again, and I can feel the openness in the air that exists when people are waiting for a response. I know I'm waiting for my response as well.

"I'm ready."

"Amen!"

"AMEN! AMEN!" Their Amens batter me; I bow beneath the harsh blows of their spiritual desperation.

"My son, you are ready to receive your gift from God."

His two attendants scramble from his side, drag me to my feet, and bring me down to the floor. One positions himself next to me, the other behind me. When I look over my shoulder I see the attendant standing there with his arms extended before him.

"I feel something very powerful coursing through my spirit," the prophet yells. "This is going to be a big miracle. Bring me to the boy!"

The attendant beside me strides up to the stage and helps the prophet down the steps. He positions the prophet before me, and I notice that the prophet seems even shorter than before. He is only a few inches taller than me. His hot breath causes my eyes to water; I resist the urge to reach up and rub them.

The prophet suddenly pulls off his sunglasses. He stares at me with his sightless eyes. I become uncomfortable, so I lean slightly to the right and his face follows. I lean slightly to the left and his face does the same. A sly smile begins to unfurl itself across his face. My heart begins to beat itself to death.

"Do not be frightened. I can see you through my spiritual eyes," he says. "And after this miracle, if you are a diligent Christian, you will be able to do the same."

Before I can respond, his right hand shoots forward, and he presses my temples. I stumble backwards but maintain my balance.

I turn to gaze at all the people in front of me, and though I can't see individual faces I see befuddlement in its many, various forms. I see random expressions contort themselves into a uniform expression of confusion. I actually manage to separate my brother from the masses because his presence is the only one in the room that seems to match my own. We're both confused, but our confusion isn't laced with fear.

The prophet presses my temples again, and again, and each time I regain my balance. His attendants are ignoring me now. They're both looking down at the prophet, inquiring with their eyes about something. I'm not sure what. Then I hear the shuffling feet, and I know that the people are becoming restless.

"The spirit of bad sight is very strong in him, and it won't let go," the prophet yells.

Life returns to the church like air filling up a balloon. I see the prophet's attendants nod, and the new Amens that tunnel into my ears all have an edge of determination.

"This healing will require special Holy Ghost healing power. Come, take my robe!" The attendant closest to me pulls the robe from his back, and the prophet stands before me even smaller and less imposing than before. "While I am working on this spirit everyone in this room must pray. You must pray that I will receive the power I need to overcome this spirit within him!"

I see many heads moving up and down in prayer, and I hear loud pleading, and snapping, and impassioned howling.

"That is very good!"

The prophet steps forward and blows in my eyes, and then he rubs my temples. I remain standing. He blows and rubs again. The same. He does it again, and again, and each time the praying grows louder and more insistent. The prophet moves even closer to me, and this time when he presses my temples he does not let go. He shoves my head back until I fall, and the attendant behind me eases me to the floor. I finally understand. I remain on the floor while his attendants cover me with a white sheet. Above, I hear the prophet clapping his hands, and I know that he's praying. The fluorescent lights on the ceiling are shining so brightly that the light seems to be huddling in the sheet with me. I hug the embodied light close.

After a few minutes the prophet stops clapping.

"It is finished! Pick the young man up."

His attendants grab my arms and haul me up. I hear a cheer building up in the crowd, gaining form and weight, but the prophet cuts everything off with a loud grunt.

"Not yet. It is too soon. And young man, keep your eyes closed." I realize that my eyes are still closed, and I wonder how he knows.

I begin to believe in miracles. I realize that many miracles have already happened; the old prophet can see me even though he's blind, and my eyes feel different somehow, huddled beneath their thin lids. I think about the miracle of my family, the fact that we've remained together despite the terror of my mother's abrupt departure, and I even think about the miracle of my presence in America. My father reminds my brother and me almost every day how lucky we are to be living in poverty in America, he claims that all of our cousins in Nigeria would die for the chance, but his words were meaningless before. Compared to what I have already experienced in life, compared to the tribulations that my family has already weathered, the matter of my eyesight seems almost insignificant. *Of course I can be healed! This is nothing. God has already done more for me than I can imagine. This healing isn't even for me. It is to show others, who believe less, whose belief requires new fuel, that God is still working in our lives.*

Then the Prophet yells in my ear: OPEN YOUR EYES.

My lids slap open, and I see the same fog as before. The disembodied heads are swelling with unreleased joy. I know what I have to do.

"I can see!" I cry, and the loud cheers and sobbing are like new clothing.

"We must test his eyes, just to make sure! We are not done yet!" yells the prophet, and nervousness slowly creeps up my spine like a centipede. "We have to confirm so the doubters in here and the doubters in the world can know that God's work is real!"

One of his attendants walks a few feet in front of me and holds up a few fingers. I squint and lean forward. I pray I get it right.

"Three!" I yell, and the crowd cheers more loudly than before.

"Four!" I scream, and the cheers themselves gain sentience. They last long after mouths have closed.

"One!" I cry, and the mouths open again, to give birth to new species of joy.

———

This is what I learned during my first visit to a Nigerian church: that a community is made up of truths and lies. Both must be cultivated in order for the community to survive.

The prophet performed many more miracles that day. My father beamed all the way home, and I felt that I had been healed, in a way, even if my eyes were the same as before.

That evening, after tucking my brother and me in, my father dropped my glasses into a brown paper bag, and he placed the bag on the nightstand by my bed.

"You should keep this as evidence, so that you always remember the power of God," he whispered in my ear.

The next morning, when I woke up, I opened my eyes, and I couldn't see a thing. I reached into the bag and put on my glasses without thinking. My sight miraculously returned.

"Burial and Diaspora" by Gina Mariela Rodriguez

Gina Mariela Rodríguez is a writer and performer. Her birth story appears in *Birthing Justice: Black Women, Pregnancy, and Childbirth* (Routledge, 2015) and her original works for the stage have been produced in Rhode Island and New York (*Ariel*, 2008) and Massachussetts (*Free at Last*, 2013). Gina is a graduate of the Africana Studies program at Brown University and was a 2013 Callaloo Creative Writing Fellow. She lives in Providence, Rhode Island.

When I imagine Abuela, the grandmother I never met, she is grainy like her picture, and moves in black and white. I remember the moment she died like it was yesterday. I was six and in the bathtub. The phone rang and then hung up like calls from Cuba usually do. Dad left the bathroom door open and went downstairs to catch the next call. I heard him speaking, but couldn't understand. Then he came up the stairs, slowly, and lay his body across them. "Mi Mámi die, Mi Mámi die," he said. It was the first time I saw him cry.

For the first eighteen years of my life my relationships with my living relatives in Cuba—my brothers, nieces, nephews—were as still as Abuela's photo, surrounded by candles in an 8x10 frame. Untouchable, distant, static, sacred. Our lives were pixilated through translation, calling cards, coffee-colored envelopes and strange stamps. I had no physical connection to anyone, nor to Cuba then, no understanding of how my breath would change once I walked amongst my ancestors.

Until I went to Cuba, home was an idea without place. Land was merely earth and water and buildings and trees. The daughter and granddaughter of immigrants, I am both a stranger and a settler. I walk upon the bones of someone else's ancestors, ride along streets paved over unmarked, colonized graves. I will never be home here, and, I wonder whether I will ever feel comfortable dying here, my body too becoming part of this stolen land.

When I was in the fifth grade, several of my mother's aunts, uncles, and older cousins passed away. There was a wake at least once a month, and each one was the same. Thick, weighted lilies in the Dello Russo funeral home. Black dresses, gold crosses, open caskets, a line of solemn faces, whispers, pinching patent leather shoes, perfume. Mass followed by orange flags on top of cars, funeral processions to the Oak Grove cemetery, names added to family gravesites. After the burials, we would visit the other relatives in nearby graves; Nonno and Nonnie Foti, Nonno and Nonnie Mobilia, uncles, aunts, and cousins, all buried within a conversation of one another. The adults would tell stories of how Papa Dominic used to kneel at his mother's grave, at her feet, and weep for her. They would talk about their card games until three in the morning, of Papa catching clams on the beach and eating them raw. Burials were times we wept and times we held onto one another, passing memories through the generations like stones. Receptions followed, and we would eat pasta and eggplant and cake and coffee. No political conversations allowed, on my mother's orders.

I was seventeen when Nana, my Mother's mother, passed away on Papa Dominic's birthday. I started to think about the generation gap closing, about my parents, aunts, and uncles becoming the oldest tier of the family. I started to wonder where my father would want to be buried, if he would want to be buried in this land of exile, his enemy turned refuge. I asked him once. He said, "I don't care where I end up." But I know he lies. When I ask my mother she says, "I'll go wherever your father goes." When I ask her what she will do if he wants to be buried in Cuba, she says, "I'll guess I'll go to Cuba then." We both know this is impossible. It's hard enough to send a package. A body? Two? To be buried? Forget it.

"But Ma, what about being buried near Nana and Papa Dominic?"

"I can't be buried at Oak Grove. Can we stop talking about this?"

"I don't understand."

"You have to be a town resident to be buried there."

"So, none of us can go there?"

"No. Can we please stop talking about this?"

At Oak Grove, our Sicilian community and extended family remain intact underground. There is a sense of comfort in this. I can hear them laughing, I hear their cards and poker chips hitting felt topped tables, wine being poured into glasses, Nana's scotch on the rocks clinking against her glass. Yes, we are generations of foreigners in this stolen land. I try to rationalize my sadness with this fact. But we would have been together, there.

"See that spot right there? That's where I want to be buried." He points to a bed of leaves fallen at the base of a tree whose bark leaned towards the water, her thick green leaves providing us shelter from the sun. We are standing at the mouth of the gorge that snakes through the land behind his parent's house, our feet on a bed of thin, moss-covered shale. Eyes bright, he traces roots that weave themselves in and out of the shale cliff. There is a bond between him, this young man I am just starting to get to know, and the earth that cakes under his fingernails and sweeps across his forehead. He communicates with her, loves her, trusts her, and she him. We stare at the spot for a while in silence. This is before our marriage, before moving to the coast, before companies started raping shale for natural gas.

He never mentioned the spot again and I have not forgotten. Every time another company builds a rig or gets a neighbor to lease land nearby, I think about his future grave, and whether or not there will be any land left to bury him. I think about how he already has a spot in mind to lay his bones. How there is no room for me.

In death we continue to be separated by oceans and governments and embargos. There can be no one ancestral lying place, no burial community for me. Or my parents. Or my husband. Or my children. We will take little plots of many lands. My body, their bodies, will become part of the earth in foreign soils. I wonder how to ask permission.

"Meet the Parents" by Matthue Roth

Matthue Roth helped create the voice of the Google Assistant. His picture book *My First Kafka* is a retelling of classic Kafka stories for kids. His most recent novel, *Rules of My Best Friend's Body*, is a young adult novel about gender politics, hormones, theology, and video games. He lives in Brooklyn and keeps a secret diary at matthue.com.

I was shimmering drunk. I was coming from Shabbos dinner at a stranger's house, and afraid like I always am of opening up, of showing too much of myself to well-meaning but inexorably straight-laced people who were being kind to me—the kind of people who volunteered at the end of Friday night services when the rabbi asks that, if anyone has extra seats at their Shabbos dinner table to please let him know. I'm not the sort of person most of these people want crashing their family meals.

I'm in the Pico-Robertson district of Los Angeles, five blocks east of Beverly Hills. I'm unkempt. I've been living on a couch for a month. I don't even own a suit. But these Jews, these Orthodox Jews, take me in anyway.

They meet me after services, introduced by the rabbi with me standing next to him like I'm helpless, like I need a translator, either that or a wheelchair. They look peaceable and innocent. The husband with a clean-shaven baby face, a paunch rolling out over his belt, covered by a white short-sleeve button-down shirt. He looks pregnant, but it's a cute sort of pregnant. You know he will be the type of father to pull his own weight with chores and never ignore the kids. The wife has a young face, a pretty face, even though they're both my parents' age. She wears a glorious, monolithic pillowcase of a dress, loud purple and yellow paisley, a matching head scarf.

They nod politely when I say I'm a professional poet and they inquire politely how I became Orthodox, because they can tell from the way I look that I sure as sugar didn't grow up this way. I tell them

I just sold a book and the title sounds like a joke. "Never Mind the Goldbergs," I say, but they recognize the name of the publisher. This gives me a momentary legitimacy—I'm not a bum, I'm really not, I just don't know many people and the place where I'm staying doesn't have a kosher kitchen—but how impressed can these people be? I mean, this is Hollywood. Their congregation president has won Emmys. The fact that I wrote a novel about punk-rock Orthodox Jews and somebody actually published it doesn't make me famous. It makes me one-time lucky, a loser who's just been asked to prom. Only now, I'm a loser in a tux.

So I drink.

Shabbos dinner, when we feel obliged to talk about the Torah, alcohol gets pulled out of the liquor cabinet and passed around. It makes the pretense of God go down easier. We say *l'chaim*, which we say means "to life" but really means "to lives," as a way of wishing each other good health, when really we're hoping that the drink doesn't kill us, that we will behave with some amount of honor once it goes to our heads or, failing that, that we won't remember what went down. What is it about us, a normally tight-assed and mind-your-own-business people, that so incline us to feeding each other and getting each other trashed? Perhaps it's an outgrowth of this hospitality toward strangers. Or perhaps it's just we fear alcoholism, and this is a way to avoid drinking alone.

I sit there looking restless, squeezed next to the candle tray and poking at my food.[1] The husband is talking about the Torah portion that week. It is Vayera, right at the beginning of the Torah, where Hagar left her infant son Ishmael to fend for himself in the desert.

---

[1] Poking at my food. One more occupational hazard about being a freelance Shabbos-meal crasher: You never know what you're going to get. And if you're a vegetarian and you don't warn people ahead of time, your plate may end up looking like mine: covered half with potatoes and half string beans. I didn't mind—beggars can't be choosers and all that, and also, I am a major potato fan—but your hosts will inevitably watch you, feeling bad they didn't think about this earlier, and asking either themselves or you what they could possibly defrost that would make you a little less hungry.

There is a meaning, some G-dly point that he is talking toward, but I can't quiet my mind enough to get there with him. Tiny plastic tokens, black and orange, dangle from candlesticks. They had legs. They are spiders. I flick one of them with my finger.

The table gives a general sort of laugh. That couple and their two sons, white-shirted and black-pantsed, and the family of guests, are all smirking at me. It hadn't even made a sound.

"You've found out our little secret," says the husband, dropping out of his Torah talk without missing a beat. "It's Shabbos *erev* Halloween. We tend to go, uh, a little overboard."

"Spooky Shabbos," the smaller of the boys explains to me.

Everybody laughs generously.

The wife pulls herself up in her seat, stiff-lipped. "Are you insinuating that I only hang spiders from my candlesticks on Halloween?" she demands, not unkindly.

"I'll be right back," I say.

I wander through the dining room and walk the length of their place. It was as big as a house but it tried to be a mansion, with oversized couches crammed into every room. All I remember is that every piece of furniture and shelf was beige. There were chandeliers that shone rainbows and should have pulverized the rest of the room in color, but didn't. It was like the beige won.

I stand alone in the living room like a burglar, feeling even more stiflingly awkward than usual. Even when there's no one watching me. I look at their family pictures. Jealous of the size of their house in the pictures. Jealous of its size in real life. The boys with perfect skin, the girls in their tight but long-sleeved sweaters and big boobs. Jealous especially of the father and his sons all wearing yarmulkes, which just doesn't seem right in my head. How could they all be religious? I felt like it was always supposed to swing one way or the other. Either the parents don't know anything or the kids don't care. I wished for an Orthodox family.

My eyes zoom in on the daughter. She is the oldest, you could tell: shorter than the boys, but more comfortable in her body, I know her. Her name is Rebecca. She lives in New York, in Washington Heights; she went to Shabbos meals at my friend Alej's house. She wears glasses and had long thick hair as curly and bright as a Hasidic rabbi's sidelocks. She is out-of-my-league beautiful.

And now that I knew her parents, and that they liked me, I knew that I would never stand a chance with her.

Standing in that living room I felt more lost and pathetic than I had in awhile. I was going to live like this forever, a stranger at synagogue, drifting through the houses of kindly strangers. Even if I was rich, or famous—even if my book became a bestseller, and a movie, and it caused half the Jewish population of the continental United States to question why they were living an empty meaningless existence and become Orthodox, I would still be the same person. I would always be the kid who showed up at her parents' for Shabbos dinner at random. It wasn't a money thing. It wasn't even a power thing. It was just being that kid, the one who doesn't fit into the established schematic of normative Jewish life. I was a charity case. No matter what I did to change that, to these people, I would always be a charity case.

I returned to the dinner table and took my seat. They were just starting to hand out the prayerbooks, singing the song that comes before the prayer after meals. It was the polite way to ask you to leave. It was the holy way.

"Runnin' With the Wrong Crowd" by Andrew Shirley

Andrew Shirley is a freelance writer, middle school English teacher, and developmental writing instructor. He has a B.A. in English and an M.A. in Writing and Linguistics from Northwestern State University of Louisiana. A student of cultures both high and low, his writing is informed by everything from classical philosophy to horror movies. He lives in Louisiana.

I wasn't shocked when we got arrested. It doesn't matter what anybody tells you, when you decide to break into a house and start takin' things that don't belong to you, you ain't shocked when they catch you. In fact, you start to get so paranoid that some people might say it's a small relief once they finally pick you up. I ain't one of those people, but I'm sure they're out there.

So naw, I wasn't shocked when we got arrested. I was mostly just pissed off that I'd have to go through the whole booking process again. Like I don't have better things to do than sit in the police sta-tion until my bail gets posted. They brought me in and sat me on the bench near the front desk, then took my cuffs off. One of the benefits of bein' a frequent flyer is that they trust you not to run. Some people might take advantage of that, but I didn't see the point. I didn't have anywhere to hide and runnin' would just make it worse.

"Rufus why is it every time I turn around, somebody is dragging your sorry hide through that door?" I looked up to see Chief Turk walk into the office. He was laughin' as he talked. He'd always been fat, but he had to be pushin' 350 now. His gut fell over his belt and his uniform buttons looked like they were gonna pop any minute and his bald head was shiny with sweat. Turk was always sweatin'.

"Guess they just think I'm pretty, Chief," I said. He laughed. It was loud and fake, like his laughs always were. His laugh sounded so phony you could never be sure if he was fakin' it or not.

"Well, let's see here," Turk said. "Looks like my boys caught you and Tommy Shane inside of the old McCarver place at the corner of Pine and Lakeside. What on Earth would you two be doing over there, Rufus?" Turk laid his hands on his gut and smiled. He knew damn well what we were doin'.

"Cleanin' house," I said. Turk laughed again. That was the song and dance here. Turk found cute answers amusin', and I played it up. I didn't know if it did me any favors, but it couldn't hurt. Worst part was pretendin' that I actually liked that fat sumbitch. I figure deep down he knew I couldn't stand him, but sometimes you gotta play ball.

"No shock to see you in here, but I've got to say that I'm surprised to see the Shane boy involved. Normally you don't see folk like that running with dogs like you," Turk said. He liked callin' anybody he picked up a dog.

"I ain't a man with a lot of pride, Chief, but that still ain't no reason to be callin' nobody a dog," I said. Turk didn't laugh. I didn't expect him to. He didn't like it when people pushed back.

"You're a dog if you're dragging people from good families down to your level," Turk said. "You know how many acres around town the Shanes own? Hell, you know how much of the actual town the Shanes own? They're good people, unlike you."

"You don't know what kinda person I am," I said.

"Ha, bullshit!" Turk shouted. "There's no mystery with you Rufus. My boys have been picking you up since you were 16. You're sitting on that same exact bench twice a year, at least. Hell, I played football with your old man, and everybody knew back then that a trailer trash tree like Bertie Wells was never gonna produce anything but rotten apples. I know *exactly* what kind of person you are."

"And what kinda person is that?" I asked. I already knew the answer. Turk wasn't as smart at he thought.

"A dog!" Turk exclaimed. I could tell he was proud of himself.

"Yeah, sure," I said. I was gettin' irritated with the back and forth and just wanted to get finished. "So you want a real answer or are we gonna sit here bullshittin' all day?"

"What you got?" Turk asked. We were playin' ball again.

"So you wanna know what can get a good person to run with a dog like me? Let me ask you a question. How long you been doin' this, Chief?"

"Thirty years," Turk said, smilin'. He was proud of his answer.

"Thirty years," I said back. "Thirty years. So in thirty years, what is the number one reason that causes people to steal things?"

"Drugs," Turk said.

"You ain't as dumb as you look, Chief!" I said. Turk was pissed off, but I couldn't help myself and laughed anyway.

"Watch your mouth, fool," Turk spit back at me. Everybody knew that if you wanted to work Turk's nerves, you called him dumb. "And you're expecting me to believe that Tommy Shane is using?"

"I ain't expectin' you to believe or not believe anything," I said. "I'm just tellin' you what happened." I looked up at the clock. This was takin' longer than normal.

"I don't believe that," Turk said. He sounded like he was convincin' himself. "Nobody from the Shane family is using, and they're sure as hell not committing B&E's with dogs like you."

"Ha!" I laughed. It wasn't one of those fake laughs, either. "The only person here lyin' is you, and the person you're lyin' to is yourself."

Turk leaned back in his chair again and stared up at the ceiling. He set his hands back on his swollen gut and rocked back and forth for a few minutes. He was thinkin', or comin' as close to thinkin' as a guy like Turk could.

"So here's what we're gonna do," Turk said, like we'd been workin' out some kind of plan together. "We're gonna tell everyone that Tommy Shane was forced to aid you under duress. If I had my way, we'd make his name vanish completely from this, but too many people saw him get picked up. Everybody's already talking, so I can't make it go away...but I can do the next best thing."

I'd dealt with Turk's bullshit for almost two decades, but this was a new one. I thought he was jokin' at first, and waited a second for him to follow it up with one of his big, fake laughs. When he didn't, I couldn't help myself. "So you're gonna throw me under the bus so you don't have to explain why the golden boy out there is actually a tweaker? You're gonna turn all of this around on me?" I asked. I tried to keep my voice calm, but wasn't sure if it was workin'

"I don't know what you're talking about," Turk said, grinnin'. "All I have to go on is facts. And fact is, you were forcing Tommy Shane to run with you under threat of death. That's what this report says. Or what it will say when it's officially filed. You know how paperwork goes."

"Oh, that's great!" I yelled. We weren't playin' ball anymore, so there was no point in tryin' to suck up. "That's a great story. But one question, why would I be doin' that? What possible benefit do I get from that? I might be a thief and occasional user, but I ain't a murder or kidnapper and I sure as hell ain't no psycho."

"Rufus, here's the thing," Turk said. His voice was calm. "It doesn't make any difference to people whether you're a thief or a user or a murderer. As far as the law-abiding, keep-earning people in this town are concerned, the world is very simple. There are people like you, and people like Tommy Shane. People like the Shane family are who they aspire to be. Skinny, scraggly-bearded trash like you provides them an explanation for everything that's wrong with the world. In a way, you provide a valuable public service."

I was clinchin' my fist so hard that my fingernails were diggin' into my palms. Turk had screwed me over before, but he was talkin' about serious stuff now. He was talkin' about turnin' what should have been a B&E in an empty house into kidnappin' and attempted murder. He was talkin' about sendin' me away for a long time.

"Here's the thing," Turk said. "I'm not naïve. I've been doing this a long, long time. I know people like Tommy Shane use. I know people like Tommy Shane steal. I know people like Tommy Shane murder. Hell, if I felt like it, I could show you that Tommy isn't even the first member of the Shane family to do any of those things. He won't be the last, either. But that's not the point, Rufus..."

"What?" I mumbled. I was grittin' my teeth and starin' at the floor.

"In a town like this, we just can't be having that kind of thing happen publicly. There's an order to things, and people don't like having that order upset. So if we have to shift some blame to keep things in order, that's fine. Hell, I'd say it's more than fine, it's expected."

"You really believe the garbage comin' out of your mouth, Turk?" I said. "Are you really dumb enough to believe any of what you're sayin' is true?"

"It don't matter if I believe it or not," Turk said. "It's about what the people outside of this office believe. And if I've got to fudge the truth to keep them able to sleep at night, I'll do it. As far they're concerned, by this time tomorrow all their worries about precious little Tommy Shane will be over, and instead everyone will be talking about that trailer-park dog Rufus Wells and how everyone knew he was bad news, but nobody knew it was *that* bad."

"How many times have you pulled crap like this before, Turk? How many innocent guys you got sittin' in jail to cover somebody else's ass?" I asked. Truth was I didn't much care about what had happened to anyone else right then, but I wasn't sure what else to say.

Turk smiled. "None of them are innocent, that's the thing. They're all people like you. They've all done *something*. They were all going down river for some reason, so what's a few more years? If people need a scapegoat, it's better to use one that's already being punished, right?" He laughed as he spoke.

"That's sick, man!" I yelled. My pulse was racin', but I knew I was up against the wall. "This whole thing is sick. If I'd recorded just one minute of this, you'd be done!" I knew it was an empty threat, and, unfortunately for me, so did Turk.

"But you didn't, did you? I'm no idiot. I know what I can and can't do. You want some advice, Rufus? If you don't want to be screwed over, don't be a dog. Like I said, there's an order, you're at the bottom of it, and shit always rolls down hill. You spend enough time doing the kind of things that you do, and eventually it comes back to bite you."

Turk waved his hand and an officer came in and slapped a pair of cuffs back on me. Now there was a part of me wanted to fight it and make a run, but there's was no point in makin' it any worse. If I did that, I'd just give Turk more fuel. So I stood up, put my hands out, and the cop started to lead me out the door.

"Oh, uh, make sure you put him in a cell. Turns out Rufus here is more dangerous than we thought. I can't believe we were letting him run around free all this time," Turk said, smilin'. I turned away from Turk and gritted my teeth as the officer led me out. As we walked out the door, I finally knew what Turk meant, cause just then I'd never felt more like a dog in my life.

"Crawlspace" by James Yeh

James Yeh is a writer and features editor at the *Believer*. His work has appeared in the *New York Times, Tin House, Harper's, VICE, Dissent*, and *GQ*, among others. A 2011 Center for Fiction emerging writers fellow, he was a 2014 writer-in-residence at the Hub City Writers Project. A native of South Carolina, he now lives in Brooklyn.

Christmas morning, and I'm hunched over on my hands and knees, dragging a pair of twenty-pound bags through the crawlspace beneath my parents' house. From one of the bags I pull out a roll of bright pink foam insulation and I shove it in between the wooden joists and use small metal wires to hold it in place.

My father and I sit hunched and cramped. Upstairs I can hear my mother slippering around, preparing the turkey we eat every Christmas. Because of the thick layer of dust that is suspended in the air in front of me, I am trying to avoid taking deep breaths and I am moving slowly.

Nobody wants to be down here all day, my father says to me.

Nobody wants to be down here in the first place, I say back.

Even though I have my glasses on like I always do and a dust mask as well, it doesn't help. Repacking insulation, because of the way you have to put it in, lying on your back with your arms up, is a messy process. Scraps of the old stuff almost always fall out. I taste dust. Dirt. Sometimes, like now, a gritty metallic flavor enters my mouth. Probably fiberglass, I imagine. I roll over, lift up my mask, cough, and spit.

Don't do that, says my father.

Or what.

Be careful! he screams.

I'm not doing anything, I say. I don't even live here anymore, I add. I am jetlagged, having just flown in last night, and my temper is short.

Good, he says.

Work, he says.

———

Twenty-three, fresh out of college and miserable. Living in a beautiful, coastal city–San Francisco–two thousand miles and three time zones away from my parents' house. While going through my bags one night, I find a stack of old photographs in a thick envelope. It occurs to me they were put there by my mother.

The first couple of pictures are of my parents looking much like they do now. My father, with his engineer's eyeglasses (function over form) and shiny bald forehead, stands with his arms folded behind his back, his legs slightly apart, slightly martial, a remainder from his required year of service in the Taiwanese army, which he's never really told me about, though I suppose I've also never really asked. My mother, looking pretty with her bangs and understated black and white dress, is also unsmiling, afraid to show her slightly uneven teeth.

The pictures that follow are similar: my mother and sister at a Chinese restaurant; my father with his three younger sisters in front of the ocean; one of my cousins with his chubby little sister and me in line at an amusement park; my father's sisters and posing on top of the Empire State Building, all of them wearing striking red blazer and skirt combinations. These pictures I skim through. I've seen my parents every day for the greater portion of my life. I know what they look like, I know what my parents and sister and aunts and cousins look like. I've seen these places and people and scenes before, have memorized and become bored with them. Even though my family doesn't keep a photo album and photos like this are rare, I am mostly unmoved. The ones that interest me are the ones where strange transformations of the familiar have occurred and suddenly you are looking at parties full of strangers.

One of those photos: My mother, my aunt Imelda, and myself in a place I do not recognize. We are all standing. Nothing particularly memorable about the background. No signs proclaiming Chinese New Year or Merry Christmas. In fact there is nothing festive about anything in the picture and why we took it in the first place is a mystery to me.

But there's something about it. My mother and aunt have on their Jackie O sunglasses (like the ones they still wear today), but are dressed in drastically different fashions. Auntie Imelda is wearing a bold white dress with crisscrossing blue and orange stripes. The collar is large and strange in that way things from the '70s are. My mother is wearing an elegant blazer made of what appears to be purple velvet. Her skin is wrinkle-free and firm over her face and she purses her lips in a way that is reminiscent of certain movie actresses. Her hands are on my shoulders because I am the perfect height for that. There is a date on the picture, those little clunky yellow scripts in the lower-right corner: August 15, 1986.

I do the math. My mother and aunt are forty-five. I am four.

———————

Thirsty, I complain. Can't breathe. My father doesn't look back at me, just continues picking up trash. Some wadded up paper, an empty pack of Winston Lights, remnants from the workmen he had hired from the classifieds to originally install the insulation. He tosses everything he finds into a bag. Never do good job, he mutters.

———————

Once, a few years ago, while I was home for the holidays, my mother found a short story I had written, entitled "The First Time Brad Li Huang Had Sex with an Asian Girl." It was for a freshman creative writing class. The story contained a few autobiographical elements, which my mother picked up on. She shook her head, concerned. Jem, she said to me, her way of saying my name. *You should write something more romantic.*

This is what I am telling the girl I am seeing casually, here in the city, and she laughs and gets up to change the music to something slower.

Your mother's cute, she says.

Yeah, I say.

And then suddenly I feel serious and tell her how things are going with my father.

Last time I was home, I say, he was completely nuts about everything. My parents were having a new hardwood floor put in and he kept yelling that I clean out my old bedroom and pick out the few things I wanted to keep or he would "take it all to the dump." And how he was yelling the whole time at my mother, it was kind of fucked, I say, leaving out the part about him picking up a shoe and hitting her over the shoulders with it. There are some things I don't want to admit to anyone, these things about me and my family.

That sounds horrible, she says, touching my shoulder. But there must be some OK moments, too, right?

Well sure, I say. But still. I mean, he's never even told me he loves me.

Maybe he's trying?

He took me golfing.

That's something, isn't it?

I don't play golf, I say. I kind of hate golf.

———·———

Up ahead is my father's khakied ass. We are crawling to the next spot, below the dining room. In one hand my father is carrying a half-filled trash bag, in the other a heavy-duty lantern, which is really just a bare bright bulb inside a small metal cage, attached to a handle. The lantern is, as I said, heavy-duty. It requires a direct current and, because of that, an extension cord. I am in the process of crawling ahead when I accidentally yank on the extension cord.

What's going on? demands my father.

Nothing, I say.

Keep eye, he says, his back turned to me as he continues crawling ahead.

What?

Cord! Cord!

Fine, I say.

I follow behind him and behind the cord. As he inches forward, it bounces along after him, like a pet. I follow and we tunnel into the darkness beneath our house.

Earlier that morning. My father, standing in the doorway of my bedroom. Me, still in my bed.

Him: What's going on?!

Me: Almost ready.

Him: Hurry up. Put on clothes. Work, work. Don't have time.

Me: Why? Can't we just hire somebody? Can't they just do it? Why do we have to do it?

A long silence.

Some things, he says, you just have to.

Me: I don't understand.

Him: Nothing to understand! Just do.

Once a month in the city, my extended family and I all go to Chinatown to eat a family dinner. Fifteen of us in the party and almost as many conversations going on at the same time. I watch us in our noisy action: my aunts on my father's side, their husbands, their children—my cousins—who are all my age or older, my one cousin's husband, my other cousin's husband, their kid. I imagine what it would have been like, growing up here, immersed in so much family and motion. It's a feeling of presence, right there in the moment, and also one of absence, of what could have been, but is not. Auntie Imelda, dressed in this gold shimmering and utterly foreign-looking

thing, gesticulating wildly at her calmer, more conservative sister
as that sister's husband smiles absently (I wonder if his hearing aid
is off). I catch every third word or so of their Mandarin. They are
talking about my cousins when they were younger, something about
the foods they would or wouldn't eat. My cousin Alvin is not paying
attention. He is arguing loudly and making fun of my other cousin
Denis.

Look at this guy! cries Alvin. Look at this guy! Come on.

Denis sits there, doing something on his phone. After a long de-
lay, he looks up to find everyone waiting for him to say something. He
smiles stupidly as a way of response. Wha-at? he says, pronouncing it
in two whiny syllables, then goes back to his phone. Denis, it must be
said, is the sad sack of the family, mercilessly picked on and corrected
by Alvin and, really, all of us. It's just too easy. Denis, who is thirty-six
years old, has never had a girlfriend and still lives with his parents. In
the bedroom he has occupied since he was a small child (he went to
college in his hometown and lived at home, even then) Denis hoards
packing supplies and cashes in on free magazine subscriptions for
magazines he has no interest in. Although he doesn't particularly care
for music, he has the phone numbers of several local radio stations
on speed dial, so he can be the whatever caller to win free tickets
to the whatever show. He wins with surprising frequency. On these
occasions he will invite one of his few friends or, once in a while, his
mother. If he can't find someone to go with, he just sells the tickets
on Craigslist. This is what Alvin is mentioning and we all laugh, then
eat some more.

During times like these, I usually just like to watch. Alvin will
try to get me to agree with him on something negative about Denis,
about how he's always "browsing for deals" on his phone while we're
at dinner or needs to shave (occasionally Denis will show up with a
small patch of hair above his lip, not quite a mustache, yet not quite

an accident, either). A lot of the time my aunts, wanting to include me in the grown-ups' conversation, will tell me stories about my father. What he was like as a "kid," by which they mean someone around my age.

You know, Jem, Auntie Imelda says to me while grabbing a piece of roast duck that's just arrived. Your father loves to dance.

Really? I ask, surprised. My father, with his squinted, angry eyes and tucked-in shirts, I cannot imagine on the dance floor.

Yes, yes, she says, chewing and smiling.

Huh, I say. Wow.

He's not bad, she says slowly in Chinese.

Hmm.

He is not bad, she repeats in loud, slow Chinese, as though I had not understood her before. Your father . . . *tiao wu* . . . dance . . . You don't believe me? Ask him to dance for you sometime.

You're kidding, I say. What's his favorite kind to dance to?

Popular music, she says.

You mean like Britney Spears?

Sure, she says. She makes a loud laughing noise.

You can't be serious.

Just ask him, she says, grabbing another piece of duck. You should ask him to dance with you!

No way, I say—and I won't. But by now, I'm laughing too.

———————

Another visit home for the holidays, another scene of work. This time it's Thanksgiving. My father wields a small green chainsaw. He's ripping off the limbs of several large maple trees that he says are too close to our house and I am assisting him, applying pressure with both arms to a particularly large branch so that when it falls, it will not crush him, or me, or the house.

For a moment my father idles the chainsaw and inspects his work.

80

Then he pulls the trigger again and continues. The contrast in sound makes me suddenly conscious of the chainsaw's high racket echoing into other yards of the neighborhood and I wonder what the neighbors must be thinking. Do they know it's us? The story of my life, trying not to have attention drawn to me for the wrong things.

Dad, I say. Don't you think it would be nice to have some peace and quiet on a holiday?

What? he asks. He squints at me and idles the chainsaw, but it still makes a loud noise.

Should we be doing this? On Thanksgiving?

We're almost done.

I suppose I don't really believe I can get him to change or even to stop. But I still ask: Why are we doing this, today?

Some things you just have to, my father says, in a flat, automatic voice. But for a moment he appears to think about what I've said and I wonder if I've gotten through to him.

And then he revs up the chainsaw again and a gust of smoke shoots out the back of the chainsaw and up into the air.

———

Here in San Francisco, people are always surprised to find out that I was born and raised in the South. But you have no accent, they say. I watched a lot of TV, I say, and their reaction usually goes from shocked, to impressed, to sympathetic. What was it like? Were there any other Asian people there? they ask, and I laugh because I like these kinds of questions. If I'm feeling good, I can run with the answers and the conversation descends into cartoony accents, hee-haws and hoedowns. It is a satisfying thing, to make fun of those who make fun of you while they are unable to defend themselves or get angry or become suddenly complicated and human.

Sometimes though, like now, outside this dirty Mission dive, there is a pause and things are different.

So you were born there, a thin girl with blue eye-makeup asks me, suddenly serious. We have been talking intensely in a dark corner booth for the past hour or so, referencing obscure music, movies, and books. In South Carolina? she asks, leaning against the graffitied wall outside.

Yeah, I say.

The girl breathes out an elegant line of smoke and I turn slightly away. And your parents?

They were born in Taiwan.

But wait, she says, making a confused face. How did you end up there? I mean, in South Carolina. Why'd your parents move there? I don't mean to pry.

I don't know, I tell her, and I don't, really. Work, I guess.

The idea of it makes me confused and resentful. It's as if they had chosen South Carolina as some kind of punishment for all of us. There are a lot of other places where they could have gotten jobs— better places, like here. So why there?

Hmm, says the girl.

Yeah, I say, and then: Want to go back inside?

————

The actual answer is, well, it's a little complicated.

When I call my mother the next day to ask her about it, she starts to tell me the story.

Daddy, she slowly begins, as she's slowly begun so many times before. He was in engineering school . . . At Georgia Tech . . .

And I, as I've done so many times before, begin to tune out. Truth is, the way my mother tells stories completely bores me. She cuts out any interesting or surprising details and personal opinions, leaving only the sanitized, vague explanation, the kind of thing you might relate to a child, because you didn't want to scare or excite him too much.

Which is also why I don't like listening—who wants to be talked to

82

like a child? Even children don't like that. More than that, she never acknowledges that maybe I've already heard some of this before, from her, or from someone else.

I mean, I get it. I know I should know these things about her and my father, that in some ways I really ought to and need to know these things about them. That there's only so much time left. And yet I cannot bring myself to actually listen, in order to know. And it's in this way, I realize, perhaps she is at least partially right: I may not be a child, but what I am doing is, indeed, *childish*.

I laugh and I think about calling her, but don't.

Before my father and I continue on into the next area—a narrow corridor linking the dining room to the family room—we take a moment to rest. We sit together, necks hung low, tired from breathing the stale air.

In the bright light of the lantern, my father's face is surprisingly clear. The expressionless cheeks, stub nose, lipless and forever-frowning mouth. The only things we have in common are the thick eyeglasses that we wear at all times and the blind eyes that they are supposed to help, an inheritance for which I curse him almost daily. I am still staring at him like this when he notices and gives me an inquisitive, almost tender look.

Work, he says, half order, half statement of resignation.

When it happens for the first time, I am in middle school. In the hallway between the dining room and guest room. My mother stands watching. My sister is gone, away at college. She hears about it a couple days later when my mother calls her. Not that she has much to say. The whole thing doesn't last very long. He punches me, once, and it doesn't hurt. The blow is harmless and soft, like a little kid's, and we are both embarrassed by that.

Other times when my father gets angry, which are often, I am sitting at the kitchen table with my headphones on. Dinner is being prepared. My parents yelling as I pretend to do my homework. I can hear their shouts over the music and I can see it: the angry shape of my mother's mouth, my father's movements, like a wave. Magazines flapped across the room.

But back to the photos. The next one I pick up is of my father and my aunt Imelda. Imelda, I notice, has strikingly clear and cataract-free eyes. Wearing a sleek black dress she looks oddly, well, *sultry.* My father looks not much older than I am now. A head full of thick black hair on top of his head. On his face, dark black-framed eyeglasses I've never seen him wear before. Startling how similar the glasses look to my own these days. My father is looking at the camera with his chin tilted upwards and his brow furrowed. But it's more playful than threatening: it's youthful.

I cannot tell what the date is, but it looks like 1981, a year before I was born. Which would make my father forty.

I pick up another photograph, this one a Polaroid. It's of my family together in front of a giant church somewhere in Canada. Later research tells me it is St. Joseph's Oratory in Montreal, the largest church in Canada. Because of the lay of the ground–or the tilt of the photographer (that stranger, whoever it was)–the mammoth copper-green dome appears to leaning to the slightly to the left. My family and I are directly in front of the church, posing in its flower-filled garden, perhaps a hundred yards up. Strangely, we all appear to be the same height. Some kind of optical illusion going on. On the right my father is wearing a gray polo shirt and khaki pants. He holds his hands together in front of him, smiling in the way he smiles, which isn't so much a smile, so much as a look of temporary non-aggression. My mother, wearing her usual Jackie O sunglasses, has her lips pulled inward, trying to keep herself from laughing from embarrassment. My sister, also wearing sunglasses (but less glamorous and more practical; function over form, that inherited trait from my father), has her head tilted slightly, as though she had read of this flattering angle in a teen magazine and was now trying it out for the camera. I am on the far left, in cargo shorts, a baggy T-shirt, and a San Francisco Giants baseball cap. Because of what I am wearing, I know that I am in middle school or high school, those in-between ages. Appropriately, I am not smiling.

But maybe it's not teenage angst or rebellion. I'm not wearing my glasses. Maybe I'm just squinting, trying to see into the camera. It is unlikely, but maybe, in the tiny circle that is the lens of the camera, we are being reflected and I am straining to see what we look like to the outside eye.

My father and I move into the crawlspace beneath the kitchen, the final area we are to re-insulate and clean. Again we hear the sound of my shuffling above. The turkey must be about ready by now, but still here we are. In front of us is a tangle of low-hanging wires and a large heating duct that we will be forced to clamber over, hands and knees.

The crawlspace here is the darkest yet. Unlike the areas we cleaned earlier, where bits of daylight had been able to splinter in, here it is completely dark. My father shines his lantern, surveying the concrete perimeter of the room, where halfway fallen-out sheets of insulation hang like great yellow webs.

My father crawls to an area he estimates to be the middle of the room. Here he fastens the lantern to an overhead pipe and suddenly we're able to see, strewn along the ground, piles of soggy, unusable insulation, rusted metal and trash, dead roaches on their backs.

My father crawls towards the largest pile and picks up an old foil-faced insulation board. With a sudden, violent motion, he snaps it in two, cursing in a mix of Mandarin and English, something in between the English word "sick" and the Mandarin term *"si zhen,"* which means "dead person." He is again referring to the workmen he had initially hired from the ad in the paper.

Can't do anything right! he says, then picks up an empty beer can and chucks it in the trash bag he's been dragging around. He curses them again and again, never seeming to realize that perhaps it was his fault to hire them in the first place, or to refuse full payment until he thought the work was satisfactory. The work never was and our family ended up getting sued.

My father is quiet for a moment, even calm. Then he finds another large pile of trash, previously hidden along the wall.

Stupid dumb! he snarls.

I creep over to my side of the crawlspace to make sure I am keeping occupied. In the corner I come across a few large balls of dirty crumpled-up paper. Inside one of the balls there seems to be something stiff–digging around with my wire, I discover a small, half-decomposed mouse. After the initial shock, I examine the body with the wire, prodding it around a little, then poke it into my bag.

Need hand, my father calls out.

Can't, I say. Working.

Hand, hand! he barks. Hand!

Fine, I say in a complaining tone.

I tie up the trash bag and drag it along the ground, inching toward my father as he eyes me contemptuously, and I consider pulling the dead mouse out of the bag and flinging it in his direction.

And then the lantern goes out.

I didn't do it, I start to say. Look, I'm not even close to it. I'm right here.

Don't make me laugh, he says.

Nobody's trying to, I say.

For a moment everything is dark and silent, as if we were no longer there. And then my father takes a deep and noisy breath, the kind of deep breath he takes to try to calm down, or begin to scream.

———

And then it's his retirement party. In the grand reception area of a hotel forty-five minutes away from my parents' house, together with my family and a bunch of people I don't really know, we celebrate my father. Everyone there is Chinese except for one white person, an engineer who had married one of the Taiwanese women (and who I had, once, gotten into a particularly irritating political argument with). Towering ceilings, flutes of champagne, sunlight streaming in from the gigantic windows and the glass dome above. Me, standing. An improvised speech, not entirely different from the wedding toast I will give to my sister and her husband a year or so later. At the end, something I have never said to my father before. *I love you, Dad.* The words feel awkward and new. A couple of people in the audience are crying. These are the people who will come up to me later and shake my hand and say, *What a good speech, Jem,* and I do not care for these people. I do not know where my mother or sister are or what they are doing and I do not really care either. What I want to do is watch my father's reaction. His face flushes a little. He nods.

Good, he says, patting my arm, once.

———

There are times when I wake up from a dreamless night and I look out the window at the fog and hills and houses atop those hills and I wonder where the hell I am. I listen to the ocean against the cliffs and open my window and breathe in salty air.

Other times, while eating with my aunts or sitting on the toilet, I am more certain. I think about events to come. I think about my future as a happy person, I think about what my wife and kids might look like.

Sometimes I think about my father's inevitable death. And I am terrified. It occurs to me that although I probably love my mother more, the person I think about more often is my father. I have not seen him in a couple years. Only a few times have we spoken during this period and it was in grunts and obligations.

And yet I still wonder what I will be thinking about when I hear the news. Last I heard from my mother was that he was OK. But what will happen when I hear that he is not? Which sad scene will I recall? And which will he? In that split second before everything stopped, could he have ever imagined I might still be trying to talk to him?

"Girls on Ice" by Alia Yunis

Alia Yunis is the author of the novel *The Night Counter*. She grew up in the U.S., Greece, and the Middle East, particularly Beirut during its civil war. She has worked as a filmmaker and journalist in several cities, especially Los Angeles. She currently teaches film and television at Zayed University in Abu Dhabi. "Girls on Ice" was originally published in *Guernica*.

I was in the bathroom stall at the Armenian chicken place in Anaheim when I overheard Sarah say to her even more annoying friend Abeer at the mirror, where they were both putting on gobs of makeup, "I'm just going to kill myself, *habibti*, if I don't make the triple axel at the championships next month."

"Yeah," I thought, "I'm going to kill myself if I don't lose twenty-seven pounds next month, you straight-haired, straight-nosed, shallow bitch."

Of course, I didn't lose any weight. I even gained a couple of pounds because I became a vegetarian to save the animals and started eating a lot of hummus and pumpkin seeds. But Sarah killed herself. Which didn't make sense because she landed that triple axel perfectly. Twice. And won the championship.

She won in grand style. From the *LA Times* to all the local TV shows and trendy blogs, she was toted out as the first Arab-American-Palestinian-Muslim-Southern Californian-vegan-left-handed champion skater. I understood where all the Middle East and Southern California labeling was coming from, sometimes with exclamation marks after them–there wasn't a whole lot of ice in either place, and there was no time in Palestine for figure skating, and so many other more logical ways to spend your time in Southern California. And I know Sarah hadn't eaten meat or dairy since seventh grade. However, I'm not sure that Sarah was really left-handed. That was probably a story my aunt made up so she wouldn't be shamed by having a daughter who always stuck out the wrong hand to shake hands.

But you couldn't tell which hand Sarah favored when she waved at bystanders from all the parade floats she was asked to be on, usually wearing a rhinestone tiara, usually speaking on behalf of an organization that helps sick or poor kids and sponsored her last competition. She looked like another perfect young, beautiful, talented, primed-for-TV, all-American girl, which, trust me, is nothing newsworthy in Orange County.

Things changed when the journalists, via touting from all those useless Islamic and Arab civic organizations, discovered her Muslim defect. They loved it. That made her a big underdog story. In return for all the media coverage, she smiled for the cameras when TV reporters asked her questions like, "So is there a particular kind of freedom you feel on the ice as a Muslim female?"

Yesterday, she became the first Muslim-Palestinian-Arab-Southern California-vegan-left-handed champion skater to kill herself. That was the flaw mother lode, which was why there were many news trucks outside our house.

Inside our house, at Sarah's condolences, things like the dishonor, the sorrow, the sin of suicide were all being whispered while my other cousins and I went around serving people Diet Coke and apricot juice. No one was talking about her success on the ice.

I offered Ramzi's mom the lone mango juice on my tray. She wore a *hijab* and had thought Sarah should, too, if she were going to keep dating her son, who was going to Princeton in the fall to be an engineer.

My father had called earlier and said Ramzi was at the men's condolences, which my uncle in Garden Grove was hosting. "How is Ramzi doing?" I asked his mom.

"Why?" she said, afraid. I couldn't tell if she meant why was I asking about Ramzi (I think she was worried of someone else in Sarah's family wanting to date her son, especially another one who didn't wear a *hijab* and was kind of fat for a vegetarian) or if she was asking *the big why*–the "Why had Sarah killed herself?" why.

"She's dead because she knew she and Ramzi would be apart soon, and she couldn't bear the thought of him meeting someone else," I felt like saying. I was just making this up from a Russian novel we were reading at school. I wanted to be able to say something aloud that would make sense, even if it weren't the real why. But Ramzi's mom scampered away before I could give her an answer.

"She was probably slipped those pills by a Muslim hatemonger," I heard one mom tell my mom between two kisses on the cheeks. My mom was crying so much her eyes were shrunk all beady and blood-shot like a pistachio. I hadn't known she felt that much for Sarah.

"Thank you," my mom said to her because there was delusional comfort in knowing Sarah hadn't done this on purpose. "I'll tell my sister you said so."

I went to the bathroom. It was locked so I waited my turn until Ramzi's mom came out. She jumped back, like I had said boo.

"I hope it was clean enough for you," I offered. "I scrubbed it myself this morning. My mom made me. With bleach."

She squeezed herself past my twenty-seven extra pounds, and I went into the bathroom. There was a silver soap dish filled with seashells on the counter from when we all went to San Diego last year for another cousin's wedding, months before Sarah became the first Muslim-Palestinian-Arab-Southern California-vegan-left-handed champion skater. Until almost dawn that night, Sarah was dancing and laughing along with everyone else. Except for one moment. I was hunkered down in a corner so no one could see me downing the half-finished beer my uncle had left at his table when I saw Sarah suddenly stop dancing, just like that–just stood there quietly, face blank, not feeling the rhythm of the music. Then Ramzi tapped her on the shoulder and she turned to him and smiled and started danc-ing again, like a wind-up ballerina does when you open a music box. Until today, I'd almost thought I'd imagined it all.

"Instead of killing herself for nothing, she should have gone to Palestine and killed herself for something," I heard a woman waiting her turn say on the other side of the bathroom door.

Palestine. It always comes back to Palestine in our family. That lady on the other side of the door wasn't being mean and nasty on purpose. Palestine was what had given the past three generations of our family its breath. But somehow it had failed Sarah because she didn't have any breath now.

I wish Sarah had said, in that bathroom at the Armenian chicken place, "I'll just kill myself, *habibti*, if I can't do something to help Palestine." Palestine always needed help, so living to help it could keep you alive forever. That would have been better than any old triple axel, at least that's what our grandfather, who spent more than half his life in an Israeli prison, would have said.

But maybe Palestine could drown you in its sorrow? What if it were Palestine that had made her stop dancing that night in San Diego? Palestine was at least a more noble excuse than my Russian novel explanation.

Sarah and I were born in the same year and we had had almost nothing else in common since then, aside from our relatives and Palestine. But she had never held that against me, like I had held it against her. See, she was nice, on top of it all. That simple, dull word "nice." I wish I hadn't thrown away the gift certificate for the facial she'd gotten me last Christmas after I told her it must be nice to have such a dewy complexion. But I'm glad I'd lied and told her on my birthday, when she got me another one, that I'd used it. She said she could tell, which was obviously an untruth that I wished I'd responded to more gracefully. Maybe by giving her a gift certificate for a foot massage in return, which I'm sure skaters could always use.

Who knows? Then she and I could have become better friends, and she would have whispered to me the reason she had stopped dancing that night, and I would have told her it—whatever it was—

would be all right. Then we could have gone on with life and saved Palestine together. We could have spent the rest of our lives trying, at least.

I flushed the toilet again so no one would hear me cry.

"Up in the Trees" by Courtney Zoffness

Courtney Zoffness won the 2018 Sunday Times EFG Short Story Award. Other honors include the 2017 Arts & Letters Creative Nonfiction Prize, the 2016 American Literary Review Fiction Prize, an Emerging Writer Fellowship from The Center for Fiction and a residency at The MacDowell Colony. Her fiction and nonfiction have published in *The Southern Review, The Rumpus, The Common, Los Angeles Review of Books,* and elsewhere. "Up in The Trees" first appeared in the *Indiana Review.* Zoffness directs the Creative Writing Program at Drew University, and currently lives in Brooklyn.

I can't sleep. My furnished apartment in Freiburg, Germany, has a TV that broadcasts a single channel, in German, and since I'm too tired to read but too wired to rest, I tune in for half an hour. I speak *nicht Deutch*—just a little Yiddish—but can still make out the tail-end of a news program on an Auschwitz survivor, replete with images of rawboned prisoners and the eminent entry gate ("Work shall set you free"); a preview for a film called "Female Agents" in which be-lipsticked vixens gun down unsuspecting Nazis; and the start of a sitcom called "Tel Aviv Rendezvous" in which a guileless guest shows up at a Shabbat dinner with un-kosher wine.

It's six hours earlier in Brooklyn, New York, so I call my husband, to tell him about the triad.

"What is it," he asks, "the atonement channel?"

In the sunniest spot in Germany, rain clouds roll in, discharge, and retreat. It's July, and between short daily storms the sun blazes. One learns quickly in the federal state of Baden-Wurttemberg to travel with protection: sunscreen and sunglasses. A windbreaker and umbrella. Shoes that won't soak through and subsequently squeak throughout the day.

I have a bag packed with such supplies on my mile-long walk to the University of Freiburg, where I instruct an English-language writing seminar. Through the canopy of trees above my head, the sky is intermittently yellow and gray, heartening and menacing. On Günterstalstrasse, the city's main axis, I pass open-faced bakeries, one after the other, whose honey-sweet smell absorbs into my clothes. I am lured in like a bee and because yahoo! I'm in Europe, I order a slice of strawberry rhubarb pie for breakfast and sit at the window and smile unwittingly at passersby.

The view is aggressively adorable: trolleys glide along cobblestone streets amidst buildings the shade and shape of lemon meringue. Narrow water-filled canals, vestiges from the Middle Ages, crisscross alleys and abut sidewalks. It seems every window has a box neatly packed with flowers and everyone, old and young, narrow and wide, rides their bicycle.

I sip espresso and watch folks outside cluster at the crosswalk. I try not to think about how I jaywalked the day before and an elderly man berated me—all consonants and knitted brows. (Reproach requires no translation.) Nor do I dwell on a German friend's supposition that the man said this: "Ordnung muss sein." Order, he'd said, must be maintained.

I let a piece of pie dissolve in my mouth and try to decide if it's more sour or sweet.

It is impossibly both. I note that I should do this more—make a meal of dessert. Perhaps I'll start baking in New York, despite my wee aisle kitchen and temperamental oven. Even though I don't own proper bake ware. Even though I'm not so good at following directions.

Above the rooftops the Black Forest seems to float, a wooded island in the sky.

———

I never expected my 92-year-old Jewish grandmother to sanction my trip to Deutschland. In fact, I held off telling her that I'd accepted a summer teaching post there in part because I didn't want to upset her. Grandma has a brain tumor. She is prone to passing out.

When I finally confessed a week before leaving—at top volume due to her near-deafness—she barely blinked. I assumed she hadn't heard me.

"Germany!" I re-shouted. Nothing. Had I stunned her into silence? Like so many Jews in the Diaspora, my grandmother's family fled pogroms and shed their Ashkenazic surname. She and my late grandfather, who helped build our local synagogue, ensured that I was thoroughly versed in the Holocaust.

"I feel guilty," I offered, hoping to diminish her disappointment—or assuage my fidgety conscience.

Grandma puckered her penciled-on brows and shooed at the air with her hand.

"Forgive and move on," she said. Then she took an uneasy sip of water, a drop of which dribbled down her chin.

———

At the University of Freiburg, where philosopher and Nazi Martin Heidegger rose from professor to chair to rector, my students discuss their short stories-in-progress. Subjects vary from loosely true to admittedly contrived: domestic abuse, amateur sex, Satanism, heartbreak. All have signed up for the class to learn how to write fiction, to learn about plot and structure and endings and beginnings. They want to master language. (Cue Heidegger: "Man acts as though he were the shaper and master of language, while in fact language remains the master of man.")

The students' drafts are raw and rough. Some are over dramatic and don't convince us. To the writer of a knife-throwing protagonist, one classmate gripes, "That wouldn't happen in real life." Other narratives lack tension. "Where's the obstacle?" I press. "What's at stake?"

Most of them hail from the States: Pennsylvania, Nebraska, Texas. A few are German. One's from South Africa.

That afternoon, Nadja, the department assistant, takes the group on a walking tour.

She points out popular beer gardens and cheap restaurants and a cinema that shows English-language films for only four euro. She guides us to the famous Münsterplatz, the center of the city, designed around the mammoth and intricate red sandstone cathedral. We tip our heads back and marvel. Gothic spires pierce the clouds. Gargoyles poise on the edge of the roof as though bracing to jump.

A student who studied the church's construction in art history points out the statues adorning the façade: prophets, saints, demons, imps. She notes that several of them feature "attributes." Like St. Catherine, who holds a wheel, the device with which she was tortured and killed.

At cafés along the periphery, diners schmooze under umbrellas and an accordion player pumps vaguely familiar tunes. Nursery rhymes, maybe. Show tunes? The sky is graying over. Nearby, a guitarist croons Red Hot Chili Peppers and several students, American and German, chime in: "I don't ever wanna feel, like I did that day!"

I tongue the salty sweetness in my teeth.

When Nadja pauses to plot her next move, I ask if we can go see the synagogue.

"The what?"

Temple, I offer. House of worship. Church for Jews. I point to the street sign at the corner: "Platz der Alten Synagoge."

"Oh!" Her face lights up with understanding. Mine does at being understood. Then she shakes her head. "It was burned down." The war, she says. The sign is merely pointing where it used to be.

———

Saturday and cloudless: U.S.-born, German-based Emily takes me on a hike along the Dreisam River. Locals loll in the sunshine.

Women go topless. Kiddies swim nude. All around us, the forest swells skyward, interrupted only by mounds of vineyard.

"Isn't it charming?" says Emily. It's not charming. It's Eden. Ducks bob on the current and egrets wade in the shade. "Here," she says. She's picked a wild raspberry off the vine. Now a blackberry. I swallow. Everything is so goddamn delightful. Isn't there some kind of Biblical story like this? A community that's comfortable, too incautious, and God strikes it down?

We emerge from a tunnel in which someone's graffitied "Fuck the police" and into a cloud of white fluff: seeds drifting on the wind. The hope of a new plant generation.

Emily tells me how the German population is in serious decline, how deaths are outpacing births. There's an incentive, she says, that provides men with a year of paid paternity leave for every child they produce.

"A year?" I shout. She laughs at my enthusiasm. My husband and I plan to have two—maybe three with that kind of offer. "Fully paid?" I fill my lungs. Freiburg. Why not? The rent is so much cheaper. Healthcare and education are practically free. Not to mention that the city's eco-friendly even by Brooklyn bohemian standards: vegetation sprouts from rooftops and solar panels decorate storefronts and farmers markets pitch tents nearly every day. The Green party has a stronghold here.

In the sunlight, the bellies of floating seeds glow like fireflies. We could hike through the Black Forest every day and bike along the Dreisam. My husband, I think, would love it.

On a nearby bench, an elderly woman watches us. She is old—older than the war.

The sight of her fills me with suspicion. Church bells echo through the trees. A duck buries its head in the stream, revealing only its tail and pedaling feet.

Dinner with friends at Oma's Küche, Grandma's Kitchen. I do not think of my own grandma's kitchen, where the menu's exhaustive pork sausage selection (listed in English! I wouldn't even need to know German to get by!) would never be served. Instead I feast on spinach-and cheese-filled crepes and sweet white wine from a local vineyard. Afterwards, we wind our way through the university square, past a clock tower and a Starbucks and a jewelry store with window crystals twinkling just out of reach. It's the weekend of the summer music festival, Schlossbergfest, and as I climb a hill into the edge of the forest, I bump into a few of my students buying shots from a veil-wearing bride-to-be—a tradition, I'm told, that helps new couples pay for their wedding. The Americans love it here. What's not to love? I say.

The festival is packed. Locals and tourists and teenagers and retirees crowd around performances and beer stands, clapping and smoking and shouting to be heard. We push our way through the mob to a paved pathway, which takes us to slightly less congested section in back. On stage, Van Halen lookalikes croon Pink Floyd's "Comfortably Numb." "Germans love American rock," someone says. We stake seats at a wooden picnic table and I seek out beer and though I can't understand what the vendor says through his discolored teeth, but I pretend I do. The stein is twice the size of a stateside mug and I walk extra slowly so as not to disturb the foam.

"So cheap!" I say when I get back.

"No," I'm told, "you got the cute girl discount." When I turn around, the bartender is giving me a thumb's up. "Prost," say my friends. It's too dark for anyone to see me blush.

I am ashamed and proud to know every song the German Van Halens cover: Aerosmith, the Eagles, Creedence Clearwater Revival. After my second stein, I sing them aloud.

Everyone's giddy by the time we tumble down the mountain, past the university, and into the desolate residential streets that are famously safe. (Is it the New Yorker in me that feels threatened by the dark?) The forest is my guide: if I keep it on my right, I'll eventually find my way home. In the full moon, the canopy is impenetrably black and formidable and my shadow overtakes the sidewalk. I note how the air tastes purer and more oxygenated than it does at home, how I'm so used to inhaling exhaust fumes (toxic!), how this town is so inconceivably quiet–no sirens! no honking horns!–how I could live here, I could totally live here, why couldn't I live here?, how I could write and teach and grow tomatoes and get a dog–two dogs!–and send my kids to the international school and there's something shiny on the pave, something glowing, and when I bend down, I see it's a cobblestone-sized plaque, a brass "stumbling block," at the base of a residential driveway.

Here lived Robert Grumbach. Born 1875, arrested, deported to Dachau, then to Gurs. Beside it is a brass memorial for his wife: *Hier wohnte Berta Grumbach.*

I'd read that some residents in victims' homes protested the installment of these Stolpersteine when a German artist first proposed the project in the 1990s. The value of their property would depreciate, they said. And who wants to be reminded of the genocide every time you go in and out of your house? It wasn't the current tenants' fault that certain groups were scapegoated. That the Grumbachs slipped away.

Beyond the metal gate safeguarding the property, two Volkswagens sit head to toe.

There's a figure watching me from in the upstairs window. Or maybe it's just a curtain stirring in the breeze. I rub my heel on the brass to help it shine. I am still humming "Comfortably Numb." I am waiting for the rain.

NONFICTION

"Jodi" by David Bahr

David Bahr is an Associate Professor of English at the Borough
of Manhattan Community College, The City University of New
York. His writing has appeared in *The New York Times, GQ, Poets
& Writers, Publishers Weekly, The Village Voice, Time Out New York, The
Advocate, Out, Boys to Men: Gay Men Write about Growing Up* and *Affective
Disorder and the Writing Life: The Melancholic Muse.* His work has been
cited by *The Best American Essays* and *The Missouri Review,* and he
has been awarded writing fellowships at Yaddo and The Edward
Albee Foundation. A different version of "Jodi" originally appeared
in *Prairie Schooner.*

The last time I saw Jodi was in downtown Manhattan, off Houston Street, during Ronald Reagan's second term.

Through the SoHo crowd, I heard my foster sister call my name.
Still chubby, Jodi stood about five feet tall, with porcelain-white
teeth, a delicate nose, slim hands and small tapered feet. Despite her
weight, her fragile features made her seem young and graceful, like a
plump ballerina half her age. Jodi was 37, unmarried, and had lived
most of her life with her parents, April and Lou. After they moved to
Florida, she remained in Queens, worked temporary receptionist jobs
and watched lots of television; her favorite shows were *All My Children*
and *Soul Train.*

Jodi rushed toward me, her smile wide, clutching a Macy's bag
with one hand, her other arm at a slight crook, finger and thumb
touching, pinky suspended, as if holding a cup of tea. Moving closer,
she glanced at the ground, chewing gum, and chuckled.

"You little shit," she said. "How come I never hear from you?"
Her gum snapped and popped.

I told her how busy I was. School. Work. "It's good to see you," I
said.

Dressed in blue jeans, she was on her way to a job interview.
"Unemployed again," she said. "But I'm tired of working for jerks.

You know?"

I knew. She rarely held her gal Friday gigs long, a source of frequent friction between her and my foster parents. But Jodi had her reasons: the receptionist or filing position was boring, the work demeaning, the boss abusive. *Work isn't supposed to be fun*, Lou would yell. *And what are you going to do for money now?* April would add before Jodi slammed her bedroom door and turned on her stereo.

Jodi was happy to see me that afternoon. She told me about some guy from Europe she was dating and pointed to one of several thin gold bracelets, the sort of the dainty jewelry that she bought and stole for as long as I knew her. "He gave me this." She blushed.

I nodded.

"So what about you?" she asked. "Seeing anybody?"

"Me? Oh no."

Shifting uneasily, I said I had to go and then gave her a kiss. She frowned.

"Call me, you little brat," she shouted as I darted across the street. "I'm listed."

"I will. I will."

I didn't.

It was April who called me a year later.

My foster mother rarely phoned, even on holidays; I knew something was up.

"What's wrong," I said.

Jodi had AIDS.

I sat down.

"She had been sick for a while," April said. Fevers. Strange bruises. No one knew what was wrong.

I took a deep breath.

It had been months since I had spoken with April, years since I'd seen her.

"And we always worried it would be you," she said.

Jodi became my sister when I was two, fresh from the foundling hospital, where my troubled single mother left me six months earlier. It was the year of Jodi's Sweet 16. The party was held in my foster parents' furnished wood-paneled basement. Jodi had her hair teased high, she wore false lashes, her lids were powder blue. Her friends, girls in miniskirts with kohl-lined eyes, passed me from lap to lap, posing for the camera. In one snapshot, my foster sister's straw sombrero rests on my head, nearly covering my eyes, and I suck on a corncob pipe, grinning, my early childhood captured in a moment of photogenic bliss.

When I was five, Jodi took me with her to Main Street, Flushing, to visit her dirty, bearded boyfriend. He worked at a headshop and I remember how she disappeared with him into the back, behind some beaded curtains, while I stared at the black-lit velvet portraits of Jimi Hendrix and Janis Joplin and two thin salesgirls with long straight hair made fat faces and laughed, their teeth glowing like radioactive snow.

I own no photographs of Jodi, only a drawing by her sent to me soon after my mother reclaimed me, five years after she left me at the hospital, convinced that this time things would work out. I'd been in my mother's paint-chipped, one-bedroom apartment in Flatbush, Brooklyn, three months and already truant for two. I spent my days listening to game shows and eating junk food, gazing out the gated window, watching black girls jump rope. At night I heard shouts, sirens, and, once, a shot. I refused to leave the house, was convinced kidnappers were coming to get me.

"I have a stomach ache," I said most mornings, awakening with a slight fever and swollen glands, both usually gone before lunch, a meal which I managed to stretch for several hours, until late noon.

It was during one of those lazy, long days that Jodi's drawing came folded in the mail: a charcoal sketch of a cocker spaniel with huge black pupils and a glistening nose. It resembled less a living animal than a stuffed toy, the sort of shedding, matted thing I'd brought with me to my foster family when I first arrived. Jodi signed it with four big X's and three large O's, *to my little brother, a pair of big brown eyes just like yours.*

I cried when I saw the sketch.

This was before my mother's suicide attempt and my time at the group home, where my foster parents finally found me, five years after I left them, and brought me back to the tree-lined street in Whitestone, Queens, where they and Jodi lived.

"It'll be just like it used to be," April said with a frown. "You'll see."

Decades later, I close my eyes and still remember: I'm thirteen years old, home only a year, sitting on the daybed in the dim-lit basement, knees pressed against my chest, listening to a song coming from my foster sister's nearby room. I'm not sure of the singer. I barely hear the words. But the coda I hum: *Oh Georgie stay, don't go away. Georgie please stay.* I hum and sway and imagine it's about a kid who runs off to New York City. I imagine it's about me. But where will I go? Back to my depressed mother? The group home? All I know is that I must leave: I'm not the boy that April remembers. No longer cute and quiet, I'm bushy haired, pimply, anxious. I run around for hours like a kid on speed, tormenting the dog, making loud farting noises, demanding attention. Or I sulk, quiet and blank, a pre-teen lobotomy. Now a sleepwalker, I try not close my eyes while in bed at night, afraid that my body will rise up against my will and I'll awake in some corner of the house, in a drenching sweat, screaming.

April's welcome has waned. Her excitement has turned into frustration. She flares into rages, bars me from the house when I don't have school, blames my mother for ruining me. My social worker explains that the instability of the last five years has affected me. April listens, eyes plaintive, lips flat as a line. "I don't care," she later tells my foster father. "Normal boys don't behave like that."

But this afternoon it is raining and my foster mother has let me stay in the house. Sunny days, she makes me play outside. She says that's what boys my age do. But all I do is sit on the front stoop, staring at people and cars going by. Sometimes, I hide in the backyard. April knocks on the rear window, opens it, shakes her head, and sighs. "Just gonna sit there doing nothing? On such a beautiful day?" I get up from where I'm crouching and circle the block, then tour the neighborhood. After a few hours, my feet hurt, but I keep going. When I walk, strangers don't regard me curiously the way they do when I sit on the porch doing nothing. Walking, I have somewhere to go.

But today the rain falls furious, pummeling the sidewalk and house. I don't own any books or games or records so I just sit, downstairs in the den, next to Jodi's bedroom, gazing at the television I'm not allowed to watch. Nothing but music and the scent of lavender incense coming from behind Jodi's door. Guitar riffs roll over me and rain taps the small window by the ceiling. A glass record cabinet with April's Sinatra and Streisand, and two shiny vinyl Lazy-Z boys, reflect the fluorescent glare of my foster father's fish tank. I watch the iridescent fish do their aquatic figure eights. And Jodi plays the song a fourth time.

I finally recognize the voice of Rod Stewart and realize he's singing about the murder of a young gay guy, Georgie, by a bunch of New Jersey thugs. Suddenly, I don't like the song so much, and am glad when she turns it off during the final refrain, *Oh, Georgie staaaaay, don't go awaaaay.*

———

"When are you coming?" my foster mother's older, tired voice asked from my answering machine as I stood in the middle of my East Village apartment. Jodi's on medication. She's doing better and would love to see me. Everyone would. It's been a long time.

I again promised myself to book a flight. But for days, weeks, I stared at the phone, unable to pick up the receiver, to actually do it.

Finally, four months after April's first call, I purchased a round-trip ticket to Fort Lauderdale, where Jodi has been living with my foster parents since becoming ill.

April was excited: When was I arriving?

In May.

"Two months?"

It was the best fare I could get. I had classes. I had to notify my job. I had to pack.

Right before Jodi's diagnosis, I'd been doing fine. No more night sweats. No more swollen glands or fevers. I had successfully managed to block out everything concerning AIDS and its now-familiar symptoms. Those first years on my own, during a brief and failed attempt as a waiter in a predominately gay restaurant in Greenwich Village, I heard agitated bits of conversations. *You really have to sleep with over a thousand men to get this. If you don't use drugs, you'll be fine. Just stay away from hustlers. It really only affects Haitians. Pleeease, Reagan's in office! Next year we could all be dead!* I tried to ignore these men—older, lecherous, no doubt with a roster of sexual encounters I couldn't even begin to match. The little sex I did have was cautious, quick, sparked with fear.

Recently I again tried to date someone, an Irish-American guy around my age with a broad, defiant smile.

"I don't understand," he said the last time I slept over his place and he tried to kiss me and I didn't respond. "What's wrong?"

"I got a lot of things going on," I said. "My sister. Work. I'm sorry."

It was the same excuse I had used the previous two nights that

I'd been with him. He let out an exasperated breath and turned on his side. I wanted to place my hand against his back and curl into him with a kiss. But I didn't. My body wouldn't budge, as if I were thirteen again and stuck on the front porch, too frightened to enter the world around me. It had been the same with the last few guys I briefly dated, before I even knew about Jodi.

Instead, I lay there, silent and untouched, estranged from my own skin, watching him drift off, his freckled pale chest facing the wall.

The date of my trip approached; I had trouble sleeping. I imagined Jodi, skin like tree rot pressing against her bones, the air sucked out of her as she slipped from consciousness, unable to dance, barely free to move. I imagined my foster sister twisting her head into a hospital pillow, like the sterile stiff sacks I had at the group home, her sheets threaded with needles, the fever unbearable, freezing, as she blackened out, exhausted, a small patch of raspberry lesions embossed on her thigh. I imagined Jodi and I imagined myself, trapped and alone, in the very same bed.

The night sweats, the swollen glands, the fevers: they all returned. Although I had taken the AIDS test four times, each instance convinced I was dying but always testing negative, I again believed I was infected.

The week I was to leave for Florida, I developed a crushing flu with a temperature of 103. I dragged myself to a clinic, took another AIDS test and, finally, to April's disappointment, canceled my flight.

The next day, my symptoms were gone.

"There But For The Grace of God," by Machine, "Let's All Chant," by the Michael Zager Band, "Get Off," by Foxy, "In The Bush," by Musique. I first heard these songs on those rainy days I camped outside Jodi's closed-off bedroom, when, in the shadowy light, I danced alone, briefly liberated, humping the air to lyrics about screwing, surrender, and salvation. The music was manic, primal, a throbbing syncopation of desire and despair. A few times, Jodi's door opened and she came out and we danced together, like two children imitating grown-ups, a pair of superstars. I'd pretend we were at Studio 54 or Xenon's, places I'd heard about but which Jodi couldn't get into, resigning herself to a club in Queens called *Triangles.*

It was at *Triangles* that she met the muscular Latino guy that she led from her room late one Saturday morning. They did The Hustle just for me, a few side breaks and turns. I was transfixed. His thick thighs flexed within his tight pale jeans and his broad back strained against a small red polo. The way they looked at each other, so intimate and knowing, I knew that they had had sex the previous night and probably that morning. I envied my foster sister. But Jodi beamed at me, giggling in his arms and rolling her eyes, as if she too couldn't believe her luck.

My senior year in high school, I found a part-time job at a local dry cleaners and was given a small role in a in a school production of *Carnival.* I no longer had to roam the streets alone. I hung out with my cast mates at school or in their homes, a reserved, observant teenager, not quite belonging but no longer an exile. We listened to show tunes while surrounded by posters of *Tommy, Hair,* and *Funny Girl.* Parents offered me soda and snacks, and from one dad, a hit off a joint. I returned to my foster parents' house to sleep and said little to April or Lou. We all knew that I had ceased to be a part of the family and no one pretended. I was on my own. Free. After graduating high school, I would be moving into the Manhattan, to become an actor, I informed everyone. Lou nodded. April said nothing, unable to look me in the face.

While I mapped out my future, Jodi hung out with our next-door neighbor, a girl of seventeen. April was not pleased. *What are you doing with a girl almost half your age?* she would yell. One afternoon, I returned from a cast member's house and saw Jodi hanging out of our neighbor's second-floor window, laughing and flirting with several young guys on the street. *Hey*, Jodi cooed, waving to a guy in his early twenties as Foreigner's "Hot Blooded" blared from the room. I was embarrassed. She was thirty-two and pals with a bunch of teenagers. I was tall and lean in my Jordache Jeans and Members Only jacket. It'd been months since I hid in the backyard or strolled the streets. I had big plans. I had saved a thousand dollars and would soon leave this family, strangers to me now.

A few weeks after my canceled flight, April called again. She no longer asked when I would be arriving, which, to my surprise, made me sad. Our conversation was short. Jodi was deteriorating. In three weeks, she would be dead. And I would fail to make her funeral. Few people had.

April wondered if I were acting anymore.

That didn't pan out, I explained. I didn't say I was temping–filing, answering phones–doing the sort of work Jodi once did. "I'm in college."

"That's right."

I told her the courses I was taking. Shakespeare. Virginia Woolf. I made dean's list again.

"It's been so long," she said. "What do you need for that, a B average?"

"I'm an A student."

"Jodi was an honor student, weren't you?" she said, her voice drifting from the receiver.

But I knew: Jodi had attended only a single semester of college, to take an art studio class, not enough credits to qualify for honors. She'd earned a B.

The night I learned that Jodi died, I went to a nearby gay bar, and I stood against the wall, hidden in shadows, away from everyone. "Last Dance" by Donna Summer played. For a moment I was sure that that was the song that Jodi and the Latino guy had Hustled to, so easily and with such openness, so fucking free, although now the connection seems too obvious to be true. Still, I can see his muscular chest against her back, his tan arms across her stomach, sheltering her. He glances at me, holding my stare, his pupils dark and inscrutable, and he presses his full lips to her neck. Jodi smiles. She is so happy that the sorrow within her eyes is amplified, the sorrow of a someone who never had a steady boyfriend or friends her age or the thin body to match the fine prettiness of her face. She looks up at him and then at me. *Can you believe my luck?* The music swells, defiant and hungry, fueled by loss, and I can feel his large hands pull her closer, his crotch against the base of her spine and I'm so jealous and ashamed I can barely breathe.

"Past Burying" by Aaron Barlow

Aaron Barlow teaches English at New York City College of Technology (CUNY). From 2012 to 2018, he was Faculty Editor of *Academe,* the magazine of the American Association of University Professors. He publishes on film, popular culture, new media and science fiction.

Sometime during the spring or summer of 1988 I buried the ashes of Ethel Clift beside the graves of her two sons, one of whom was the actor Montgomery Clift. I did it alone, using a post-hole digger. Rumor had it that the ashes of her older son, William, had been buried in a World War II artillery shell when he had died a couple of years earlier, scandalizing the Quakers whose cemetery it was. I never confirmed that, being generally too drunk at the time. Perhaps for the same reason, I don't remember what Ethel was buried in.

I don't really remember, either, exactly when I worked in the cemetery, some twenty acres hidden inside a fence in Prospect Park in Brooklyn. I know I left before 8/8/88, a hard date to forget and my first day in Peace Corps. And I know I started after Friday the 13th of May, the day I defended my doctoral dissertation. The time between is something of a blur, my only clear memory being the cemetery and its tottering headstones.

The cemetery was my oasis. That may seem odd to you, especially since I spent a great deal of my time there as an onlooker to tragedy. That summer, you may recall, was one of daily AIDS death in New York. For the Quakers, with their high gay concentration, even more so. I don't know how many times I escorted a man who had arrived alone clutching a plastic or paper bag up the slope from the gate to where the gravel road divides around the steep central hill of the graveyard. Me, with a shovel and a post-hole digger and a map of available sites and he with the remains of a life and a relationship. We, walking through the trees and bushes, seeking a spot, a finality that is almost impossible to find, there or anywhere else. I hated it: When most people die, there is a burial ceremony. Family arrive, and friends. But the relatives of gay men, in those days, commonly refused them—and many of their friends were already gone.

My memories of those burials mainly consists of a composite image of a man leaning his head against his arm against a tree, sobbing while I, as quietly as possible, dig as neat a hole as I possibly can. Once I am done, he gently removes an urn from his bag and lower it in. Sometimes, but not nearly always, he wants to fill in the hole by himself.

When I wasn't burying ashes, or mowing or trimming, I spent most of my time recovering headstones. Because the cemetery was unusually hilly, uneven most everywhere there were graves, the stones were more likely to slide and fall than in a nice, flat graveyard. There were areas where all of the stones seemed to have disappeared, but I found them, generally under a couple of inches of grass-covered soil or beneath dirt and debris. I would clean them up where they lay and, after establishing exactly where they belonged, I would set them back upright. I would also straighten tilted ones, and there were plenty of those. I became intimate with the stones: even the straight ones needed to be clipped around by hand, every other mowing or so.

I think I worked from about eight until four each day, heading back to the house where I was staying—my parents' house—to get drunk and pass out until I got up to go back to the cemetery. I wasn't happy, and blamed it on being back in America. I had only returned to finish my PhD. Until July of the previous year, I had been living in Africa, having spent a year and then a renewal as a Fulbright Fellow at the University of Ouagadougou in Burkina Faso. That's an almost unknown landlocked country just below the Sahara Desert. Though I had been a drunk for almost twenty years, it was there I could indulge with greatest ease, the privilege of the expat. As I really liked Africa, too, I couldn't wait to get back.

Peace Corps had offered me a place as an animal-traction Volunteer (I would work with farmers, teaching them to use oxen for plowing) in Togo, the country just south of Burkina Faso. I knew I would be able to be posted in the far north, close to my old country and far from the clutches of 'Mama Peace Corps,' allowing me to drink in relatively familiar surroundings, and in peace.

But I had to get through the three remaining months in the States.

The past year in North America had been difficult. Yes, I had managed to complete my dissertation. It was on the science-fiction writer Philip K. Dick. He really should be named the patron saint of bewildered substance abusers. He got me through that winter, at least. But it cost me. I was drinking a case or more a day of "light" beer as I wrote. Once too drunk each evening to continue writing, I spent the remainder of my waking hours alienating the few acquaintances who were still willing to tolerate me. I took a job working for friends in their head shop, a throwback to the sixties where one could buy "smoking" supplies and underground comix, but bailed without telling them. My housemate was a very nice poet in the Iowa Writers Workshop, but I saw her rarely, having, I suspect, freaked her out. In the house, I stuck to my little room—the only one on the second floor. I ruined a research fellowship project and ended up leaving Iowa City months before my defense, running for my life. I snuck back that May but left without seeing anyone but my committee.

In Brooklyn, having had to land somewhere for the months before Peace Corps, I learned from my mother that the man running the cemetery was leaving for some months, at least. So, I asked the Quaker administrator if I could replace the custodian, needing something to do but drink all the time (though I didn't tell her that). I had plenty of yard-crew experience, so got the job.

It's been some years, now, since I've been in the cemetery. Though I am back in Brooklyn, I've parted ways with the Quakers and, though both of my parents and an uncle are buried there, I have little interest in braving Friendly disapproval on my way to getting through the gate. Sometimes, however, I do think of doing what Montgomery Clift fans did, every once in a while, while I was working in the cemetery. He, his brother and mother, are buried near the outer fence. His grave, if you know where to look, can be seen from the other side. Occasionally, I would see someone peering through, trying to identify his grave. I imagine walking up the hill to that spot, holding onto the chain link with my fingers, and staring in toward the grave I once dug.

"Memory Lapse" by Maurice Emerson Decaul

Maurice Decaul is a former Marine, a poet, essayist, and playwright, whose writing has been featured in *The New York Times, The Daily Beast, Sierra Magazine, Epiphany, Callaloo, Narrative* and others. His poems have been translated into French and Arabic and his theatrical works, *Holding it Down* and *Sleep Song*, collaborations with composer Vijay Iyer and poet Mike Ladd, have been produced and performed at New York City's Harlem Stage, Washington DC's Atlas Intersections Festival, in Paris and in Antwerp. His play, *Dijla Wal Furat, Between the Tigris and the Euphrates*, was produced in New York City by Poetic Theater Productions.

A while ago, I was going through my files when I came across a cache of partly crumbled photographs. One was of me holding the sight box for the M252 mortar in Garden City, N.Y., parking lot. In another, I sat with Oum in the open hatch of a UH-1W at Camp White Horse, outside Nasiriyah, Iraq. There was another of me and the guys at the 2003 Marine Corps birthday ball. I looked like a boy in those photos. At the bottom of the stack I found one photo of us standing with First Sgt. Allen. I was wearing a set of borrowed Alphas; she wore a black evening gown, First Sergeant stood adorned in dress blues, everyone was smiling, teeth shining. I stared at it and whispered to myself, "very different times."

I'd forgotten about these photos, until one night when I was at her house searching a shoebox and I came across the mangled photo album that had stored them for years. They were all there, near the letters we had sent each other while I was overseas. The photographs were wrinkled, crushed and forgotten like the discarded notions that had once been the impetus for "us." Very soon after, a sentiment of resentment splashed with a bit of melancholy began to rise within me so I gathered them and took them when I left.

The parking lot photo showed me standing gaunt and blank wearing woodland camouflage the afternoon I left Garden City for Camp Lejeune to prepare to go to Iraq. This was a picture of a young man who was anxious about war but too indoctrinated to acknowledge it. My photo was taken by the woman whom I had married months before, certain that we would grow old together. The day she took my photo she had worn indigo sweatpants, a canary yellow hooded sweatshirt and plain white Converses. Her hair only lightly grazed her shoulders. As I looked at myself in the photo, I began to remember that as the bus departed Garden City that evening, what she had been wearing that day would become my singular unaided recollection of her. From then, I would need a photograph to remind me of the contours of her face. I was puzzled why but time was too precious then to ponder such things. So I let the question slip, promising myself to ask again at another juncture.

II.

I had forgotten her facial features as soon as the bus started rolling. As much as I tried to recall her face, it was as if I had never stored it in the infinite expanse of my long-term memory. But this of course is not true. I recall her face with ease now and I would describe it as round, with high cheekbones and eyes brown and intensely intelligent. She was then and is now quite beautiful. But the evening I left, remembering such details became an exercise in both frustration and futility.

As I began thinking about the answer to my question, I thought that it would be helpful to first define what memory is, so I consulted a text for an answer.

According to "Psychology," a textbook by Schacter, Gilbert and Wegner, "memories are the residue of [those] events, the enduring changes that experience makes in our brains and leaves behind when it passes." According to the authors, "if an experience passes without leaving a trace, it might just as well not have happened." In a sense, our memories define who we become.

Socrates describes memory "as a block of wax":
Let us say that the tablet is a gift of memory, the mother of the muses; and that when we wish to remember anything which we have seen, or heard, or thought in our own minds, we hold the wax to the perceptions and thoughts, and in the material receive the impressions of them as from the seal of a ring; and that we remember and know what is imprinted as long as the image lasts; but when the image is effaced, or cannot be taken, then we forget and do not know.

While Aristotle, speaking on memory and recollection, notes:
It is obvious, then, that memory belongs to that part of the souls to which imagination belongs; all things which are imaginable are essentially objects of memory and those which necessarily involve imagination are objects of memory incidentally. The lasting state of which we call memory- as a kind of picture; for the stimulus produced impresses a sort of likeness of the percept, just as when men seal with signet rings.

Hence in some people, through disability or age, memory does not occur even under a strong stimulus, as though the stimulus or seal were applied to running water; while in others owing detrition like that of old walls in buildings, or to the hardness of the receiving surface, the impression does not penetrate. … We must regard the mental picture within us as both an object of contemplation in itself and as a mental picture of something else.

But we did have experiences that left behind traces that I could recall easily. The trip we took around lower Manhattan on the Circle Line. The day we were married. Us walking to the subway to take the No. 2 train the afternoon of the West Indian Day parade in 2002. These were all pleasant days that come to mind without any retrieval cues and I believe that the idea of a pleasant day has much to do with why it was so difficult for me to remember her face that other day.

State dependent retrieval is defined by Schacter, Gilbert and Wegner as the tendency for information to be better recalled when the person is in the same state during encoding and retrieval, or more simply when I tried to retrieve an image of her face from that day filled with uncertainty and angst, I found it hard to do so because for the most part, my most vivid memories of her face up until that point included some sort of cheerful experience. Certainly, that day my state of mind, and I suppose hers too, was not the same as the day we were married. Still eight years since, even as our relationship and marriage have collapsed, I find it hard to remember more than what she wore for my grand send off and maybe it is O.K. that that day an image of her face was not imprinted on my block of wax.

III.

After the initial weeks of settling into Nasiriyah, the sergeants had devised a structure for the platoon's day-to-day operations. One day of guard. One day spent patrolling. The third day spent as quick reaction force, aka, the rest day. This cycle was repeated until the morning that we left Iraq for Kuwait. That morning, Frank Sinatra's "New York, New York" streamed from our Humvees, moving us along like running cadence. That morning I smelled the smoke from our burn pit which rose from the desert like a date palm, for the final time and saw the men of the Italian carabinieri sitting in front of the compound without cover but not without cheerfulness. We waved to each other and I wondered how they would manage the monotony and defend against complacency.

Routines have a way of creating the impression of security. But in

Nasiriyah one had to be hypervigilant. One's weapon had to remain serviced and accessible. One never left the compound without a helmet or an interceptor vest or an interpreter. One stayed on edge awaiting that rare skirmish.

To relieve stress and pass time we would often pontificate about how different life would be once we returned home. For inspiration most of us relied on pictures of wives or girlfriends to ignite recollections or to stimulate dreaming. I taped the picture of her I'd fished from my cargo pocket in Garden City to the roof of my Kevlar and over the months my sweat and the sun's rays quickened its fading. The morning that we left Nasiriyah, I shared this photo with an Italian who shared with me his talisman, a picture of his small daughter. He asked whether I had children and I said no, but we still joked about how in the future my son would marry his daughter.

There was scuttlebutt about Britain's Royal Marines habitually burning all traces of home before going into combat and I remember thinking how stoic of them, but I could never bring myself to do it. I correlated her fading image with my tenuous conception of home. I wanted to get home; therefore I wanted to get to her. The photo was my talisman. I sealed it inside a Ziploc bag to stave off continued deterioration and there it stayed until I lost it.

In October I saw on the news that a suicide bombing had occurred in Nasiriyah, not far from where we had been relieved by the Italians, and that the bombing had killed more than a dozen of them. Maybe the Brits had it right all along. What good is sentimentality in the face of circumstance? I had not learned that Italian's name but that night I got on my knees and prayed for all of them and for him and his family. I haven't spoken with God in a while but I truly hope that he heard that prayer.

IV.

The problem with writing from memory is the problem of truth.

There is a concern when writing nonfiction, autobiography, memoir etc...about truth and relating truth to one's readers. Truth, of course, is paramount. The reader expects it and it is the writer's obligation to remain truthful to experience and memory but this notion of truth is not truth with a capital T. It can never be.

In fact, the notion of what is true will be colored by the author's experience, perception of that experience, his biases and his own fading memories. Stories regardless of genre should be read with these parameters in mind. A piece of nonfiction can never be truly devoid of untruths. What is important is the author's intention to relate the facts as he truthfully recalls them and the readers' acceptance of the limitation imposed by nonfiction. Because our memories define who we become, when writing from memory subjectivity though not ideal will color the writing. How one perceives the self will undoubtedly inform how introspective a piece of writing culled from traces of experiences will be.

V.

Several days ago we sat at a diner to talk a few things over and she looked at me squarely and asked, "Did we not have good times?" As I spread jam on my toast, I thought back to the day we took the Circle Line, how at ease she had looked. I thought to myself, "Yes, sometimes." When the bill came she insisted on paying her share, then we went our own ways.

The next day, I bent to scrub soap scum from my bathtub, half kneeling, half praying. I wanted to inter the unshaven face I regarded in the mirror. I turned the tap and water splattered about the sink and a few drops splashed haphazardly into the cup I was holding. Off. Water from the cup rinsing the loosened soap scum was an earsplitting contrast to life's insufferable silence. If I succumb to the stillness, I thought... but there is not a soul to talk to in the house except, me.

It was late and the day had slipped unhurriedly by. I walked back into my bedroom and looked down at the chaos of papers and photos strewn across my bed and decided it was time to put it all away.

"Best of Both Worlds" by Sunita George

Sunita George is an Associate Professor of Geography at Western Illinois University. She enjoys travelling, gardening and drinking tea. Lately she has been working on developing her creative side, and has promised herself that she would take up her childhood passion for sketching, and non-academic writing. She loves teaching, and is passionate about gender issues, particularly as it relates to preventing violence against women.

One of my earliest childhood memories is that of my sister holding my mother's watch to her ear. She may have been about five years old and I, four. She was obviously very excited about her discovery: that time had a voice, and that the voice said, "tick, tock, tick, tock." She pressed the watch to my ear. I listened, hopefully. Nothing. I pressed harder. Nothing. I tried the other ear. Again, nothing. My sister snatched the watch back and pressed it to her ear one more time. It spoke to her again reassuringly, its steady rhythmic voice, tick-ticking away. The next iteration of the experiment was carried out on me, but the results did not change. I imagine it was one of those "whatever" moments—soon forgotten, revisited much later, and only sometimes, when things start falling into place, and the "whatever" moments wrap themselves around full circle to become the "Aha, that was it" moments.

To have partial hearing loss is to live in the margins. In this twilight zone, perfect hearing in some frequencies gives way to reduced or complete loss of hearing in other frequencies of sound. This oscillation between hearing and not hearing is a world that people with normal hearing may not understand in practical terms. "Are you deaf?" is a question that is asked rudely to people like me, the exasperation in the tone suggesting, "I know you are not really deaf. So, quit acting like an idiot." To straddle both worlds—the world of hearing and the world of not hearing—from the margins as smoothly as possible, without having to ask, "what did you say?" repeatedly, elaborate schemes are sometimes hatched that are variously called on when need arises. It is a constructed world put together from fragments of conversations, facial expressions and lip reading, where context is key to understanding what is said, but only partially heard. It is a world of guessed inferences many times.

In the India of my context, dichotomy ruled the day–Good/bad; night/day; sweet/sour; bland/fiery; deaf/not deaf. It was a culture that was not comfortable with the margins. There were no annual hearing exams when I was child. The "mother knows best" approach was the primary yardstick used to gauge hearing (and many other things). If a baby did not flinch when an air horn was tooted near its ear then the verdict was deaf, and, all else, not deaf. The "in-be-tweens" like me were the invisibles that did not fit well in this binary world. I was in a limbo zone; I was hearing, but not hearing, which was translated as, "You are not listening!" I remember, much later, when I suggested I could not hear certain things, and certain people's speech well, I was told, "Children only hear what they want to hear. There is nothing wrong with you." An early effort by me to explain my predicament was met with ironic deafness to my plight by the well-hearing majority.

A central part of what connects us, one to the other, is hearing. I listen, I interpret, I reply, and so on, like a ball bouncing back and forth. The play of words and meanings need movement. If one play-er holds on to the ball to examine it, the game loses its gameness, and the players lose interest. Without hearing, speech may just be gibber-ish. Hearing is what keeps the ball rolling, and when the ball does not roll smoothly there is judgment many times. How did I figure out I was holding the ball too long? Were the failing grades in the spell-ing tests I took in elementary school an indication? I like to think it was. I had a spelling test phobia. At my school we were never given a shortlist of words we needed to know for the spelling tests. We were told only, "You have a spelling test from chapter X on day Y." It was up to you (or your parents) to figure out the strategy. The smart ones could read the clues–a word like "conscience" was definitely going to be there on the test–and they did very well. I did not have a strategy; I had an excuse, and my parents had a philosophy: children should figure out their own learning strategy. The combined effect of my excuse and their philosophy proved to be lethal to my spelling grades. The teacher would call out the words a couple of times, and we were to write the spelling down. The word would not be used in a sentence, so good luck to you if you were depending on the context to guess what the word was in order to guess what it's spelling could be!

I failed each and every one of those tests. The consonant sounds of s, f, and z were particularly hard to hear. So, when the teacher called out, "sleep", I would write down "leap," or worse, "leep"; "fast" could be inferred as "asked," and so on.

Labeling our ailments can move us from the margins to the lime-light. And if it is a label that is certified by medical science, then, you had arrived. My hearing loss was my own problem until then. It was a dirty little secret that was not acknowledged, and it suffered from an identity crisis. "Name me! Name me!" it cried out. At twenty-three, I finally got a hearing test.

I was accepted to graduate school in the United States. This was a big deal in my circle of family and friends. New beginnings often start with checklists: get all documents in order ☑; visit family and friends to say goodbye ☑; read up all you can about life in the U.S. from Newsweek and Time Magazine at the American Consulate library ☑; Shop for new clothes and shoes ☑; Miscellaneous. At the bottom of the list, in the low priority category of "miscellaneous," was the hearing test. I think it was my mother who suggested that I go for a hearing test, "just to make sure that nothing was wrong." And so we went. The tests confirmed what I already knew–Acute

High Frequency Hearing loss in both ears. It was recommended that I use hearing aids for both ears. While I felt vindicated, I had a panic attack for an entirely different reason. What would it do to my appearance was all I could think of–image was central to my universe then. Visions of me in a bright colored "bib" with a big clunky hearing aid tucked into it, and white wires running across my chest to my ears from the aid, proclaiming to the world of my hearing inadequacies gave me the creeps.

As a child growing up in India, I had seen (and I think they still exist) schools with names such as "St. Bede's School for the Deaf and Dumb." The archaic use of "dumb" to refer to hearing impaired mute children was common practice in much of India at that time. The children in these schools were required to wear colorful "bibs" to make known to the world that they were hard of hearing. "The bib" was the "white cane stick" of the hearing impaired children. It was meant to identify them, and to alert the well hearing masses to their handicap, and prompt them to act appropriately. There was no way I was going to abide by the label "dumb" and assert my deafness. Luckily for me, time was on my side. I had to leave for the U.S. in less than week after my hearing test, and there was no way I was going to be fitted with a hearing aid by then.

And so, I landed in the land of opportunities, eager and ready. The new context presented new problems, and prospects. My immediate problems were twofold: to understand and be understood. The accents of the "new world"–the southern drawl, the Yankee accent, and other accents that I had never heard before–threw my old frameworks of making sense into complete disarray. The body language was new also–lip-reading the almost lipless mouths of many white folks was awkward. The deadpan mumblers, whose expressionless faces, thin lips, and speech in frequencies that were inaudible to my ear was my new communications nightmare. The usual challenges of graduate school were compounded by my hearing impairment. In my first semester, I had signed up for a seminar class in which students were expected to critically read assigned materials, and engage in meaningful discussions. I remember being in that class feeling like I was watching a foreign language movie without captions—all emotions and gestures, almost comical. What I got out of some of these discussions were certain words, phrases, and some sentences. I would then toil to extract coherent meaning to what I knew I had heard within the given context.

As part of my assistantship duties as a graduate assistant, I was assigned to teach a lab course in physical geography. Unlike seminar classes, where I could always remain quiet with the "no comment attitude" in the classroom, I was thrust into center stage, and had to perform. I had to engage in the "ball game" again—teach, ask, react, respond, answer. When student's asked questions, I would often ask them to repeat it several times before I could understand what they were saying. "Oh! never mind" some would say in irritation, while other students would snigger. While I could infer sarcasm of certain comments from the body language and tone, the details of what exactly was said was often not heard in their entirety. The beauty of the margins is that it affords ambiguity in meanings, and offers you a choice of meanings and intentions. Dulled hearing suspends judgment. I see it as a benign force that has sheltered me from insults and slights, whether deliberate or otherwise. The default setting in my mind when I haven't heard something properly is, "Maybe I didn't hear it right" or "that may not be what they meant." In the margins there is room for accommodation, there is room for reinterpretation, and so, a safe sanctuary from ugly words and intentions.

As a teaching assistant I was always anxious about the end of the semester student evaluations of my teaching effectiveness. A recurring theme in these evaluations was "instructor can't understand

English." Given that I was a foreigner, deficiency in English was interpreted as the plausible cause for my teaching inadequacies. This assessment bothered me deeply, because I knew it to be untrue. Yet, I never thought to acknowledge my hearing problems. The power of habit in conditioning our thinking is so compelling so as to render simple alternatives unimaginable. Why was I so secretive about my hearing impairment? Was it vanity or why it something else, I do not quite know. But, when the comments became a staple in my evaluations, I changed tactics.

In my final years in the graduate program, I was assigned to teach large independent classes with nearly two hundred students. I decided to come out of the closet then. In the introductory first class period, I said, "I am hard of hearing. I read lips, so I might come up to you to take a closer look. If I ask you to repeat what you said, it is not because I don't know English." I felt free. I felt liberated. The "don't know English" comments never happened again, but more importantly, I learnt that having a handicap was not the same as staying handicapped because of it.

Over the years, after I graduated and found a job, I continued to navigate my world through the same methods of lip reading, guessing and context. What would it be like to hear normally? I have always thought that I was robbed of all the best conversations, jokes, and connections people make through deep communications. I decided, finally, to find out. It was a bright, sunny July morning when I went for a hearing test at the Speech Language and Hearing Clinic at the university where I now work. A cheery student clinician, who seemed impressed to know that I was a professor at the university, administered the test. She was, however, not so impressed with the results of my test. She looked perplexed, as if wondering how I had managed to get this far without hearing aids. Once again, the test confirmed what I already knew, and binaural hearing aids were recommended. This time I followed through with their recommendation.

At my hearing aid fitting appointment, the audiologist did what is called Real Ear Measures, which allowed her to program my hearing aid to ensure that I was getting the appropriate amount of amplification I needed. Amanda, the audiologist, warned me that it could be disconcerting to hearing certain frequencies I may not have heard in a very long time. At some point, I heard so many things all at once, and I found it hard to focus. There was this really loud sound that grated on my ears. I snapped, "What is that?" and Amanda said, "What?" "That sound" I said. "Oh! That's just paper noise," she said, pointing to a group of students working on something nearby. I did not realize crumpling papers, and turning pages could be so annoying to the ear. The world was certainly a loud place, it seems. I requested that the volume be turned down. I wanted a more gradual entry from the margins to full hearing. I had imagined, rather naively, that hearing normally would be a glorious thing, an instantaneous miracle that would magically alter my world, and improve my relationships. Instead, I found that I was a bit shaken by the experience. "My God! How do these normal people focus with all this noise?" is what I kept thinking. After adjustments were made, and I felt workably comfortable with the amplification levels, Amanda proceeded to bring two boxes of Starkey hearing aids. It was nothing like the "bib and white wires" thing I was afraid of. It looked small, and unobtrusive. One of the aids was a pale pinkish white color, and the other was Mauve. Amanda explained that they were "designed to blend with your skin tone." It didn't exactly "blend" into my dark brown skin tone, but I chose the girlish mauve color because it matched my nail polish!

It has now been two years since I started wearing the hearing aids. Emerging from the margins, I felt like a toddler beginning to walk–thrilled by the prospect of exploration, but challenged by the newness of the skill. I floundered at discerning what sounds to focus on, and what to tune out. The first couple of months with the hearing aids made me very irritable, and gave me constant headaches. But I kept it up, and slowly I grew accustomed to it. I found class discussions less of a guessing game; I was hearing TV programs without having captions on, and at social gatherings where I was once shy to jump into discussions because I did not trust my hearing, I now felt more confident, and so life improved in small tangible ways. Yet, like a faithful companion who sees you through hard times, I carved for the old ways of the margins. I felt like a *nouveau riche* person, acquiring exhilarating experiences, and participating in a social class that was not my own. Inexplicably, I longed for the solitude that deafness provided me—the forced quietude that made inward reflection easy.

The other day my five-year-old son came running up to me, and said, "Mommy, I wish I was deaf like you."

"Now, why would you want that?" I asked.

"When Macie starts her singing, I can turn off the switch in my hearing aid," he replied. The margin is a place of comfort for me. After long days at work, teaching, conferencing, attending meetings, and trying to mediate truces between my constantly bickering, two wonderful kids at home, I long for quietness from the mundane, and I know that mine is only a switch away! When I put by hearing aid back into its case, I feel safe, cocooned, and at rest. A storm may be brewing all around me, and I hear but a dulled, subdued version of it. And I heave a sigh of relief, and rest. It is the best of both worlds. Indeed.

"Twelve Days" by Camille Goodison

Camille Goodison is an associate professor at New York City College of Technology at the City University of New York, and the author of *Chance Wanderer and Other Tales of Hunger.* "Twelve Days" first appeared in *Relief Journal.*

June 23

K meets me at the airport, and I greet him with a kiss on both cheeks. He returned to Athens, a year ago, after we separated. Back in New York I still see friends we have in common, and they always appear to me as if they were seeing a ghost. His friends, who'd become my friends, in the several years we'd been together, show signs of mild panic when they see me without him. Because I am pleasant during those meetings, these friendships remain semi-intact, with never a mention of the elephant in the room. The one exception was Markos, who literally scratched his head when he said, "You guys were so close!" Of all K's friends, Markos was, to me, the most dear. I hired him as my language teacher, and he took to his role. He took delight in me, and was both gentle and firm. I placed my confidence in him, as I had a lot to confide in those early days of love. He'd say something wry or pithy, and it was sufficient for me to laugh off my concerns. Today at the airport, I told K about the memorial, and that I left almost immediately. The scene felt unreal. Markos can never be still. This was K and I's first time seeing each other since last year. After hearing about Markos, I swallowed my pride, and reached out in hope. I invited myself to Greece, and before I left, I mentioned what I had in mind. We arrive at K's house, and he tells me his mother has cooked up a storm; and really, she couldn't be more kind. She tells K she doesn't think I should travel alone, and although I have my own doubts, I decide it's better this way. Whatever my ideas before leaving, I realize this was best. We plan my itinerary, before I decamp to K's old childhood room, where a figurine of a boy at prayer is defaced with his scratchitti. I ask him about this, and he surprises me by thinking it over, and giving an earnest answer about what it was like returning from his first freshman year in college in the states, back to this place. He reminds me of what I need to pack in the morning. I tell him I'll be fine, and he nods.

June 24

The bouzouki player's name is Anastasis, and it is he I first hear as I enter the inn. Totally unbelievable, I'm thinking, me, here in the mountains with this young bouzouksis[1] playing rebetika[2]. So it is, eh, I say to him, and he says, I do my own thing. I'm here to see the monastery, I tell him, and need a room. Have you got anything? I take the first thing he shows me. I figure sometimes having a choice is more trouble than having none at all and so I pretend this is all there is and sign in. Not too bad. There's a slip of a terrace, some fine old-timey wooden furniture, and a mini-bar.

Before dinner, I plan on heading hillside to watch the sunset; so, I scrub my face, change my shirt, and head out on foot. Mentally replaying Anastasis's plucky rebetiko, I walk along the narrow village streets aware of the curious glances. Ya, I would say with a big smile if someone seemed particularly curious, and they'd shyly look away. By happenstance I walk right into the town's center after I make some turns through the main alley and past some old abandoned houses with far-gone roofs. And what a ruckus. Speaking of luck, all the village youths I'd spotted earlier, listlessly kicking around a soccer ball while complaining of the most terrible boredom had replaced their complaints with rib-jabbing clucking and wonder anew. It turns out that my little teenaged innkeeper, the budding bouzouksis, and from what I could tell a bit of a character himself, living his young life as if he were some poorly understood figure from a romantic long

---

[1] Someone who plays the bouzouki (a stringed instrument, like the lute).

[2] A kind of Greek blues.

132

ago of war, sea and pain, had adopted this monkey given to him by a Spanish tourist. Well it sounds like one of the bored village youths, none too impressed by what he considered the innkeeper's taking on of airs, had let the animal loose, the same one now tragically trapped and screaming in the center of the square. In a desperate grab for the juicy seeds, the monkey had fitted its hand through a small hole in a melon the boy had given it, and was now making every attempt to break free. Such crying you've never heard. How the monkey fought with that melon jammed onto its one clenched fist. I wanted to shout, you just have to let go the seeds and slip free my friend, but what was the use. The creature held on, forever it seemed, spinning around with the breeze, until our bouzouki friend came to recapture his pet. Then angrily facing the youths he says: I know the village is nothing but old people and children so why don't you go on then. Find something else to do.

June 25

Today I make a quick stop at the grocer's for a breakfast of koulouri[3] and cream, then pick up some cheese, tomatoes, and bread to take with me for lunch. With the fuzzy signals of some laiki[4] chorus playing on the car radio, I set out for the monastery on what immediately feels like a daredevil's journey. On the long winding road to the mountain's peak, what was this, stopping me in my tracks? I meet a flock of sheep, nearly eyeball to eyeball. As if receiving and subsequently overcome by some profound mystery, right there, in the middle of the road, the sheep all gather in an immobilized configuration. What are they looking at? Devil I could tell. Arranged in concentric circles they huddle close, eyes focused downward in deep concentration, listening to a silent hymn. At the eye of this maze stands a small delicate ewe. She balances gracefully on three legs,

---

[3] A flat, circular bread with sesame seeds, or a bagel-like pastry.
[4] A popularized form of Greek folk music.

her right front leg upraised and bent at the hoof. Her eyes seem to flutter up acknowledging my presence, and by some imperceptible movement of sheep I am able to continue through. After more miles of winding road, I make it to the mountaintop as a giant busload of tourists leaves. A woman stands arms akimbo in halter top and shorts looking out over the precipice across to the monastery on the rock. A fellow comes at me from the mountainside, ripping through on his motorbike. He speaks quickly and easily and for some reason addresses me in French. When I answer back he returns in English: Where are you from? America? What city? New York? In vain I try to let my answers keep up with the pace of his questions. The monastery closes early today, my friend, he says. They're still making repairs. Come by my restaurant. There's a campsite nearby. You can eat, sleep, come back tomorrow…. I take his flyer, and thank him as I think about where to go for the night. On my way out I decide to check out the campsite and come upon the restaurant; a large dining hall – immaculate – with upside down crystal glasses set out on white frou-frou tablecloths. Except for the short-haired fellow in mirror shades playing around with a rifle, whom I'd passed a quarter mile down, the place is completely empty. Just then I see, next to the hall, pretty much hidden from view, a small house of sorts and sitting outside a group of people, young and old, with hair bleached and skins darkened by the sun. A family of gypsies. Where are you from, they ask me. Oh, they say, in great surprise, as if recognizing my home city as wildly exotic yet so familiar. And where are you going? they say. Where are you staying? Do you know anyone here? Did you eat? And that's when I remember. Let's eat then, they say. Watermelon? I have some after my lunch of tomato, bread, and cheese. The fruit is unbelievably moist and sweet. Greedily digging in, I ask them about the guitars. We're a family of musicians, they say. During tourist season, and when the restaurant is full, we play. It's the same songs over and over again. Our children hear them as we did.

The same old stories, again and again.

Tomorrow, it's Delphi. I've been on the road all day, and it's time to
find a place for the night before continuing on to see that city's ruins.
I stop over in the mountain town of Arahova. This time I settle for
the second room I see. It's a cozy old inn and no cause for complaint.
As I sign in I notice a hammer and sickle on the wall. A real hammer
and a real sickle. Black iron ore. However exotic and strange they
seem, the tools blend inconspicuously with the other rustic doodads
on the wall. I would have never noticed them if my host hadn't kept
me waiting, like a fool, as he engaged in tea talk with a young comrade. Comrade looks like a visiting student-intellectual type, making
his rounds and paying his respects as he kicks around the provinces
on his long summer vacation. For a loose instant, when not thinking
about it too much, the Saint Nicolas icon over my bed, and the old
almond treasure chest at its foot feel in perfect unity with this big
iron anachronism resting on the wall. I find a moment to ask the
innkeeper about the hammer and sickle: Were there communists in
these mountains, too? Were you one of the rebels trying to rout the
Germans from Greece? Though he appears as one of those men
too old to feel the least timid or self-conscious of anyone or anything, he goes about his desk duties as if he didn't hear me well. I
don't bother to repeat myself, but instead turn and wish him a good
night. When I get to my room, I look through the window and down
at the streets below. We're way up high here, and I can see it. The
efficiency of the fascists, keeping the village peace, as they'd put it.
All's quiet now, including the hungry stray stalking every pedestrian
who crosses his path. You'd at least expect the cur to growl for his
supper. So, some decades ago, down Main Street, villagers would've
stood by and watched, as some excited sort, broke through the
crowd to tear at the fighters who'd been rounded up and were now

being paraded through the square: It's you who are the source of our misery, she'd cry. You could almost hear the attacker's stomach shrivel from hunger, and late at night, listening to the quiet mountain terror, she'd know better. History records hasty executions for many of these rebels. I picture the innkeeper as one of them, half the time coolly plotting strategy with his comrades, and the other, getting into petty squabbles born of fatigue and irritation. Even now he gives the impression of a man who carefully keeps his thoughts to himself, and doesn't suffer fools too gladly. In the morning I run out, leaving my passport. When I finally drive back to get it, he is standing outside the door, his face hard to read as usual. Sheepishly, I take it from his hand, and he says nothing.

June 27

Today I make my way to Delphi passing through groves of olive trees on both sides of the street. As I near the edge of the city the groves grow thicker and then thin as I climb to the site of the old ruins. Desperate to escape the sun, I sit on a stone in front of Apollo's temple. My pagouri's[5] water runs warm and I drink only so much before pouring the rest on the dry earth. I see the caretaker, an old man with a rod, shoo away a group of tourists who have similarly made themselves home on one of the loose rocks. Respect the site, he says. Can't you see the rope? The area's protected. And so on and so on. They move away in their own time, and the old fellow, fuming and full-throated as he is, doesn't seem inclined to move from his old rock, a prime piece of real estate situated directly under the shade of a large tree. Behind him I notice some trees–black leaves, black branches, black roots–and I ask him, Why are they so black? Is it from fire? No, he says, with a mournful shake of his head. Lack of water. I check out the ruins of the old stadium when I hear someone singing. What is it? A loud hymn of praise? I look below and see a worshiper

---

[5]A flask or igloo water cooler.

sitting cross-legged by the temple. He wears a black cap and shorts and sings more loudly in a language I don't recognize. He closes his eyes, and I wait for him to finish his song.

What is this? I ask him. Sanskrit?

Close.

Are you a pilgrim? I persist. What religion?

Where are you from? he asks me.

New York. Brooklyn. What about you?

Curitiba, Brazil, he says.

Yeah, I've heard of there, I say. They're trying some new ways of living. Building the city of tomorrow.

Yeah, he nods. But no one talks like that anymore. He adjusts his bag for leaving: The song's Indian.

I assume it's been around since the time of these ruins.

I'd say so, he says. I'm anxious to know more but our conversation drifts predictably toward language touristiko.

The mountains are incredible, aren't they? I say.

What else have you seen?

I've heard of the Parthenon. The lengths Greeks go for beauty and perfection.

The heat…

I know, I say, feeling for my pagouri. Unbelievable isn't it? I'm likely to pass out if I keep forgetting to drink.

June 28

I've been driving for hours listening to table songs and the occasional Amanes. It's supposed to be another scorcher and I make my way towards Vergina in Macedonia, drinking my fluids and trying to avoid the Turkish toilets. It's untidy, let's say, trying to pee standing up. But they're common in the north where the Turks held rule longest. The last roadside pit stop wouldn't have been the worst if a big shit dog wasn't cooling himself, lying around the hole. Vergina resembles desert, but instead of sand you have dry earth. The living things that thrive here adapt to the heat, and I find myself captivated by the open space and feeling of desolation. I'm here to see Philip's tomb, but then I remember it was around here, too, where Apostle Paul proselytize and was jailed. I try to find some unity in these disparate facts but decide it's too hot. I enter the tomb, buried under a large mound of earth. It's dark and cool underground, and I'm relieved to be inside. Displayed about the museum are recently recovered artifacts of gilded armaments and satyr-decorated utensils. I read a caption that mentions the old gravestones here with their Greek names, proving once again that Macedonia has always been a part of Greece. Strange how ancient feuds persist, wholly unaffected by any passing of time. Sometimes pride forces you to choose honour over transcendence. While there's still some light I reconsider searching the area where Paul met the woman at Philippi, where he healed the mad teen, captured wide-eyed and screaming. But there's barely anyone else around, and since it's off-season, everything closes early.

The only other tourists are a group of Germans hanging on to their young guide's every word. Realizing that her entirely true hand-pat, 'you can't see everything,' would not calm me, the museum clerk eventually assures me the tomb was the better treasure. I sit in the diner across from the museum pouring over my map. And after another long late lunch of chicken and potatoes and some unsteady driving around, I try to find a place for the night. As the sun sets, I take out my map and cross off a quadrant. I refold and look to the next.

June 29

Finally. I make it to Mount Olympus. I hear you can reach the summit in six hours. Most quit halfway, for food and rest, then continue on the next day. I take a swig from my pagouri, and brave myself for the journey. I take the low-lying bridge unto the path and follow the red arrows leading into dense forest. It's said, travellers dash up and down this place in no time on a regular basis, but I choose going slow. At one spot the sun floods in, without mercy, no trees offering you shade. Close by is a waterfall, where I sit on the rocks listen to the sounds of the water and daydream, like Homer, of nymphs and other toy forest creatures. I fill my pagouri with fresh river water until I notice the tadpoles and three-legged frog. I continue on, as the path now grows crazy wild. Now I worry about the kid who I believe's been following me. I stop so he can find me and I can ask, what's up. He says he strayed from his grandpa. "Maybe trace your steps back," I say kindly. "He could be looking for you." I continue, renewed. One hour of walking through wild thorny bush and crawling up cliffs of crumbling rock on all fours, my legs are streaked with blood. I slip and take a tumble, landing on my back. At this point I see the kid standing over me,

"The monastery where I was to meet my grandpa was supposed to be only twenty minutes away."

I tell the kid, "Look, you'd really better turn back."

I continue alone, looking for signs, arrows pointing to something. I fall again, this time hard, landing on my backside. This doesn't add up. No one mentioned thorny bramble and crumbling rock, and so I return, and it's then I realize all that climbing, crawling, falling was in vain. An illusion. The real Mount Olympus was across the way, on the other side of the street. I ignore my stinging legs, and jealously look across at the mountain peak, the real one, with its bare apex of stone. The naked throne of Zeus. Across from the tavern where I sit for lunch, not far from the mountain's foot, two free donkeys with loudly clanging neck bells drink from the fountain where I'd just refilled my pagouri. Just bring me something good, I tell my waiter, a slight ruddy-faced boy of no more than twelve. I watch the donkeys, road, and tourists, and satisfy my hunger with some bean soup, bread, village salad, and giant beans. But still, I can't stop looking back and thinking how, despite its presence right under my nose, I managed to miss the real thing.

July 1
Monemvassia. Standing high on the rocks overlooking the sea, I watch the rough waves smash the rocks, the sound muted by the distance, and I space out for a bit. Earlier in the day, I stop by the canal to check out the bungee jumpers, the valley echoes with the voices of the youths: *Malaka*[6] and *Etsi Bravo* but mostly *Malaka* because you only do this if you're a tough. The bungee operator suggests I take the plunge. I'm in the mood to forget myself and so I do despite my fear of bridges, water, heights and, now that I think about it, people. My feet bound by the rope, the rest of me free, I feel my hands and the back of my legs catch the sun, and it warms my whole body, except for my face, which is ice-cold. My forehead and temples spring drops of sweat, and patches of my windblown hair stick to the cold skin of my face, as my teeth chatter. I dangle there for a bit, over the blue-blue water, between the Peloponnese peninsula, and mainland Greece, unaware of the youths' shouts for me to climb back up. My heart beats loud and deep—my head, chest and legs a drum—and I wait to see how much I can stand before fading.

July 2
Driving along the peninsula's northern coastline I stop for an evening swim near the town of Therveni. You can smell the sea, salt, and catches of the day as the last of the fishing boats draw close. Everyone's enjoying their last swim as the tavernas and nightclubs come alive with student hedonists and other children of summer holding their own over the lyre-inflected disco remixes. I take a quick dip and watch the sun set behind the mountain. After my swim, I shower and

---

[6] Etsi bravo! could be translated as, Way to go! Malaka basically translates as masturbator or wanker. But its ubiquity, and particularly in a context like this, is functionally more akin to how some black youths may use the n-word among themselves.

dress for the Karagiozis shadow puppet theater I saw advertised at the local demotiko[7]. Maybe I'm the only adult there without a kid. I buy some popcorn and take my seat near the back. One kid takes a seat near me and sneaks looks. I turn around and he quickly looks away. Ela! Pame! Opa! Karagiozis bucks wildly to the puppeteer's canned stadium music, as he makes his entry on stage. I laugh at this, a lot of the act lost to me because my Greek's lousy. From what I figure, Karagiozis talks up his children but it doesn't sound like they're doing too well. He asks one son, did he finally get promoted, and to what grade. The son replies, Friday. This one I get because Monday is first day, Tuesday second, Wednesday third, and Thursday fourth. But, as Paul would have it, Friday is not five but Preparation Day, Saturday being Sabbath. Poor Karagiozis: We eat, we drink, and we go to bed hungry. This is his steady refrain. He takes his wife to the doctor because for some sad reason she's using motor oil in place of cooking oil. Tough times are more common than village dandelion. Such good intentions and modest desires, yet the fellow can't ever, can never catch a break. It's a world for schmoozers and others so royally self-appointed. A wayward ball lands near Karagiozis's little house. In his temper he sends the ball through the topmost window of the sultan's castle. Scared as he is, Karagiozis doesn't run or hide. The sultan's men find him and name him the culprit. True to his nature, Karagiozis talks his way out of trouble. But in a dilemma befitting the trickster he is, Karagiozis conjures a way of refusing their invitation to play for Turkey. It's a sweet offer laden with all kinds of goodies for him and his needy family. A real bind and far hairier than the first. The story anachronistically taking place now and during the time of the Ottomans, the Greeks have just won the Cup, and proud Hellene Karagiozis must say no. Never mind the riches the Sultan throws his way.

"We drink, we eat, and we go to bed hungry", the audience says,

---

[7]Elementary school.

along with their proud Everyman. From behind the screen speakers blare the anthem of the Greek soccer team. Beside me I hear some uncle murmur the unofficial words: We're fat, we're clods.... But your boys won the championship, I say. Back at the hotel I go to sleep with the sounds of my neighbour's television. The Euro cup final. Germany versus Spain. And it's Spain, 2-0.

July 3

The meat market, Athens. Thanks to the scorching asphalt, some blood's coagulated under my shoe. *Thyxk, thyxk.* For two steps my foot sticks to the floor before the blood dries. Emboldened by the Millionaire Club's flyers, posted all around in Slavic scripts and touting suggestible blonde dancers named Nadia and Sveta, the mutton seller starts acting the rooster. Now, how do I get from here to Mount Lycabettus? That will require some doing and so I circle it on my map. I set off in the direction of the narrow café-lined streets. A tranny wearing strappy heels and a long satin skirt split way up the sides asks me for money. I give her a euro and tell her all I have left is to last me a couple of days. In patchy English she asks two men drinking coffee al fresco. Her sarcoma blisters mottle her arms and shoulders. Her beehive is a tangle of swirls and curls. After a dramatic pause to stare her down then slo-w-ly blow smoke from his mouth, the muscle-T-shirt fellow says "Ohi".

And right then it did sound like the strongest word in the Greek language. Passing through Syntagma (Constitution Square) I ask two workers sitting on the steps of the National Bank for the best way to Kolonaki. Their thin khaki shirts stained with sweat. They respond faintly in Punjabi-accented Grenglish and that's when I notice one fumbling for the syringe now rolling down the steps. Before I could thank them they're back to that clumsy tussle, two kittens at play, softly flailing, flopping over themselves and on each other. The needle glints in the sun, comes down in an arc, and lands in the crook of an arm. Immediately the needle-bearer collapses in the lap of the other who, likewise, takes the occasion to close his eyes and drop his head.

Kolonaki is a window shopper's treat with glamour stores named Soho and Robert Redford, but it's the dessert houses that win my heart. A thousand uses for walnut and honey. So, Greece's Turkish heritage isn't all sour. Leaving Kolonaki, I walk upslope to the funicular which will lift me to the top of the city. On the way I stop at the language school's bookstore. I'm midway between downtown and the mountain which overlooks it. I'm standing at a slant and looking across at the language institute. I stop and think about Markos. This must have been the place he'd told me about, where he took extra lessons. We'd fallen out of touch, until recently, when I heard the news. He'd managed doing better for himself, becoming a playwright of some note. According to the obit, he'd been depressed for a while, and on meds, then went off last summer because of side effects. After the hospital, he went back on the meds, but this time they were no good. Imagine being so sick, that nothing you do, can drive the demons out. From the mountaintop I see the chichi Kolonaki apartments with pools on the roofs. I see the Acropolis, Syntagma, the national bank, the market. And, Pnika. Earlier when I explored its quiet groves I checked in with a woman walking her dogs and she said, yes, this was it. This was where Paul preached to the Athenians and healed the sick through faith.

July 4

The Antiracist Festival, Athens. I sit at the edge of the open theater and listen to the lyre-player. He bows his head towards his instrument as his fingers pluck like mad. I imagine a wild horse galloping. Dust clouds rise from its hooves, which hit the ground hard. One, two, three, four. A gritty fast-track loop. The brisk pace holds steady as the intensity rises. We're all quiet here, me and my friends sitting on the grass. Not friends really but we're here together. The strumming quickens until it's just one long sustained vibration. Everyone's moved, their faces tense with anticipation. My foot quivers with the strings. Very rapid. When the strumming ends, I bicycle-kick, from the remaining built-up tension, the lone star hanging from the sky. In the near distance, a five-piece band plays more traditional music, and a young man takes an older woman and shows her how it is done. She's got her own moves however and pretty soon the couple's in sync. Every two steps I find myself less than a hand's width from some stranger arguing politics and banks. I wait for a cab by the hospital, and head across town to my room for the night.

Late night, or early morning, I ask the hotel clerk where's the best place to get something to eat. Ah, kind of late he tells me and I say well it's well into the night, so the customary dinnertime around here. He suggests a place by the water and says it's pricey. From his expression I figure it's not a natural recommend for his hotel's clientele. I go to bed hungry and in two hours am back up.

"Can't sleep?" he asks me.

"On a night like this?" I say, bravely.

"You fired up on ouzo?"

For the first time, I notice the fireplace in the room behind him. Although the temperatures have been scorching, I secretly wish that it worked. I sink in the couch by the doors and look out at the streets. We're quiet for a while and then he turns up his radio and says,

"Ever heard this song?"

It's a Cretan classic about a golden eagle that plays with thunder and lightning as it flies across the farthest ends of the skies.

"Imagine that", he says to me. I recognize it from my papou. Just the thought. Flying across space. It leaves you ecstatic!

"So what do you do?" he asks me.

"I write", I tell him.

144

"It's like that poet," he tells me, "who wakes with this marble head in his hands. It's wearing down his elbows but he has nowhere to put it.

"I can see that", I say.

I'm starving now and again ask for the best place to get something.

"It's really too late now", he says. We rummage around and find some grape leaves, olives and bread.

"You're in luck", he says, as I clean the plate.

"An empty stomach's no good at a time like this", he says. "Now you can dream".

"How To Be a Swimmer" by Racquel Goodison

Racquel Goodison has been a resident at Yaddo, the Saltonstall Arts
Colony, and Millay, as well as a recipient of the Astraea Emerging
Lesbian Writer's Grant and a scholarship to the Fine Arts Works
Center. Her stories, poems, and creative nonfiction have been
nominated for the Pushcart and can be found in various journals
online and in print. Her chapbook, *Skin*, was the winner of the 2014
Creative Justice Fiction Chapbook competition.

It helps if you grow up on an island. Then you will be surrounded by water and, if the island is small and poor enough, there will be
not much to do and a lot of reasons to learn how to travel water with
nothing but your arms to carry you.

Be a little girl from a pretty poor family. Let the sun set your pale
skin on fire and cause your mother to complain that "you too sensitive". She will beg your father to "take you someplace to cool off"
so that the heat rash will get a break from burning so much. She will
tell him to take you to the only place they know for a girl like you. It
is not the pool. Remember you are poor and there is no pool anywhere around. It is not the bath, though you do have one bathtub
in the small orange house you live in. Like the house, it is small and
not enough to quench the fire that burns you from the inside out and
the outside in. Maybe you will begin to wonder, how come you were
born in this skin and how come you were born into this place, into
this family and onto this tiny island.

Have a dad who listens to his wife, your mother, more obedient-
ly than you do. He will pick you up like a bag of oranges. You are
nothing in his large arms. You are thin and light. The biggest thing
about you is the "head of hair" that grows like wildfire from your
scalp. Even that seems not built for this climate. Your dad will tousle
this hair and say, "come, we going to the beach."

Have a dad with a car. It will be the same car he's had since the
year before you were born. He will think that it is also his baby. He

will keep it well. He will keep you well. He will put you in the front seat beside him and he will let you play with the radio while his baby takes you and him to the beach that is less than fifteen minutes from your house. Even the radio stations will remind you that you are stuck on a small spit of land. You will turn the knob back and forth between Radio Jamaica and the Jamaica Broadcasting Corporation. Then you will look out the window and think about when you will live someplace else.

The ocean hems you in when you get there. Let your dad scoop you up while you are standing on the shore, scratching your itchy rash, and feeling like there is no escape across that much endless sea. Let him use his giant arms and throw you like the light thing you are into the biggest stretch of anything you've ever seen. It will catch you and cover you and then let you float to its surface.

Relax or it will drown you. Breathe easy or it will snake into your lungs and choke you from the inside out. Let your arms and your legs float out, like a starfish.

You will feel like a part of sun and like another drop in the ocean. Your skin will be relieved.

Let it carry you on its own rhythms, but keep your eyes open. This is one way to travel on water – and to begin to swim.

"Girl's Camp" by Meredith Guest

Meredith Guest lived the childhood of a boy named Hank. It wasn't a bad childhood, just not hers. Guest is an out of the closet male-to-female transsexual living in Northern California. She speaks, teaches and writes; as well as, gardens, hikes and reads a lot. "Girl's Camp" is an excerpt from Guest's memoir, *Son I Like Your Dress.*

The summer after sixth grade, neighbors up the street invited me to accompany them on a vacation to pick up their two daughters from camp and afterward, spend a week traveling and camping. It seems they wanted a boy along to help with the manly camping chores like collecting firewood and helping set up the tent, chores two belles-in-training could hardly be expected to do; they might, after all, break a nail. It was my first and only visit to an all-girl's camp.

I don't know what I expected to find, but when we arrived, the first thing I noticed was not the idyllic surroundings, the rustic log cabins nestled in the woods, the beautiful clear blue lake complete with diving platforms and a flotilla of canoes. No, what struck me speechless was that the place was crawling with – you guessed it – girls! They were everywhere, and I mean everywhere! James Audubon going to sleep and waking up in Bird Heaven could hardly have been more excited than I was.

Of course, I had seen crowds of girls at school, but this was different. Here no boys contaminated the surroundings, sullied the view, or spoiled the splendor of girls. Yeah. This place was nothing but girls. The camp buzzed with a palpable force field of pure, unmixed, unadulterated girl energy. Had I been less shy – a LOT less shy – and prone to musical outbursts, I might have thrown my hand over my chest and belted out the old Ginger Rogers-meets-Fred Astaire tune "Heaven…. I'm in heaven!"

What I *did* do, right there on the spot, without even thinking about it, hell, without even knowing I was doing it, was execute a feat of great intellectual acuity: I performed a near perfect Aristotelian syllogism. And in case you don't remember what a syllogism is, well, according to Will Durant in *The Story of Philosophy:* "a trio of propositions of which the third (the conclusion) follows from the conceded truth of the other two." Aristotle's famous example goes like this: Man is a rational animal, and, Socrates is a man, therefore Socrates must be a rational animal. Or more mathematically, if $A=C$ and $B=C$, then A and B must be equal. In my case it went like this: Only girls can be at an all girls' camp, I am at an all girls' camp, therefore I must be a girl. It was perfect! It was foolproof! It was inarguable! In no time at all I would be running around with the other girls, screaming and chasing and diving into the lake clad in my adorable girl's bathing suit, and, of course, I'd magically have pigtails! A little suspension of disbelief is a suitable reward for a twelve-year-old who has just performed a near perfect Aristotelian syllogism, don't you think?

My few moments of overwhelming joy were short-lived, however. Soon the presence of a boy was noticed, and I was suddenly the object of unnerving, unwanted and unwelcome interest. Like a nail being struck by a hammer, I was impaled, crucified on the reality of what I was – a boy, an alien in this world of girls, an invader from the Other Galaxy. I pulled inside myself like a turtle and tried my best to become as small and inconspicuous as possible.

This and countless other experiences, individually as invisible as the dots of a pointillism, taken together created "No Trespassing" signs across the entire landscape of my identity, barring entry into all those places that felt like me.

"Illegal Paris Love" by Kenita Jalivay

Kenita Jalivay is a writer, literacy activist and indie filmmaker in Philadelphia. She dreams of one day designing a service/travel/film program where she leads underprivileged youth on volunteer missions abroad while training them to document their stories through video and still photography.

My twenties and early thirties can best be described as a cultural carnival on an international scale. For nearly five years, I was involved in a serious relationship with a North African Arab Muslim in Paris, France. His name was Ali, and he was my best friend. He was also an illegal immigrant. Ali was one of millions of undocumented workers propping up France's robust tourism industry, all while existing in the shadows.

We met one afternoon in the restaurant on Rue St. Antoine where he worked as a bartender. I was in Paris on a personal journey to retrace the steps of the black literati that had influenced my youth – Richard Wright, James Baldwin, and Chester Himes. My flophouse hotel was across the street, so I dropped in to the restaurant often, its combination of cheap salads and pastas in sync with my budget. As I sat at my table, poring over a book, Ali descended a flight of steps from the second floor dining room, a tray of glasses balanced in his hand. He looked sharp in his crisp button-down shirt and black dress pants, his skin the sunny brown of Saharan sand. A smile, a lightness, radiated from his core. Our gazes met and held, just steps before he reached the ground floor. Something was happening. Our eyes began conversing at once, searching, whispering, sharing secrets archived in the deepest regions of our hearts. I forgot my book. Ali's tray, on which he was no longer focused, wobbled jealously in his hand. We gasped, laughing in unison as several glasses toppled to the floor with a crash.

Our introduction forged in the warmth of humor, Ali continued the tradition that night, inviting me out for a drink while his cousin, Mokhtar, who spoke English, accompanied us as a translator. In our funny, but awkward exchange during lunch, we had learned that connecting was going to entail somewhat of a communication impasse, as he spoke only "tourist English" (read: "Hi, how are you?" "Thank you very much," or "Would you like to eat here or take-away?") and my French was all but non-existent (though, I'm happy to report that, after years of hanging with Ali, I am "street fluent," or a little stronger than intermediate.) I admired Ali's decision to have his cousin tag along so that we could talk. From the very beginning, he wanted me to know him, to see him for what he was. He shared stories of his life in Paris, how he worked six days a week to earn money to support his parents back home in Tunisia. He had had little time for fun. Ali felt his youth slipping away, and was happy when I agreed to accompany him that evening. For the first time since he could remember, our date gave him something to look forward to.

The maturity with which Ali was able to express his vulnerability touched me. He seemed to me an old man, one packaged in the lean, fit form of a twenty-something that slaved 75 hours a week. I wanted to know more. We finished our tea, eager to take part in the hustle-bustle of Parisian nightlife. As we traipsed through the gaily lit streets of the Marais, and hurried past ear-shattering nightclubs in the Bastille, Ali stretched across the cultural divide to reach me, proving that language was no obstacle. His cousin, however, *was*. As is typically the case with budding love, the two of us, bashful at first, only wanted to gaze at each other, minus the intrusion of a third party (albeit a helpful one.) We said our *mercis* and a*u revoirs* to Mokhtar at a nearby Metro stop, clasped hands, and strolled off into the headiness of a Parisian night, our imaginations ripe with the possibilities.

Over the next several years, Ali and I learned and shared so much. We spent a small fortune on phone cards and plane tickets to stay close. Our love – separated by six time zones and thousands of miles – was an unorthodox, bohemian arrangement, hip in a way that only twenty-somethings seem able to pull off (indeed, now in our staid thirties, we've laughed on occasion at how fearless our commitment was to each other.) After we pooled our resources enough to fly me back to Paris again and again (he couldn't visit the U.S. on account of his status), we often had little money left over to go out. Instead, we devised our own activities to accommodate our broke budgets. We would hop late-night buses and marvel at the beauty of Paris's arrondissements, the city opening for us like a 24-hour museum. Ali and I would stroll and share ice cream bars, noting the human tapestry of passersby as we stopped to rest on slatted benches. On Sundays, since our neighborhood near Place d'Italie seemingly slipped into a coma, he would take me to a massive, outdoor Arab market in Choisy-le-Roi, a suburb several miles outside the city. We would stock up on halal lamb, fish, spices, onions, potatoes, peppers, olives, and fruit, staples we needed to carry us through the week. Living in our cramped studio together, we discovered that meal preparation was a mutual passion.

It was during these quiet moments that Ali revealed to me the true pulse of the immigrant experience in France. We observed how Africans in Europe (both North African Arabs and West African blacks) appeared to feel most comfortable amongst one another, as their race in France – paradoxically exalted as the place where black Americans fled to slough off racial abuses in the States – solidified their second-class citizenship. After France lost many of its former colonial strongholds in the African independence movements of the 60s, a number of these immigrants – already familiar with French culture and language – moved to France in search of greater opportunities for their families. Upon arrival, however, they were met with a xenophobic backlash, the likes of which has stifled their access to socio-economic possibilities that would enable them to move out the ghetto and better educate their children.

Today, while many people of foreign origins in France were born there (and are often third-and fourth-generation French citizens), they still struggle to overcome the bias that deems them cultural outsiders. The Paris that Ali showed me – one replete with harassment, the inability to get hired for non-menial positions, open discrimination from shopkeepers, and a general resentment of foreigners one could practically taste in the air – shocked me. Once, when picking me up at Charles De Gaulle, it hurt me to see random baggage claim workers interrogating Ali as to his "reason for being there," until I walked over, embraced him, and acknowledged them in flawless English. They were taken aback. While I knew French at the time, I purposefully spoke English when addressing them, as I had learned the concept of being an "American" could carry some heft abroad; it was likely to make prospective bullies back off, as they perceived us as assertive and unwilling to go down without a fight. Sadly, my suspicions proved true. Dumbfounded and ignorant, the pair peered at my passport for several surprised seconds, the indignities magically drying up. Instead the staffers legitimized Ali's humanity by quickly moving on.

I never saw myself as privileged until I fell in love with Ali. I grew up a black girl in the rural Midwest, my childhood a struggle to prove I was as good as my white peers. It took leaving my country to realize that I had brought with me, or even possessed, the special benefits that being an American abroad entails. I walked around Paris for years – gullibly? – at all hours of the night, never suspecting any harm would befall me. It never did. Ali, on the other hand, has to be conscious of the streets at all times, the locations where the police congregate. As a lone Arab male, he can easily be scraped against a wall, cuffed, and tossed in the backseat just because they're in the mood. Indeed, when the riots of 2005 occurred, he nearly had a nervous breakdown for fear of the gendarmerie (and their notorious reputation for beating the shit out of Arabs), as they had issued a curfew ordering everyone off the streets by sundown. I remember the strain in Ali's voice as he prepared to leave work every night around 11:00, wondering if *this night* would be the one where he found himself face to face with enraged cops determined to make an example of an immigrant flouting the law.

I look back with wonder at how Ali and I made it through such challenging circumstances, and for so long. Although we came from vastly different cultural backgrounds, I attribute our happiness to the devotion that we showed each other, the time and patience we took to learn about each other's background. These experiences enriched my life beyond any lessons I could have acquired from books, and made me much more knowledgeable and sympathetic to the struggles that people face across a broad, geopolitical spectrum. After nearly five years together, sadly, Ali and I called our relationship off, both of us worn down from trying to figure out how we could move forward on a permanent basis. I wasn't ready to relocate to France, and he had no interest in coming here, fearful that the United States deplored Muslims, evidenced, he felt, by its unjust occupation of Iraq.

Though our relationship hit a stalemate, the lessons that I learned from Ali are eternal. He taught me the value of giving people a chance, and that the greatest happiness you'll ever know might come at the hands of a person completely foreign to you. He also showed me how to see beauty in the tiniest of moments, and that the most exhilarating experiences will occur when you think you're down on your luck, poor, and without options. I learned some of the most powerful lessons in my life from a broke bartender in Paris. As it turned out, he happened to be the richest man I've ever met.

"Learning to Speak" by Anne Liu Kellor

Anne Liu Kellor is a multiracial writer, teacher, editor, and mother living in Seattle. Her essays have appeared in publications such as the anthology *Waking Up American: Coming of Age Biculturally* (Seal Press), *Fourth Genre*, *Vela Magazine*, *The Los Angeles Review*, *Literary Mama*, and more. Anne has received support for her work from Hedgebrook, Jack Straw, 4Culture, and Hypatia-in-the-Woods. "Learning to Speak" was previously published in *Duende* and is adapted from her memoir manuscript, *HEART RADICAL*. This book explores Anne's migrations between China, Tibet, and America, and was chosen by Cheryl Strayed as 1st-runner up in Kore Press's 2017 memoir contest.

I.

When we break silence at the end of the meditation retreat, I am surprised by the sounds of others' voices. How the pitch and inflections of the woman who sat next to me do not match the person I had imagined when all I knew was her presence, the way she entered the room, took off her shoes, and settled onto a cushion to sit. Her speech feels too human, somehow intrusive, and I wonder if mine will sound this way too.

Once words are allowed, we feel pressured to speak. Nervous laughter, bristled edges of defense, or notes one octave too cheerful creep slowly back into conversations as we recall the task to assert who we are, to announce our individual selves, to form unique narratives and opinions. We return to old patterns, imitations of self, because words are worth more, or so we've been taught. Because too many in this world have stayed silent.

II.

The voice of my mother. The voice of my grandmother. As an infant, the first tones I heard were Chinese. The soft murmurs of the women who held me and rocked me and sang me to sleep. Soothed by their voices, I drifted in a world without language, and yet I was already learning the sounds of Chinese. The voices of my ancestors, passing again from mother to child, rising and falling, imprinted their memory in my cells.

English, the language of my father, was also familiar to me, but it was less prominent, somewhere on the periphery, somehow more connected to the world of people who lived outside the intimacy of my home. In preschool I understood the language that floated around me, but I had little experience asserting myself within its midst. This world was something else, something I was a part of and yet somehow removed from. At first, my teachers were worried because I was so quiet. Then slowly I learned how to play and talk in a world of English. My teachers happily reported to my parents that I had been caught with the other girls peeking into the boys' bathroom. It was a sign of progress. But I never stopped being quiet.

III.

In college, I wanted to be invisible. I longed to dissolve into the moss-laden trees of the forest, to slide into a room like smoke and dance through its crevices, then slip away before anyone could ask my name. Hiding behind thick glasses and under long ponchos, I wanted to discard my old ideas of self, built around image and beauty. I spent days alone, taking long silent walks, reading mystics like Rumi, and writing pages about loneliness and God. More than anything I longed to be seen, but I was still too raw to risk full exposure.

IV.

In China, my struggle to communicate became more elementary. First I needed to relearn the basics: how to introduce myself, make small talk, order food. Yet the longer I stayed the more I wanted to say. Language was my passport, my key to belonging. If I could master the words, then I could share my full self. So much vocabulary was new, yet the sounds of Chinese had never left me.

Every day people stared like I was an alien. I caught their whispers, trying to place me. They'd hear my fluent tones, yet see my sharp nose, my big breasts, and brown hair, a shade lighter than their own. Some might venture a guess: hun xue, mixed blood, or I might volunteer this myself. But as time passed, the less I cared to give a simple answer. *Let them whisper, let them guess. I am tired of trying to prove that I belong.*

V.

Through silence I know how to listen. Through silence I gauge when to speak. Through silence I have learned how to sense when a channel to exchange meaning is open, or when I am caught in a volley of empty rounds. In silence, I remember how to give and receive, let go of the need to have something to say, the urge to cast myself in relation.

But silence can also suffocate, settling in my chest in layers like silt, a sign that I have waited too long. I want now to speak more than anything, yet it feels more comfortable to stay hidden. A web of gauze winds circles around my face, even as love song trembles through my body.

For years I went on, restraining, withholding. But the more I learned to reveal, the less I could bear to hide. Slowly, steadily, a line was drawn—a desire stretched taut across my throat, an old and tired seam splitting open.

"Motherless Mother's Day" by Cheryl Klein

Cheryl Klein is the author of a story collection, *The Commuters* (City Works Press); a novel, *Lilac Mines* (Manic D Press); and a monthly column for *MUTHA*. Her stories and essays have appeared in *Blunderbuss, The Normal School, Mom Egg Review, Razorcake*, and several anthologies. Her work has been honored by the MacDowell Colony and the Center for Cultural Innovation. She blogs about the intersection of art, life and carbohydrates at breadandbread.blogspot. com.

1.

I was pulling a flouncy eyelet sundress over my head when my sister called. The dress seemed right for a Mother's Day tea, and thanks to the spaghetti straps, it meshed with my current favorite look, which could be summed up as Things I Couldn't Wear Back When I Had Real Boobs And Had To Wear A Serious Bra At All Times.

"I'm leaving now to come pick you up," Cathy said. "Adam and I went to brunch and neither of us had a watch. I'll probably get to your place at about noon."

It was 11:45. She was at her boyfriend's house in Long Beach and I lived in the very opposite corner of Los Angeles County.

"It takes more than fifteen minutes to get from Long Beach to Highland Park," I snapped. "I'll meet you at the party."

Adam had come to represent—happily for her, bitterly for me—a world of no watches, no disease, no disagreements. Where bodies were only used for hot sex. When she'd made me look at a "rash" on her hip, it seemed like one part hypochondria, one part humblebrag—because it was clearly a bruise and, yes, now that she thought about it, she and Adam *had* had thrashing sex the night before.

When Cathy and I were kids, we gave our mom the standard construction-paper art projects and gold-plated #1 Mom charms for Mother's Day. But our real present to her was being nice to each other for one whole day. We were both invested in performing the role of Good Daughter, and we had chemistry as co-stars.

This year, our mom had been dead for almost ten years, and I was six months into treatment for Stage 2 breast cancer, caused by the same genetic mutation that had caused her ultimately fatal ovarian cancer. Cathy had the BRCA-2 mutation too, according to a lab somewhere in Utah, but she was still healthy. And that seemed like everything.

A couple of months before, she'd started dating a new guy, a firefighter who did yoga and went backpacking and sent her sweet, goofy texts. I hadn't met him yet, but he sounded perfect—for her and in general. After their second date, she'd told me, *He has a gay brother.* Homophobia was a dating deal-breaker for her. *His brother is HIV positive, and we had this amazing conversation about how neither of you let the stuff you're going through keep you down.*

She'd meant it as a compliment, but I'd felt demoted to the status of Queer Friend Who Dies Nobly To Make The Real Main Character Seem Deep And That Much More Beautiful.

"I'm glad we're going to this," she said on the phone. "I think we could both use the distraction."

Things had been civil but tense between us lately. I'd avoided calling her for a few weeks. I was testing her: How long would it take her to call me? And I was denying her: *If she doesn't want all of me, she doesn't get any of me!* I didn't tell her about my first radiation appointment or my nude photo shoot with an artist named J. Michael Walker. (And wasn't that just the sort of gutsy, artsy thing she'd *never* do?)

When she'd first started contemplating a preventative Angelina Jolie-style mastectomy, *she'd* wanted to compare notes on types of implants. I felt like I'd been sentenced to prison, and she'd shown up wearing a striped Sexy Jailbird uniform from a costume shop, wanting to talk about our matching outfits.

2.

I parked on the steep hill next to the little yellow house Michelle's sister shared with her Austrian cameraman boyfriend. I wiped the tears from my face and the sweat from my bald head. Alissa had orchestrated her usual perfect spread. I'd made a fruit salad to her exact specifications (mixed berries and fresh mint leaves) and put it in my nicest green melamine mixing bowl, but she immediately emptied it into a better bowl. There were buttery scones, a tomato and prosciutto tart, tea, prosecco.

I helped myself to the items that seemed the most vegan. I put butter on them so I wouldn't feel deprived. Cathy asked me if anything was wrong. I gave my head a slight shake and hid beneath my floppy straw hat. I was determined to suffer mysteriously.

Alissa and Cathy traded stories about teaching high school. Michelle and I often commiserated about how our little sisters sidestepped family obligations and avoided confrontation, but somehow they'd both ended up teaching teenagers in tough, confrontation-heavy neighborhoods. It was not uncommon for Cathy to begin a story with, *So, we were on lockdown the other day....*

"What are you wearing to prom?" Cathy asked with only a touch of irony.

"My friend is loaning me a dress," said Alissa, who was long and lanky and had worked as a fashion publicist before getting her credential. "She's Persian and has to go to formal family things all the time. She's actually bringing it by today."

Today Alissa was wearing a short jumpsuit and a chunky necklace that had belonged to her and Michelle's mother, who'd died of breast cancer in 2009. Michelle was still mad that Alissa had raided her jewelry box the day after their mother's death, while Michelle was sleeping off her grief.

The party moved outside to a brick patio amid flowering trees. Michelle was complaining about the girl she was dating.

"She gets high every night, and then she makes insensitive comments like a drunk person and won't have sex with me," Michelle said. "And the sex is my only reward for tolerating the insensitive comments. Actually, sex is the main reason I got back together with her in the first place after she was so thoughtless to me the last time, so what's the point if I'm not even getting laid?"

This was why I loved Michelle—she could be so brutally honest about someone she was in fact completely smitten by.

Alissa's other two motherless friends—a brother-sister pair who'd lost their mom just a month ago—smiled abstractly. They had the stunned look of the newly half-orphaned. The look of, *Wait, so the world is still here?* Cathy sipped her tea. I was sure she was thinking about sex with Adam.

She'd spilled her BRCA-2 news to him early on, just in case he wanted to dump her right then and avoid getting to know her small natural breasts only to lose them. She tended to be reserved, and it was a rare moment of disclosure. For a minute, she'd been scrubbed raw by life just like me, she'd had nothing to lose just like me—only she was sharing it with Adam, and not with me.

Adam had responded kindly: "That's such a hard thing to go through. We'll get through it together. I'm into *all* of you, not just one specific part."

When you get very bad, improbable news, there's a tiny part of you that believes an equally improbable antidote must be close at hand. Certainly if I was unlucky enough to get cancer at thirty-five, the universe would make up for it by allowing my partner to get pregnant on her first trip to the sperm bank, right? C.C. didn't get pregnant on the first try or the fifth try, but for Cathy—whose biggest source of insecurity had been her single status—the math of the universe was apparently true. How fantastic it must feel to have a firefighter rush in, all sirens and ladders, to save you from your fears of dying alone and boob-less.

"Is there anything you *like* about this girl?" the sister half of the brother-sister pair asked Michelle.

"Yeah. When we *do* have sex, it's hot. And when she's not high, she's really thoughtful and sensitive."

Cathy ate another one of the Trader Joe's rugelach bites she'd brought. She'd put on some weight in the past few months. I'd chalked it up to the constant dinners out that came with a new romance, but maybe, I thought now, she was also indulging in a favorite family habit: comfort eating. I was no stranger to it, had spent my late teens and early twenties chubby, but the combination of anxiety, Effexor and a hyper-obsession with my health had landed me at my skinniest adult weight. Sometimes I felt smug, sometimes extra vulnerable. The world could see my skull and the ladder of my sternum and my soul. Cathy was creating a soft layer of padding between herself and its cruelties. The bumpers of her hips pulled her green dress tight; her arms looked solid, as if her very bones had thickened to the point of un-breakability.

Now, I can see that she was struggling, piling sandbags against a river of overwhelming information: her sister sick, her own body a time bomb.

The prom dress arrived. The butter melted in the sun.

3.

As soon as I got in my car to go home, I called Cathy on my cell. I couldn't stand giving the silent treatment to someone who welcomed it.

"I'm mad at you," I said.

"For being late?"

"Well, that was the final straw. But I'm mad at you for not calling me and for being fake when we do talk."

"I'm not being fake," she protested. "I just try to talk about other things, things we can agree on. But then you act like I'm shallow."

"I never said you were shallow," I shouted. (And while that was true, hadn't I sometimes comforted myself with that thought? That maybe she owned a house and was on her way to domestic bliss, but wasn't I an artist who listened to more NPR?)

As I made my way from the 2 freeway to Eagle Rock Boulevard, past the Rite Aid and the emergency vet and the homeless encampment, Cathy unleashed a years-long list of grievances. After our mom had died, we'd made an unspoken pact to support each other unconditionally, but now that the treaty had been broken, she let me know how mean I was. I'd been dismissive of her last boyfriend, she said, and unsympathetic to her best friend's fertility problems.

"Because Jenny *already has three kids*," I said. But a part of me was hovering above myself, watching the eight-year-old whose herd of My Little Ponies had ganged up on Cathy's lone baby pony.

"And there are some things about your health I don't want to talk about, and I don't think I *should* talk about with you," she said.

"What, that you're afraid I'm going to die?" I said it loud because I believed in climbing on the back of the elephant in the room and riding it as it bucked.

"Yes," she said.

"You think I don't know that? You think I haven't thought about it? Not talking about it just makes me feel those terrible emotions all by myself, which is really lonely."

"When Mom was sick," she said, "she tried to talk about death with me, and I turned her down. It was the right choice then, and I'd make it again. No one talks about that stuff." She said it the way you might say, *No one dry cleans everything that says "dry clean only."*

"Yes they do," I said.

"No they don't! Whenever Dad brings up financial stuff, you tell him you don't want to think about him dying."

"I'm trying to tell him that our priority is *him*, not getting a big tax-free inheritance after he dies. But yeah, maybe he could use someone to share those thoughts with," I said.

"Well, I'm glad that you're at that point," she snapped, "but I'm not."

Again I felt a little triumphant. Maybe I had to be the crazy one, but I would be the crazy one who was Brave Enough To Look Death In The Face.

Then I remembered the meeting I'd attended at our church in the raw first days after my diagnosis. All Saints was Gothic Revival on the outside, but the community meeting rooms were all wood paneling and dropped ceilings. In the one that housed the cancer support group, two older women were examining the tags they'd chosen from that year's Angel Tree.

The meeting started. Diagnoses and updates were shared. One man had stopped bleeding when he used the toilet. Another was annoyed with his landlord for not fixing something. Cancer was their every day, not so different from a leaky roof that was hard to patch. Their matter-of-fact attitude struck me as both enviable and terrible. As it turned out, they were all Stage 4, officially dying, if not all at the same speed.

When it was my turn to talk, I cried so hard my sinuses nearly swelled shut as Susan, a calm, motherly woman with metastasized pancreatic cancer, handed me tissue after tissue. Would I ever have kids? I wondered aloud. Was anything ever certain? God's love, maybe? Then where was God's love, and how could I get my hands on a giant slice of it?

When it was Susan's turn, she said, "I'm putting things on my calendar. I wasn't even supposed to make it this long, but I figure why not make plans? I'll either be here for them or I won't."

I left the church with a pale green prayer shawl crocheted by one of the parishioners. It hung in my bedroom for months, a symbol of the night I'd seen God's love and my mom in the form of a woman named Susan. Touching it made me feel sick and heavy, but I was too superstitious to put it away. I never went back to the group. Despite the front I was putting on for Cathy now, I wasn't ready to be Susan.

I told my sister fuck you. We both said I love you and hung up.

"Step One" by Alexandria Marzano-Lesnevich

Alexandria Marzano-Lesnevich is the author of *THE FACT OF A BODY: A Murder and a Memoir*, recipient of the 2018 Lambda Literary Award for Lesbian Memoir and the 2018 Chautauqua Prize. Named one of the best books of the year by *Entertainment Weekly*, Audible. com, Bustle, Book Riot, *The Times of London*, and *The Guardian*, it was an Indie Next Pick and a Junior Library Guild selection, long-listed for the Gordon Burn Prize, and a finalist for a New England Book Award, and a Goodreads Choice Award. The recipient of fellowships from The National Endowment for the Arts, MacDowell, and Yaddo, as well as a Rona Jaffe Award, Marzano-Lesnevich lives in Boston, where she teaches at Harvard. "Step One" was first published in *Alimentum*.

> "The general condition of the soul, therefore,
> is stoic hunger, stoic loneliness."
> — Stephen Dunn

Step one, chop the chocolate, the recipe begins, so you unpeel the gold foil from two large bars of Ghiradelli semi-sweet, snap the glossy brown-black bars into squares, and stack the squares like dominoes. Then you choose your biggest knife, a discount store find, and your widest cutting board, because you know from experience the chocolate will shard. That is always your struggle with this recipe, the recipe you otherwise believe to be perfect: the way the chocolate shards. You stack the squares. You lift your knife.

Step one, chop the chocolate.

For a long time, you did not like chocolate. You did not like chocolate when you were in college, and the women you knew were forever confessing the chocolate they'd eaten: the HoHos, the Hershey's, the cupcakes they'd peel icing from. From their lips the all-American list sounded exotic, an easy, guilty love you did not share. Your boyfriend then, a short Israeli man, called you un-American for your dislike. The vowels came out all wrong, but that didn't matter because he loved chocolate and you did not and in some essential way that made him American and you not. This became a joke between you, a fine joke because it took what belonged to him—the world—and gave it to you, and took what belonged to you and gave it to him. The Towers wouldn't fall for three more years still; New York, where you lived, hadn't yet erupted in a rash of American flags; and the word carried no suspicion, just his gleeful claiming. And for you, when you heard it, a kind of pride. Three years later, done with college, the boyfriend long gone, you still wouldn't like chocolate. But no one would call you un-American for it then.

As a young child you had loved chocolate. Then your mother, alarmed (the story goes) at the size of a glass bowl of chocolate pudding your father's mother had brought to the house, told you that you were allergic. You can imagine this: your mother's quiet, nervous parsimony then, her fear you would be fat. Maybe she really was that afraid you'd eat the whole bowl. More likely, though, she was just sick of the woman who'd worn white to her wedding to your father, insisting that the wedding wasn't really a wedding because everyone knew that second marriages (your father's) didn't count. More likely she did not want to grant that woman pleasure. So she said, *Oh, she can't have that, she's allergic.* Just one sentence. But you believed her, and even now when you so much as look at chocolate pudding your mouth grows slightly itchy and starts to crawl with richness. Which is maybe where the whole chocolate thing started. But you hate that idea because you're a grown woman now and ought to be over psychosomatic responses to things your mother told you.

Step one, chop the chocolate.

Once you took a woman to an all-chocolate candlelight dinner. You didn't love the woman, but you were sleeping with her because you were no longer welcome in the bed of the woman you did love, and for now that seemed good enough. (You couldn't know yet that "for now" would last longer than intended. "For now" always does.)

The restaurant was known for themed dinners, amongst them the chocolate, and when your siblings had given you a gift card to the restaurant you'd thanked them but later cried on the phone to your mother because you had no one to bring. You couldn't tell that to your siblings, who all did have someone to take for romantic dinners, because by this point you were out as gay and while no one had ever said that they were uncomfortable, not exactly, no one much liked hearing about your dates. Especially not your mother, who was the only one you ever told.

The woman you were sleeping with had recently enrolled in acupuncture school, and when the night of her first exam approached, you thought it would be a perfect chance to use the gift card. (Actually, you thought *fuck it*, because you were tired of having the gift card and no one to take. There would be other gift cards, you reasoned. There would be other dinners. What exactly were you waiting for? The woman loved chocolate.) You called the restaurant. You made the reservation. When the night came you picked up the woman at the acupuncture school. She'd brought a dress to change into, and when she walked to the car in the white cotton slip-dress you admired her slender, cool limbs and her grassy blonde hair. She ducked her head and smiled at you with those upturned lips that were either a smirk or happiness, and you had no idea what she was thinking because with her you never did, but you still wanted to slide your hand up the inside of that long cool thigh, because with her you always did. You closed the car door for her, moved to your own side, trailed your hand up her leg and asked her about the exam. She was still a beginning student and they didn't let her use needles. Instead she had to take a small white donut sticker, the kind you used as a schoolgirl to reinforce loose-leaf paper, and she had to place it on her exam partner's skin so that the acupuncture point was inside the hole. If the point was covered she failed the question.

You loved hearing about this, every time. Picturing her, with her long and slender fingers–fingers she would someday use to pierce, to make bleed, to find the relief latent in pain–delicately placing the white sticker on her partner's smooth, papery (you imagined) skin. The circles were tiny. To place them properly seemed an impossible feat of perfection. True, needles were smaller, but you'd always imagined acupuncture to be a looser art. But the woman, she had to place them perfectly or fail!

You kissed her then, in the car, your hand on her cool perfect thigh. You lived in a world of words, of messy imperfection, nothing ever in the circle or out, all things perhaps possible, which means that they felt impossible. You loved this the way you loved math homework when you were a child. You loved this the way you loved checkers. You loved this.

Dinner was venison with cocoa, dark and murky-tasting and if not delicious or surprising at least fine. The salad was dressed with cocoa nibs, a better combination than you would have expected, a bit spicy. To start there was savory chocolate soup, with shallots and orange.

That soup is the only thing that has ever made you want to wash your mouth out with soap. (And you have had fermented soybeans so sticky with rot they form strings in the air! Once you ate a fish eyeball! You've eaten Marmite! But nothing in your memory compares to the soup.) It tasted like dirt, like drinking liquid dirt. It looked like a bowl of hot chocolate and it felt like hot chocolate on your tongue and lifting it to your lips you thought of your cousins in France, and the way that, when you were children, you were jealous to hear them say that in the morning they drank bowls of hot chocolate. But this, they could have this if they wanted this. (They would not want this.)

No way to know that years from this moment you will have a girlfriend whose mother woke her every childhood morning with a bowl of hot chocolate into which she'd stirred six teaspoonfuls of sugar, a number that will make you shake your head when you hear it but will also make you think, *that is love*. To forego what is responsible for what is delight. To choose to give another such soft happiness. When the girlfriend tells you this story for the first time, you will remember the soup, the soup that was thick and murky and challenging as a bog. You didn't just not like the soup. You were offended by the soup.

The soup will make you realize that you finally, again, like chocolate. Because you hated the soup for what it was not.

Step one, chop the chocolate.

You are thirty-four and you have hips that cry out for children and a heart that cries out for children and you still do not have children. You are a long way from having children. As you stand at the counter alone, knife in hand, preparing to chop, the girlfriend with the taste for sugar is still months away in the future, and whether the two of you will ever have children is further into the future still. No way of knowing anything, really.

Like you cannot know what she will, someday, be the one show you: your knife is sharding the chocolate.

The future day you learn this she will stand at her own kitchen counter and in front of her will be your handwriting. *Step one, chop the chocolate*, the paper will say. Her hand will snap the squares. She will lift her knife, and it will gleam, sharp and shiny as yours is not. As you watch her, and watch the clean way the blade glides through the chocolate, finally cutting it into equally measured squares, no shards, you will consider telling her where this recipe came from. You will consider the question of how longing sounds.

Because longing is what you have now, standing at the counter alone. And you have this: A recipe that you found on the Internet when you decided to make a batch of chocolate-chip cookies because you realized that you had never made a batch of chocolate-chip cookies and to you this seemed an unconscionable absence. Too close to your childhood. A failure to comfort, perhaps. A failure to love. You are American, after all. Isn't this the cookie you should offer?

And in that way that some find overbearing, but that someday, if the God in whom you cannot quite convince yourself to believe is willing, someone will find charming, you dealt with the chocolate chip cookie problem the way you deal with most other problems, spending night after night over the blue glow of your laptop screen, trying to find the one perfect recipe for chocolate-chip cookies. You could not hurry the arrival of someone to love, you figured. You could not sate longing. But what you could do, you decided—all you could do, you decided—was have the cookies ready, the chocolate chip cookies that would became the ones you made. The chocolate-chip cookies that would become the cookies your children knew.

Will you tell her this in the future, standing in her kitchen, watching her and wondering if the children you hope will someday be yours will be hers, too? No. But you will let her bake. She will chop. She will stir. You will wait.

And then you will laugh. You will have to. Because it will turn out that the shards of chocolate, the imperfections introduced by your dull for-now knife, they are what make this recipe something you love. They are what elevate it, spreading the taste of chocolate throughout. Cleaved of the shards by her sharp, perfect knife, it is only an ordinary cookie.

So standing at your yellowed counter alone, in the eventual past that is now the present, you lift your dull knife and prepare to try to cut cleanly. You will fail, you know. But that is okay, you tell yourself. The knife is only the one you have for now. For the now that will last until someday can begin.

You do step one, which is all anyone ever can do. You chop the chocolate.

"How I Stopped Worrying and Learned to Love the (North) Koreans" by Patricia Park

Patricia Park was born and raised in New York City. She earned her BA in English from Swarthmore College and an MFA in Fiction from Boston University, where she studied with Ha Jin and Allegra Goodman. A former Fulbright Scholar and Emerging Writer Fellow at the Center for Fiction, she has published essays in *The New York Times* and *The Guardian*. "How I Stopped Worrying and Learned to Love the (North) Koreans" was originally published in *Slice Magazine*.

Koreans like to say they have a lot of *jung*, an unbridled sentiment of warm-heartedness they heap onto others and receive in return. But growing up Korean-American in Queens, I felt that *jung* was yet another imaginary concept I was told to believe in as a child—like Santa Claus or the Mets winning another World Series—that would only materialize into disappointment.

I belonged to a race of people that prided itself on its purity of blood and thinness of frame; as a robust child—with curly hair and a pronounced rear end to boot—I was a genetic glitch in an otherwise homogenous community. This fact was routinely pointed out by aunts and uncles, the cashiers at my parents' grocery store, even the principal of the Korean afterschool my parents sent me to. "Look at your daughter," she said each time my mother came to pick me up. "Don't you feel ashamed?"

My parents monitored my eating habits with a militant eye. When I was suspected of foul play, they rifled through the garbage for evidence. The incriminating Snickers fun-size wrapper or Capri Sun pouch would be brought forth, and my punishment was a tongue-lashing that managed to invoke the collective disappointment of generations of Parks, tracing all the way back to the Chosun Dynasty. If this was *jung*, I could do without.

172

But sometime in my twenties, I was plagued with a persistent nagging I could only describe as a sense of unfinished business. I decided this would only be appeased if I reconnected with my roots in Korea. A well-meaning cousin tried to warn me of what awaited. "Sure you want to go through with this?" she said, looking me up and down. "Koreans can be…pretty blunt." I was an adult; surely I'd developed a thick enough skin to be unruffled by a criticism or two. I left Queens and my cousin's advice behind and flew to Seoul.

In retrospect, it was delusional to arrive in a city of twelve million demanding instant camaraderie. The Korean-Koreans I met failed to acknowledge me as one of their own. They told me I was a "foreigner," that I wasn't "our country's people." I was offered the kinds of comments I initially mistook for compliments: I looked like I played golf, or volleyball; I spoke "cute" Korean; I had the kinds of eyes Westerners liked. However, I was treated like a Korean when convenient—when I botched a verb conjugation of "*our* country's language" or didn't *yangbo* my subway seat quickly enough for an elder—and was censured accordingly.

A pivotal moment came when I saw a face that looked like mine on the side of a bus: tanned, with single-creased, almond-shaped eyes and round, high cheeks. I was the before for a plastic surgery ad. The after-shot? Pale-faced and doe-eyed, with double-creased lids and an unnaturally high nose bridge; a repeat of every young female face I saw on the streets. I felt like an early prototype of the race, one that South Koreans were trying to revise, to forget.

One afternoon on the train, I saw my first Korean homeless man: hair disheveled, his face so brown, it was almost red. I wouldn't have believed he was Korean if not for his eyes—narrow, uncreased, and shining black. The same as my father's eyes. The same as my eyes.

The man began distributing Xeroxes onto people's laps. "I'm sorry, I'm so sorry," he said. It was a photocopy of his ID card and a formal apology for his inability to find a job. I never spared some change to panhandlers in New York, but this man was Korean—shouldn't that count for something? I thought of the deli owner by my old office who would comment on my bad Korean before tossing a freebie pack of gum in my bag.

I looked about for social cues; my fellow passengers continued texting on their cell phones, watching K-dramas from their portable video players, or just staring into space. None of them—none of *us*—reached for our wallets. I made excuses to myself—this man was an elder *and* a male, I'd pervert the Confucian hierarchy—but in truth, I felt no connection to him. When he recollected his paper from me, I didn't meet his eye.

As I grew disillusioned with life in Seoul, I had the chance to travel to North Korea, but harbored no great expectations for my trip. The DPRK, with its hermetically-sealed borders, represented to me an undiluted version of an already strict, militant culture. On the flight, myriad fears should have rightfully fought for my attention: that I was entering a totalitarian regime representing not one, but two enemy states; that my mother was born in the same province as Kim Jong-Il, and if the DPRK government discovered this fact, I'd be handled as they do daughters of defectors (to the gulags). Instead, my central worry was whether I'd be criticized and rejected by yet another faction of my kinsmen.

The amount of interactions I was permitted with the locals surprised me; the pleasantness of those interactions surprised me more. I met historians at Kim Il-Sung commemorative sites, school children on playgrounds, the elderly on the subway, and to each I introduced myself as an American-born *Chosun*, using the DPRK word for "Korean." I was a head taller and thirty pounds heavier than the next biggest North Korean, yet they enveloped me in their thin arms like a long-lost sister, daughter, granddaughter.

I also never imagined I'd be sitting around a fire with North Koreans, drinking homemade acorn liquor. I was on a fishing boat off the eastern coast when I said hello to a group of locals. They evaluated me—my Korean(ish) face, my American sneakers—and just when I expected to be met with a dismissive grunt, one of the men pushed a clam into my hand. It was char-grilled, as meaty as beef. A woman offered me her seat—a discarded piece of Styrofoam. She pried apart a clam shell and poured into one of the halves a clear liquid. "To your health, little sister!" she said, and I was made to drink.

We toasted to "one flowing blood line," to unity for the *Chosun* people, to the new memories we were forming. Even my tour guide, standing at the far end of the boat and occasionally glancing over, broke into a smile. I was overcome with a tingling sensation, and it wasn't just the bathtub *soju*. Was I experiencing that mythical *jung?* These North Koreans were so gaunt their cheekbones threatened to break the surface of their skin, and yet they shared all of their food and drink with me.

I wanted to do something to express my thanks; earlier, I had sent over a bottle of *soju*, but it was a production that required the guide as a go-between. If I flagged him down again, it would only draw more attention. Tourists were forbidden from carrying DPRK currency, but I remembered I had some U.S. singles I could give as souvenirs. They were brand-new bills, which required pulling out the stack from my wallet and licking my fingers as I counted...

The tone of the group immediately shifted.

"N-n-no!" they said, throwing up their hands. They turned their heads away from me, pushing back their makeshift chairs.

"I'm sorry, it's just...as a memento..." My cheeks flushed with embarrassment.

My handler pulled me from the circle, and as we walked away, I pinched the skin of my forearms. In God We Trust. Had I only confirmed the archetype of the U.S. imperialist? That fragile moment of unity, shattered.

I've since returned to Seoul, having traveled to a place no Southern citizen can legally enter. This is a fact I've taken to dropping into each and every one of my conversations. "I never felt *jung* until I went to North Korea. Oh *right*, you've never been..."

The South Koreans, in turn, shake their heads like I've gotten it all wrong. *Jung*, they tell me, takes a lifetime to develop, be it with a favorite mentor or despised mother-in-law. What I'd experienced was just "one, big, propagandized show" designed to "elicit sympathy" in the form of "cold, hard cash."

I often look back on that moment on the fishing boat, and it disheartens me to think it might have been staged. I wonder, too, about the last words the woman had whispered to me as I–disgraced–gathered my things to leave.

"Just never forget you're *Chosun*," she had said, waving away my dollar bills. "It's the only memory worth holding onto."

"Looking for Your Father... When The Only Clue You Have Is That He Was An Extra in a Shakespeare Play" by Johannah Rodgers

Johannah Rodgers is a writer, artist, and educator whose work explores issues related to representation and communication practices across media. She is the author of *52 Word Drawings* (mimeograph, 2017) *Technology: A Reader for Writers* (Oxford University Press, 2014), the digital fiction project DNA (mimeograph.org/The Brooklyn Rail, 2012), and the book *sentences* (Red Dust, 2007).

The "Facts"

I am the first Rodgers/Lowery in four generations to have brown eyes. From this, I know my father had brown eyes. That fact, that he was English, that his name was Richard Lewis, and that he was in Chicago in March or April, 1967, when he impregnated my mother after a performance of a Shakespeare play, comprise the sum total of what I have ever known about him.

My mother, a great talker and storyteller, has always been reluctant and unforthcoming when it comes to information about my father. On those few and far between occasions when she talks about him, she always reveals the same things, nothing much really, which for someone as confessionally inclined as she is has always struck me as odd.

One may think that my mother's reluctance to discuss my father, or her lack of factual accuracy—"he was either in *Romeo and Juliet* or *Hamlet* at the Schubert Theater, no, it was McCormick Place"—indicate that she still harbors some resentment towards this man for impregnating her and then leaving the next day, or that she is still in the throes of some unrequited love affair from long ago. Neither is true. My mother is a lesbian. My father was the only man she ever had sex with and, according to her version of the story, she very much wanted to get pregnant at the time because she was in love with my non-biological mother, the woman who not only attended my birth but who, along with my biological mother, I was raised by.

A Story In Search of a Vocabulary

1967 was not a good year to find yourself twenty-three, unmarried, pregnant, and a lesbian from a well-established Irish-Catholic family in Chicago. My grandparents had already sent my mother away once, to Rome for a semester abroad, to get her away from her first love, a girl named Louise whom my grandfather found kissing my mother in the backseat of his 1964 Camaro. My grandmother (the Catholic!) allegedly suggested abortion, which was not only against Church doctrine at the time, but also illegal.

My mother's true love at the time, Helen, was not only well-liked by my grandparents, but had recently accepted a new job in Southern Ohio, and, much to my grandparents' relief, my mother went to live with her and have the baby. I was born in a doctor's office in Chesterfield, Ohio in January 1968. My birth certificate lists my father's name as Richard Lewis. I don't know what arrangements were made to keep everything under wraps as far as the doctor and his assistant were concerned, but I do know that my baptism was held in the next county to preserve appearances. My godmother's brother, a Catholic priest, performed the baptismal ceremony. To this day, I still do not know how much he knew, or whether he was told, as our neighbors were, that my father was a "U.S. marine stationed in Vietnam." It was only after my birth that my mother and godmother pretended that my father, by then a "war hero," had been killed; even going so far as to stage a mock funeral at a friend's house in Chicago.

I've heard many stories about those years in Southern Ohio. I generally think my mother and Helen were happy then, and that they were a couple, as they rarely would be afterward. I'm not sure whether, in the late 60s, they were considered "hippies" or just eccentric, but I remember that—sometime in the mid-1990s—when my godmother told me for the first time about staging my father's death and funeral that the thing I was most surprised by was not their play-acting, but that they had cast him as military officer. My earliest memories are of Helen wearing outfits made of brightly colored, printed fabrics and wearing pins with "Out Spiro" or "Recall Nixon" or "Adelaide Now" slogans on them. But it was a very small town in rural Ohio where we were living at the time and the two of them had made a commitment to fitting in and having a community there, so I guess the Vietnam story was part of that.

In reality—as opposed to the world of make-believe—once my mother found out she was pregnant, she and Helen considered going to Montreal to tell Richard Lewis the news. They ultimately did go to Canada, were unable to locate him, and then sent a certified letter to some address in the U.K. after I was born. It was returned unopened. I've never taken offense at this since I have to assume they had the wrong address. In terms of how I was raised, some things my parents did were wonderful, others not so much so, but regarding their handling of the issue of my father, I don't think they could have done a better job. They always told me the truth about him (the little they knew) and I have always felt quite secure about the whole thing and free to pursue him and his family history if I wished to.

Once people find out about my curious (for the time) family set-up they are always interested to know more. They want me to tell them a story, to explain, to illuminate, what this experience of a different kind of family was like. As much as people want me to talk about the differences between my family and other nuclear families, there were and are many more similarities.

The year I turned three, we moved to Ann Arbor, Michigan, where I would live until I left for college at 18. My biological-mother and I moved first, followed Helen a year later. Both would complete graduate degrees at the University of Michigan: my biological-mother a Ph.D. in clinical psychology, my non-biological-mother an M.A. in Social Work. When I was younger, I included my biological mother's sexuality in my long list of complaints about her (my non-biological mother never identified herself as a lesbian, and sometimes had boyfriends, so in my mind, at least, she was straight). In grade school, I was woefully embarrassed by certain titles on my parents' bookshelves: "Sappho Was a Right On Woman," "The Joy of Sex" (I was pretty prurient, so it didn't matter that the latter title might also be found on the bookshelves at most of my friends' houses). I never went so far as to turn the spines of these or other books around when my friends visited our house—and they did visit—but I did make sure they stayed on the highest shelves or the ones closest to the floor as to remain somewhat out of sight.

Kids on the playground joked around about "fags" and "homos." It was always that way and I didn't take it personally or worry about any of it. Everyone knew I lived with two women—my mother and my godmother—and that my father was not around. But it was the 70s and there were lots of people getting divorces, lots of single moms, or at least I thought this was the case. I attended the faculty ghetto grade school in Ann Arbor, which was, in my mind at the time and in my memory now, a pretty wonderful place. I loved my teachers and my friends. There was only one African-American student in the class (he had been adopted by a Caucasian family) and the rest was white.

Over the years my father was ... I'm not sure exactly ... just not all that important. He didn't matter to me and he didn't matter in the least to my two mothers. Whatever stories or tales I may have invented to explain my family, I was always nothing but forthright and forthcoming about the father issue: I never knew him. He was English, a fact I was, even at a rather young age, terribly proud of, and maybe, I hinted, or just let people assume, my parents had divorced when I was an infant. The fact of his being English and residing in England just made the whole story that much more plausible.

Although, throughout my childhood and even into college, I fabricated all kinds of stories—when I was ten I explained a missed violin lesson by telling my teacher that a very close friend of my mother's had died suddenly, right out of the blue, just fell out of bed onto the floor, and yes she was so young, the same age as my mother, which resulted in an emergency trip to California for the funeral–I never made up tales about my father, for myself or for anyone else. I told people that I just didn't care, and this was the truth, however odd that my sound. In my angry teenage years I was consoled by the fact that I was not my biological mother's unique creation, and that there was another set of genes in me that counted as much as hers. But that was about it. I didn't want to be her.

Things Do Change

I now reside in Park Slope, Brooklyn, where I've been living for ten years. When my lesbian friends or neighbors, often couples thinking about having children of their own, hear about my family, they are eager to know what my experience of growing up in a lesbian household was like. "It was complicated," I say, "it was just such a different time." And it was. Although Ann Arbor was a liberal college town, it was still located in the Midwest and it was still the 1970s and 80s. There was no one out at my high school and, at least to my knowledge, only one gay bar in town. It was called The Flame. My friends and I crossed to the other side of the street when we had to walk down the block where it was located. I finally went in once, in college, and it wasn't scary in the least, which was the end of the illusion that it was a den of shame and covertness, as we had all believed as kids.

In the late 1990s, I would sometimes (though even these attempts were rather dilatory and late, considering when the technology first became available) search for my father's name on the Internet. But it was such a common name, and I did not know his place or date of birth; I did not even know the exact age he was when my mother met him ("he was nineteen or twenty, younger than me"). But slowly, I accumulated more information or just synthesized what I had, until I could pinpoint his alma mater (the Bristol Old Vic Theatre School), and, through new technology and old, figure out ways (they now seem obvious though each were singular revelations) of locating even more information about him.

Over the years, I would Google "Richard Lewis/actor," and discovered lots of things, including, one afternoon, someone I thought was my father. This Richard Lewis was a radio announcer with BBC Bristol and, in addition to running the weekly quiz show and hosting some other popular programs, just happened to have been a television actor. The Bristol/actor connections made it all seem quite plausible. I searched and searched, found this Richard Lewis' email address and sent him a brief note asking if he had ever studied at the Bristol Old Vic Theatre School. I didn't expect him to reply, but just in case he did, I went so far as to contact an ex-boyfriend who is English and who has friends working at the BBC to find out if through some connections I might be able to set up a meeting with this Richard Lewis. By the end of the day, I had even located a photograph on the BBC Bristol site! I ran home and told my boyfriend, Donald. After dinner, we looked up the photo on the Web. "He has your nose," Donald said in a rather ominous and serious tone. We were both pretty excited. The next day, I turned on my computer and found a reply from Richard Lewis at the BBC. "Sadly," he wrote, "I've never had a chance to study theatre at the Bristol Old Vic. I would certainly have liked to. Regards, Richard Lewis."

Last summer, I visited London and made a trip to the Family Records Office in Finsbury Park, just for the hell of it, to see what I might find. I had already learned from the Family Record Web site that "Births are in the Green Books; Deaths are in the Red Books" and that it is possible to order a birth certificate by faxing in a request if the exact date and location of birth are known. I had neither. Therefore, I went to the center myself and very quickly discovered that with a name as common as "Richard Lewis," a birthdate of anytime from 1947-1949 (even that was a guess), and the only known birthplace as "a town in Wales," any attempts to figure out which of the hundreds and hundreds of the Richard Lewises listed might be my father was utterly fruitless; my research had reached an impasse.

In the Spring of 2005, having paid no attention to the search for my father for almost a year, it suddenly occurred to me (the belatedness of this revelation is clearly odd) that I could simply look up a review of one of the Old Vic's 1967 performances. I went to the Brooklyn Public Library and, using the *Readers' Guide to Periodical Literature*, those big green books that I hadn't used since school in Ann Arbor, looked up "Jane Asher" (nothing), "Bristol Old Vic" (again nothing), and then "Shakespeare," which was cross-referenced to "Theater," which led to a whole section of "Performance Reviews." And there it was: a review of the Bristol Old Vic touring production of Hamlet at the City Center in *The New Yorker*, February 25, 1967.

I didn't have much time, and the reference librarian, who was new, didn't know that it wasn't necessary to fill out a call slip for *The New Yorker* microfilms and have them paged since they were actually sitting out in the metal flat files right next to him. We squandered a half-hour before he asked why the microfilm hadn't been delivered from the basement and one of the pages indicated that *The New Yorker* microfilms were on the open shelves. I quickly found the reel, had a small, predictable fight with the microfilm reader, was helped to find the power button after seeking assistance from the reference librarian, looped the film through the machine and found the review. The performance, directed by Val May, received lukewarm reviews in the New York papers. *The New Yorker* reviewer, Chinese Kookie, wrote "the gentlemen in the company have a gift for elocution, but they excite little emotional response, and the ladies are a pallid lot." My favorite comment on the performance, however, was from *Newsweek* review: "Richard Pasco's Hamlet comes on strong and confident, leaping into the action at Elsinore like Steve McQueen off a motorcycle." There was no information about any extra cast members in any of the reviews in the Brooklyn Library collection.

The next day I was kicked out of my apartment at 8 a.m. by the painter who was, that week, re-plastering and re-painting my living room. I work at home and it is usually a big deal when I am forced to work elsewhere. But I made the most of the beautiful spring day, went to the café down the street with my laptop and then, rather than going to the Brooklyn Public Library as planned, decided to go to Manhattan to return some recent purchases and go to the New York Public Library at 42nd Street. There were a few articles and books related to an entirely different project that only the NYPL Research Library would have. So, I figured, since I had the whole day, why not also visit the periodicals department and see what Chicago papers they had on file there?

The index for the *Chicago Tribune* begins in 1972; the one for the *The New York Times* in 1913. With the help of a reference librarian and based on the fact that I knew the performance in New York had been of *Hamlet*, I was able to locate a review in the February, 17, 1967 edition of *The New York Times*. I did not fight with the microfilm reader, though I did have some trouble fitting the film into the machine right away. I raced through various editions until I landed on the one for February 17, found the arts section, and there it was: not only a review of the performance but one that began with a complete cast list. For the first time, I found my father's full name, "Richard Glyn Lewis." He played the role of Guildenstern (of course).

I experienced a certain shock when I saw his full name on the grainy black and white page projected onto the microfilm screen. I also couldn't believe how lucky I was that my father would have three names, and use them; this meant I really could find him. There was a lump in my throat even as I tried to make a joke to myself about the fact of his playing the role of Guildenstern: What could be more appropriate except, possibly, the role of the Ghost? I was so excited and shocked that I backed my rolling chair across the smooth linoleum floor right into the patron behind me, an attractive young Indian-American woman who, somewhat annoyed, said "Excuse me," after removing a white iPod bud from one ear. "I'm so sorry," I stammered. I wanted to tell her that I'd just found my father's name for the first time, but then decided not to, and instead wait to tell someone who might actually be interested, like the reference librarian, for instance, who helped me look up the citation to the review in the Internet Broadway Database. *She* would want to hear about the vagaries of this research project and may even understand my shock and surprise at being able to find this information.

There's the zip zipping of the copy card being inserted into the reader and, around me, that distinct whirring sound of microfilm being fast forwarded. I'm also aware of the spitting sound the microfilm makes when it is rewound completely; it reminds me of a tongue somehow but I can't say exactly how or why. I'm shaking. I can't believe it has been this easy. And I'm dumb-struck by the fact that for so many years this review–and his full name–have been sitting on microfilm available at any public or university library (I've spent quite a bit of time at both) and yet remain untouched and unexcavated– more than that, for it is my unawareness of and obliviousness to its existence that strikes me as most surprising.

It is a beautiful spring day in New York City. We are having one of the loveliest springs in years. I print out the *New York Times* review, scan through a few issues of the *Chicago Tribune,* but give up looking because I'm late for a lunch date to meet a friend and I still have not found an exact reference to the Chicago review. I show my friend Adam the printout of the review. "I've found my father's name for the first time," I tell him. I've known Adam since college and he is excited for me; and, like me, he also enjoys looking at some of the great 1960s era fashion and travel ads I've printed out. After I found my father's name I couldn't do much but look at the pictures as I tried to restrain the temptation to print out every single page of that day's paper.

The park is crowded with people looking stunned by the beautiful weather, as Adam and I are too. After lunch, as I'm heading back to the library to Google my father using his full name for the first time, I walk past the little merry go-round in the park; they're playing Edith Piaf songs as a musical accompaniment. I laugh to myself because I'm so happy to be living in New York City at the moment, and then remember having been told that there is now wireless network access available at Bryant Park, possibly right where I'm standing. Rather than going inside and signing up to use the library computers, I pull out my laptop, which has a wireless network card installed, and turn it on. Much to my surprise, the wireless network at the park works! I open up my browser and Google my father. There is only a single "hit" for "Richard Glyn Lewis."

New Words and Definitions

I'm sitting at a round metal table on one of the green wooden folding chairs that are strewn around in the park. The chairs remind me of Paris, but this square of green, framed by tall buildings and crowded with people, is distinctly New York. The Google search has returned an excerpt from a death notice, or more exactly a listing in the Acknowledgements section thanking friends and family for their attentions after the death of Richard Glyn Lewis. It lists the town Richard Glyn Lewis is originally from (Cwmbran, which is in Southern Wales) and the town where he was most recently residing (Whitney on Wye, near Bristol). I click on the link for the one hit that has appeared and it takes me to the Family Announcements section in the online edition of a publication called *This is Hereford*. I look through the eight bolded, uppercase family names, none of which is LEWIS, then I search the page for "Richard" or "Glyn" or "Lewis" and come up empty. I begin searching the site in earnest, the whole

186

thing, by section, but there is nothing. I learn from the Web site that only announcements that have appeared in the *Hereford Times* over the past twelve days are listed, and that should I wish to email one of these listings to a "friend or relative," I need only click a button.

In one afternoon, I have found my father for the first time and, though this announcement may relate to his father and not him, or to another individual entirely, had to face his death. Internet time leaves little room for anticipation. I e-mail the editor of the Family Announcements section of the *This is Hereford* Web site right as I'm sitting in Bryant Park. Who knows if she will reply; I certainly hope so. In the meantime, I'm struck by how all of this information that I've discovered is meaningful and meaningless at the same time; how everything is different and yet, really, the same. For, to say to someone, a good friend, for instance, who accompanies me to a production of *Hamlet*, that my father played the role of Guildenstern in the 1967 Bristol Old Vic production at New York's City Center, is not to reference a family story or a certain feeling or anything more than a name on a sheet of paper.

I try to be sad. After all, I've just found out that my father, as far as I know, is dead! But I have no relationship to him. He is a biological fact that, at times, has been the subject of much imaginary speculation. For the first time, I say to myself , "my father was a sperm donor," which may or may not be the correct term based on the historical facts. Though, as far as my experience of him is concerned, and his actual place in my family's history, it IS the correct term.

I do receive an email in response to my query to the *This is Hereford* Website: "Unfortunately I have been unable to trace any family announcement in our paper with the information you have given me. Sorry we are not able to help on this occasion but please do not hesitate to contact us if we can be of any further assistance. Sincerely, Denise Kenny, Family Announcements." So I still don't know if this Richard Lewis is my father or not. In a way, I'm surprised by

Denise's response—don't they have an index?—but in another way this latest news feels not only predictable, but inevitable. It would be so strange NOT to exist in a state of "not knowing" with regard to my father.

Through the online catalogue to the theatre collection at the University of Bristol, I've been able to access my father's complete repertory history, and discovered that there are a number of photographs and ephemera on file from the productions he appeared in. I realize that my surprise and excitement at finding this information about my father relates as much to the discovery that my biological mother was not lying as it is to potentially being able to meet this man. He was a Shakespearean actor. He was actually in a production of *Hamlet*. I could travel to the Bristol library and locate photographs and, afterwards, possibly locate him. But the larger question remains: Why? With the precipitous rise in donated insemination, this is a question more and more children will face. I begin to wonder whether "father," a term that signifies so much more than the fact of shared genetic code, is really the right word for the man I have always referred to using this term. Learning to refer to my parents as "my two mothers" signaled a significant shift not only in my conception of my family, but also in my parents' relationship to me. Perhaps, in light of the many ongoing changes that are occurring in family roles and structures, for those children who, like me, never did have a "father," some new vocabulary will emerge to help clarify the terms of what this relationship is.

"Spreading Ashes for a Beat Poet" by Benjamin Shepard

Benjamin Shepard, PhD, LMSW, works as Professor of Human Services at City Tech/CUNY. By night, he battles to keep NYC from becoming a giant shopping mall. He has done organizing work with ACT UP, SexPanic!, Reclaim the Streets, and Times Up among many other organizations. He's authored several books, including, *White Nights and Ascending Shadows: An Oral History of the San Francisco AIDS Epidemic*, *The Beach beneath the Streets: Contesting New York's Public Spaces*, and *Play, Creativity, and Social Movements: If I Can't Dance, Its Not My Revolution*. He was named by *Playboy* as one of twenty professors "who are reinventing the classroom." An earlier version of this essay was published in Shepard's blog, Play and Ide.

"Off to Texas to spread some ashes," I posted on Facebook, above a picture of dad in 1945. We'd all meet in Texas to spread Dad's ashes. That was his request. Spread 'em out for the world, rather than leave them at the family burial plot at Midway Church, where Shepards have rested since 1740. Over the next week, ashes seemed to be everywhere. I remembered the first two times I spread ashes: at AIDS funerals in Washington D.C. and saying goodbye to a Stonewall veteran while dashing his ashes out in the Hudson. Bob's blew right back in my face as I poured them. But this was my Dad. Two months after his death and no one wanted to go to the service. But a few of us went. It all felt wrong. The service was painful. A stuffy, stale Episcopalian affair.

Eulogy for a Beat

"I know there was a Jack Shepard who got hanged holding up a stagecoach in 1720," Dad confessed in a 2009 oral history. He loved telling stories. "They caught and made an example of him. I like that story more than the story of the crusades," Dad confessed referring to the family history drafted by his grandmother, Irene Hewatt Shepard, who died at the age of 99 in 1981.

"Well, who were the Shepards?" I asked following up.

"Dust covered Calvinist sons of bitches. That's my roots. Dorchester England. They got their roots right from the Puritans. They came over with the Puritans in the 1680s to Dorchester Mass. There's a Shepard Street right there, spelled the same way. Dorchester, England to Dorchester, Mass to Dorchester, South Carolina, to Georgia, where they established a colony of thieves and cut throats in Savannah, Georgia in a place between something or another, settled in another fever swamp and built a church there like a New England Church. What I'm trying to tell you is you have an ancestry that you can pass onto your kids that isn't known to others, that you can trace from the people you knew to the Midway church records which trace us to 1740.

"But who were the Shepards? I asked.

"Dusty, hidebound, mean sons of bitches that lived in Georgia from 1740 until you guys had the good sense to get out of there, 250 years later.

"But you've been leaving for decades now?"

"I hit the road in 1958 and never returned for serious," Dad boasted.

Dad was a first class snob and a supporter of the Beat Movement, which challenged so much of conventional narratives of the Post War Eisenhower era in which he grew up. This movement transformed his way of seeing the world. His memories of that period, stories of learning to be his own person in an era of 1950s total conformity, went on and on. We talked about that era over and over again. These conversations inspired me. My first oral histories were with Dad, reflecting on this era. I wrote down his musings for a class on the US in the World after WWII.

In college I wrote an essay situating a young Dad among the crowd in post-War San Francisco: Among the waves of dreamers to find their way to San Francisco was a group of writers, who came to inspire a new movement for freedom…Perched in a smoky coffee house deep in San Francisco's North Beach neighborhood. Allen Ginsberg would contribute to this burgeoning queer civil society with one of the great feats of recently literary history. He first performed "Howl" at the Six Gallery on October 7, 1955. The first lines are now familiar enough, yet from the vantage point of 1950s America, they were striking.

"Howl" is a spiritual poem, full of references to the Old Testament, the sky, and illumination, Dad explained. The poem is a deadly attack on material culture. "I dropped out of college and hitchhiked to San Francisco after I read it," he recalled. "It was an apocryphal poem about breaking out of the mold that they were trying to put us in."

Dad read the poem to my friends and myself on several occasions. We talked, laughed, and wondered about Moloch. And as the years continued, the story opened up. The beats inspired Dad in ways few of us could imagine, creating a redemptive narrative he lived for decades of his life. It helped him see the road as a liminal space, opening us to experience something of a "holy America." These poems helped him see that streets and minds could be filled with words, creating an alchemy of nonsensical verse that helped us define ourselves, opening up alternate narratives of living. It transformed his life, as well as mine.

Reading it and walking through the city streets of San Francisco or Manhattan, we used to stroll, thinking of dad. It is hard not to imagine the memories as ghosts, their reflection lingering in the colors in the rain.

By the winter of 2014, Dad was less able to take my calls. I'd call and he could not pick up or when he did, he was anxious to get out the hospital, for us to read more poems together: "Next time, we'll read the Outlaw Book of Poetry. We'll just get together and read some stories." On another call, I asked if poems were still running through his head. "Less now," he confessed.

On the Road

Mom knew Dad longer than any of us, of course, meeting him in 1963, before bearing their three children. Count another twenty-five years of marriage and another quarter century of friendship. Mom took the first scoop of ashes, spreading them through the woods, with the kind of hollow ambivalent feeling which only a quarter century of marriage, three children, trips around the world, illness, betrayal, and divorce could create. We all spread them—ashes to ashes.

I saw a raindrop making its way through the ashes on the leaves of a bush where he lay.

In "Neal's Ashes," Allan Ginsberg writes about holding his one-time love's ashes, wondering if it was his friend's ass or his nose that he was clutching. One does wonder, holding the remains of a life, dust, and needing to reconnect with that dirt and rain and sunlight.

The last road trip Dad and I took, we stayed at the Bayou Cabins, so we dropped by, for a taste of some of Rocky's boudin sausage. Hot and dehydrated, we made our way to NOLA to a house where some friends from Brooklyn said we could stay on Port Street between North Rampart and St. Claude Ave. in the Faubourg Marigny neighborhood of New Orleans. I remember the colors on the street, the small quirky homes, the Spanish moss in the trees, Caribbean color, azaleas, art, crusty punks, angelheaded hipsters, jazz supporters, and other NOLA devotees, hanging out in the musky streets of the city in constant flux.

Most of our recommendations were closed so we made our way to Coop's near the quarter, where we'd been advised to stay clear. Instead of the musky smell of the Bahamas, the street smelled like vomit as we enter Margaretville. "New Orleans is a city with the clap," Dad's best friend Fred noted, decades ago. She still feels like that, I thought, waiting for a table at Coop's, where I'd dined with dad years earlier.

Over rabbit and shrimp jambalaya, several of the staff commented on Dad's urn, bringing us shots, to toast the beloved old man. They tapped the table in honor of all those who've come before, toasting to them, and splashing some beer on the floor, before drinking themselves.

Across New Orleans, we were offered toast after toast, as we traversed the streets. Sometimes you gotta travel the low road to find your way to heaven, explained Eric, recalling puking in the back of Dad's Volvo car when he asked if we'd been drinking at Jamie's house in the spring of 1983.

"No sir," he replied before vomiting.

As the evening wore onward, we made our way through the city's low roads and high, with toasts and stories accompanying our trips. We'd traveled here together in 1987. Will getting served and enjoying the streets and strippers at 15. NOLA has always been a grand city. I hustled a bit of this and that, eyes bulging and dreaming, enjoying and hoping as we made our way through the vomit lined street that night over a quarter century prior.

We slept in the next day, eventually making it out for a lunch at Frady's One Stop, enjoying the oyster po' boys and the neighborhood, before we walked to the Basin Street Cemetery, where Marie Laveau, the voodoo queen's grave, draws legions to this city of the dead.

At Backstreet Cultural Museum, the founder showed us his collection of Mardi Gras Indian suits from the social aid and pleasure societies, parade paraphernalia, roles such as the bull and the face of the future for the kids there. One man's body was held up high and paraded through the streets for two weeks after his spirit left. The point of the jazz parade, of course, was a final goodbye, followed by morning, grief, and recognition that life goes on. That's why Will and I were there. To usher Dad off in style, dancing with the saints and sinners along the way.

"You cannot police a bird," read one sign. "The streets belong to the people."

That night, we hit three sets, starting with Kermit Ruffians' band at Bullet's Sports Bar. With a cross section of NOLA in the bar, the room roared with dancing bodies. And, once again, people were buying us drinks for dad, toasting him, and taking care of us.

After a full set, we walked up to Galatoire's, one of Dad's favorite restaurants.
"Feels like home," Dad confessed when we dined there in 2009. We eat there every time we come. He took my daughter and I there a week before Katrina hit. His mom took him there in 1943, while his father was stationed in Burma.

We spent the rest of the night taking in jazz, enjoying sets at Preservation Hall, where we spread some more ashes and recalled our first trip there with him. Wandering for more tunes on Frenchman Street.

By Wednesday, it was time to finish the task, pouring the rest of the ashes in the Mississippi. As we poured the ashes from the bag into the river, we watched them mingle with our tears. It was over. Our task complete. And all was empty again. Dad was still with us, but not as much now.

Driving back to Texas, Will lit a cigar, bringing Dad's memories onto the trip. We talked about our dad, our lives, uncles, prep school, grandfathers, hopes and future plans. The sun gradually faded into sunset, the silhouettes of farmhouses and trees lingered in the distance.

As Will packed to fly back home, I saw him walking away. "Wait

Will," I cried, giving him a pinecone from the Sam Houston forest where Dad lay. He smiled and put it in his bag and turned to leave. Growing up our relationship was like the brothers in *East of Eden*, today it is more like *The Brothers Karamazov*, a redemptive forgiving space for new trips and stories of our lives. Some day our time will be up, but for now we are here.

I drove north to Dallas where we lived for a decade, harvesting a thousand and one memories. The road led me to the beltline looping Dallas, where we drove on many occasions for parties, on late night drives, some thousand Friday nights looking for anything out there to see. Dallas leaves its public tragedies and its private regrets, divorces, summer intrigue from a quarter century ago when the tanks rolled in on Tiananmen Square. That was the summer when a lust for something better took me from Dallas to Austin to Barton Springs, to the 500 Café, to Ten Hands Shows every night in the Deep Ellum, back to the Caravan of Dreams, late nights in the summer with a new friend, sucking the marrow out of life. "Look at all we have," she screamed, "look at the sun rise." Driving and looking at the many sides of the city, the way the sun shone on the reflecting glass of the city, seeing it for the very first time, everything seemed so real and possible. We jumped off cliffs into the water, danced, boogied, hung out in the car, careened here and nowhere, drove to and from Austin–the best of summer of my life. The crescendo of music and subsequent losses, the ups and the lessons of the downs, taught me more than anything. In between vivid images, the memories of my dad who made his way through the city, working to be the best father he could be, they are hard to shake, especially driving around Dallas, on mockingbird. This is where you learned about community, Dad reminded me, looking back on Deep Ellum. Those thoughts are always with me looking at the Inwood Theater where I worked, and the world came to me, tripping through the summers of a misspent, well-worn youth.

Driving back to Austin, the space between the road and sky opened up into sprawling vista of desert, flowers, caves and mystery. Conjuring Joshua Tree and the road, the space opened a space which felt very familiar and distant, something to find and something to leave behind in a Texas of memories. There is no way to completely reconcile the loss of a parent, with its savage endpoint. But the road heals.

Leaving for New York, I left something dear behind, something that was regained in the desert, between the caves just north of the Pedernales River, the pinecone from the Sam Houston Forest, the Texas Hill Country, the Lone Star Caverns, the Bayou and the streets of Brooklyn. Now when I see trees, they remind me of my dad who would sit on tree stumps with me when I was little. Our conversations continue on, taking us down that road.

"Khuli Dhari: My Journey to Beard Liberation"
by Sonny Singh

Sonny Singh is a Brooklyn-based social justice educator, writer, and musician. He has been active in movements for social and economic justice since high school. He received his Master's Degree in Social Justice Education at the University of Massachusetts at Amherst in 2003, where he studied and practiced the art of using education as a tool for liberation. Sonny regularly writes essays and articles on race, religion, and social justice for a variety of publications including the *Huffington Post, India Abroad, The Langar Hall* (where a version of this essay was originally published), *Colorlines, Sikh Chic, Left Turn, Asian American Literary Review. Race, Class, and Gender in the United States,* and *Open City Magazine.* He was also an Open City Fellow for the Asian American Writers' Workshop. He has been designing and facilitating workshops and classes related to issues of oppression and strategies for creating social justice for over 15 years, and regularly facilitates trainings for nonprofit organizations, activist groups, schools (grades 4-12), and colleges/universities. Sonny is also a trumpet player, singer, and dhol player, and an original member of the bhangra brass band, Red Baraat.

Growing up Sikh in the United States has never been easy. After years of enduring the humiliation of harassment, taunts, and jokes about the ball/rag/tomato/towel/etc. on my head as a turban-wearing child, my insecurities began to shift as puberty hit. Let's call it facial hair anxiety.

At first, having a moustache grow in at a young age wasn't necessarily a bad thing. After all, I passed as much older than I was, which was nice for a scrawny brown kid like me.

But soon enough, the complex around my dhari (beard) settled in, and no amount of time with a thatha—a thin cloth often used by Sikh men for beard styling—tied tightly around my head was ever enough to totally alleviate my beard insecurities.

Surrounded by peers for whom shaving was a rite of passage into manhood, it's not surprising that I felt a little left out (though to be clear, the idea of a razor on my face never sounded pleasant). Further, I was inundated with the voices of young women in my school casually referring to facial hair as gross or unattractive (with no intention to hurt my feelings I'm sure) and their preference for guys who were "clean-shaven."

CLEAN-shaven. The implication being that facial hair is…. dirty?

These are the messages we get from our peers and from the media every day. So naturally I assumed it was highly unlikely that any of my female classmates would ever be interested in dating someone like me. The combination of a dirty face plus a turban was enough to cause a whole lot of anxiety and insecurity for this angsty teenage Singh.

Applying a liberal dose of gel to my beard and smushing it to my face with a thatha for as much time as I had (facilitated and sped up with the power of a blow dryer) was a daily ritual for me as soon as I had enough hair on my face to do it.

There were always the "bad beard days" when a rebellious group of hairs would inexplicably pop out of place into a big tight curl on my otherwise smooth and sleek dhari. Or the humid days when no matter how much gel I put on my beard, it would just revert to a frizzy, curly mess within an hour.

The obsession of keeping my beard looking a certain way grew proportionally to the length of my beard itself. Bobby pins soon came into the mix, adding to the complexity and duration of my morning dhari routine.

My dad and older brother had similar routines with their beards (my dad keeping it old school with an Indian glue-like beard product known as "fixo"), as did all my Sikh male friends who kept their hair and beards and unshorn (with different levels of obsession). We'd exchange tips on the most recent holding products and techniques we were trying. It was actually a fun way to build community with other guys in the community and always proved to be a good icebreaker to get a conversation going.

Beard-gelling and tying was simply the status quo for the majority of my hair-faced life. I never questioned it. It's just how it was. It's just what we did.

When I look back on it now, I see a direct connection to my aforementioned facial hair anxiety. My borderline obsessive desire to keep every hair on my face a certain way was perhaps (at least partly) rooted in my anxiety around my beard (and turban) not being attractive. Perhaps it was a way to try to fit in just a little bit more.

Fast forward to my late twenties when I was attending Sikh research program in San Antonio, Texas: It was an intensive week of interpreting Sikh scripture-poetry, discussing the Sikh revolution, building community, and waking up really early. My second morning there I woke up too late to deal with my dhari so I went to the morning prayers all natural. My facial hair anxiety was creeping up even in that all-Sikh context, but I went with it at least for the morning. Later that afternoon I finally had time to gel, tie, and thatha my beard. Much to my surprise, a handful of my new friends asked me why I tied my beard back up, saying it looked nice open.

I thought and thought and thought about it, but really didn't have a good answer. I shrugged my shoulders and went on with the day, but the question continued to irk me. Why was I tying my beard? I couldn't come up with an answer that I was comfortable with, so I didn't gel or tie it for the rest of my two weeks there—a totally unprecedented move (up until that time I seldom left the house without tying my beard).

After coming back home to Brooklyn, I thought about why I chose to keep my unshorn hair and wear a turban and about how proud I am to be a Sikh and literally wear that identity every day. I thought about the boldness of Guru Gobind Singh instructing the members of the Khalsa in 1699 to wear turbans to mark themselves publicly as revolutionaries, rather than to blend into society. I thought about all the years I spent obsessing over trying to make my beard look a certain way without ever questioning why it was that I was doing that.

Almost 30 years into my life, I was finally asking myself, why? It wasn't easy to face, but when I was totally honest with myself, what I was really doing all those years was trying to make my beard look shorter, straighter, tamer, more polite. I felt a deep contradiction between my counterhegemonic aspirations inspired by the revolutionary spirit of Sikhi and my actions. I felt like I was trying to hide something, but what did I really have to hide? Since when has the Sikh identity been about hiding?

So began my path from facial hair anxiety to beard liberation.

Sure, there are plenty of additional challenges with rocking the khuli (open) dhari, both coming from mainstream society as well as from within the Sikh community. I definitely noticed an increase in derogatory comments, stares, and dirty looks in my daily life, which was frankly not a surprise. Nor was it anything I wasn't already (sadly) accustomed to. What has been especially disappointing are the some of the reactions I've gotten from other Sikhs. Certain family members were adamantly opposed to my beard transition and pleaded with me not to wear it open for reasons like: "It doesn't look nice/clean/professional/groomed/smart."

I was recently at a gathering at my aunt's house and was taken aback when multiple (Sikh) friends of my aunt's (who I did not know) practically interrogated me about my beard throughout the evening. They seemed almost threatened by my choice to leave my beard open. One older uncle asked me, "Who told you to do this?" and "What are you trying to prove?" The question came up time and time again in different ways that evening and continues to when I interact with certain (more affluent) segments of the Sikh community: Why in the world do you not tie your beard up?

But shouldn't the first question be: why *do* you tie your beard? Of course, Sikh men tie their beard for many reasons, and I am certain that for many, the decision has nothing to do with insecurity, anxiety, or internalized racism. For me, though, understanding where aesthetic practices that are now normalized come from is critical. A few mentors of who are scholars of Sikh history have explained to me that beard-tying first became a common practice after the British colonized India and recruited Sikhs to serve in the Army.

Perhaps then beard liberation takes on a whole new meaning of decolonizing my body, one hair at a time.

"Gray's Anatomy" by Aisha Sabatini Sloan

Aisha Sabatini Sloan's first essay collection, *The Fluency of Light: Coming of Age in a Theater of Black and White,* was published by the University of Iowa Press in 2013. Her most recent collection, *Dreaming of Ramadi in Detroit,* was chosen by Maggie Nelson as the winner of the Open Prose Award, and won the CLMP Firecracker award for nonfiction in 2018. A contributing editor for *Guernica,* her writing has been published in *The Offing, Ecotone, Ninth Letter, LitHub, Essay Daily, Tarpaulin Sky,* and *Autostraddle.* This essay originally appeared in *The Paris Review Daily.*

When I was visiting Los Angeles a couple years ago, I pulled my back. My mother connected me with her former chiropractor. As I stood, I told him what my symptoms were, and in one quick gesture he ripped my pants down, just below the cheek, without a word of warning. Because his eye contact had been spare, I wasn't sure how to make sense of the way he stripped me, like he was going to spank or fuck me. He used a tens machine and I left with almost no back pain. A bit over zealous, I walked several miles back to my hotel downtown. It's only now that I wonder what else might have prompted that need to wander so many miles by myself.

Later on, I went to see another chiropractor in Tucson when my back froze up again. I waited for what seemed like hours, watching other walk-ins pass quickly through to the other side. I think we were ushered in based on seniority, and I was new to the place, but I kept a close eye on the physical attributes of those who came and went.

The chiropractor listened to my troubles. He moved my head quickly and there was a click in my neck. After a few more adjustments, he told me to come back again, and had the receptionist sell me a multi-visit package. The next day, though I was still in pain, my body refused to obey when I tried to drive back to claim the appointment

I'd already paid for. I turned down a side street and pulled over.

I will likely never see a chiropractor again. Because he knows how to break my neck, I'm afraid that he might.

When Jean Michel Basquiat was a child, he got into a bad car accident and they were forced to remove his spleen. As he recovered, his mother, Matilde, got him the book *Grey's Anatomy*, which he memorized.

Art historian Robert Farris Thompson, one of the only critics Basquiat trusted, wondered if the artist's mother, by giving him this book about anatomy, "in a sense, had with affection commanded her son to study his body back together again." Matilde struggled with her mental health. She would sit still for hours and try to "imitate the whistling of birds." When she saw her son's paintings, later in life, she said, "You are moving very fast."

His paintings say "sangre," "corpus," "Diagram of the heart pumping," "cranium," "ear," "eye," "ribs," "skull," "jaw," "arm pit," "scapula," "tit," and "elbow." Biographer Phoebe Hoban says of the bodies on his canvases, "boys never become men, they become skeletons and skulls."

For example, in "Jesse," Basquiat has drawn a series of bodiless heads and headless bodies. "Neck," he writes just below where the skull would go. "Esophagus," over an open throat.

When I used to watch *Breaking Bad*, I felt seduced not despite but because of the graphic nature of the show. I felt devoted to it because of what it made me see—a perverse brand of intimacy that must explain how brainwashing works in cults and armies. There was one scene I refused to watch because I could tell it would have to do with the neck. I still remember my girlfriend's face in the glow of her computer screen as she saw what happened next.

———

Basquiat's talent seemed to irritate or mystify most critics. In *The New York Times*, Hilton Kramer wrote, "his sensibility, insofar as he can be said to have any, was that of an untrained and unruly adolescent wise only in his instinct for self-display as a means of self-advancement."

In a famous interview, Marc Miller asked the painter of his work, "it's just spontaneous juxtapositions, and there's no logic?" To which Basquiat responded, "God, if you're talking to like Marchel Duchamp— or even Rasuchenberg or something..." He was such a student of the artists that came before him, read so deeply into history, biology, anthropology and art, he could see clearly that critics were trying to disavow him of his intelligence. He called himself an art mascot. The vitriol exacted upon him by critics, the deep well of racism lurking in their response, is as much a part of his legacy as the art itself.

A white photographer who traveled with Basquiat to Europe was astonished by the level of nastiness. "He was treated weirdly, strangely, like he was an oddity. People were entertained by him, fascinated for the moment, but would sooner or later throw him away. Or he was feared, you know? Just genuinely feared." No matter where he went in the world, he was pulled over by the police. In Paris, with guns drawn, the police asked if a woman who had fallen asleep in the back seat of his car was dead.

Actor Jeffrey Wright, who played the painter in Julian Schnabel's 1996 biopic, *Basquiat,* was surprised at how much racism infused even the telling of the painter's life story: "I really got some insight into Basquiat because I really had to travel through the same doorways and rooms and hallways that he did," he explains. "The mystery you are left with at the end of the film about Basquiat is the stuff that Julian didn't know, so he assumed it didn't exist."

When I was a child, I was a serious gymnast. I stretched often, and deeply. I've long known about my body that there was a resistance at a certain point when I lie on my back and bring my feet over my head. It was a young or ancient part of me that diagnosed this kind of pain, a gray storm cloud of burning, as something I should move toward, not away from. Like bitter greens. Still, I avoided it for years.

Later in life, when I got into yoga, I became reacquainted with that sensation as I stretched the upper portion of my spine. It wasn't like joint or muscle pain. I felt as if the thing that kept me from moving deeper was particulate matter, separate from myself. An entity I should expel. The more I moved into it, the more it became a ripping fire. "Go deeper," some part of me always seemed to say.

Early on in Basquiat's career, a young, black aspiring artist and model named Michael Stewart was caught drawing the words "Pir Nema" on the subway. The NYPD allegedly used his face to break the window of a patrol car. He was bludgeoned and strangled into a coma and later died. Basquiat's on again off again girlfriend, Suzanne Mallouk, was close with Stewart and covertly photographed every wound on his body in the hospital. She helped his family bring his case to court. When Basquiat found out what happened to someone so like himself, a beautiful black artist who scribbled on the city's surfaces, he spent the night drawing black skulls. He made a painting called "Defacement."

I googled "Defacement" in order to see the painting and came upon a similarly titled book by Michael Taussig. The Google Books summary explains, *"Defacement* asks what happens when something precious is despoiled. It begins with the notion that such activity is attractive in its very repulsion, and that it creates something sacred even in the most secular of societies and circumstances. In specifying the human face as the ideal type for thinking through such violation, this book raises the issue of secrecy as the depth that seems to surface with the tearing of surface."

We live in a society wherein white supremacy, and individuals preoccupied by blood lust for the black body, use law enforcement as a tool. What is it that these men and women, masked, robed, or uniformed, seek to find when they smash the faces of our brothers and our fathers? What pleasure unfurls itself when they go repeatedly–systemically–for our necks? It is as if what is broken there holds secret symbolism. A glowing circle at the cervical spine that, when shattered, bings points for the other side.

At dinner a few weeks ago, my father told the story of a young man in Detroit he knew growing up. A group of famously rough cops told him to stick his face through the open patrol car window. "Please dad," I said. But he wanted me to hear it. That particular young man did not die. But you know what comes next: they rolled up the window. They began to drive away.

———

At a certain point, the way I felt when I curved my head forward and stretched my cervical spine became a bit of an addiction. I tried to keep myself from dipping into it too much. But I noticed that if I had been stressed out or if I consumed weed or alcohol the day before, the stretch seemed to push that lingering stiffness out into my blood, heat moving into my stomach before dissipating. I was left light head-ed. I would ask physical therapists and yoga teachers what it was. Nobody seemed to know. Some encouraged restraint. Others called it the body's wisdom. Eventually, I weaned myself off because one day, I spun my torso quickly and heard a sound at the base of my neck. A whooshing. As if I'd opened up a window.

Basquiat's antagonism toward white audiences became part of what attracted them to his art. His friend Lee Quiñones, notes, "Jean Michel's work is very anti-art world, you know. It's almost like a curse. And people still love that. They love being cursed at." But the curse seems wrapped up with a gift, somehow. Like the monk who shouts "shit stick" to awaken a student.

When he was still a teenager, Basquiat co-invented a religion called SAMO with a friend and wrote about it in the school newspaper. He saw himself as its leader or prophet. This morphed into the first act that placed him on the map as an artist. He and Al Diaz painted SAMO on walls and buildings: "SAMO as an end to playing art," "SAMO as an expression of spiritual love."

In *Widow Basquiat*, a biographical novel about his relationship with Suzanne Mallouk, the painter is obsessed with silent films. He is especially partial to DW Griffiths' *Broken Blossoms*. He memorizes a line that says, "The yellow man holds a giant dream to take the glorious message of peace to the Barbarous Anglo-Saxons." He would repeat this over and over again. Robert Farris Thompson asserts, "Basquiat's essays in anatomy, in their jazz-riff manner of exposition, are style and content in service to healing on a heroic scale."

If you watch the film *Downtown 81*, you can see the artist walking through the city chanting what was labeled in his notebooks as a prayer: "the earth was formless void/ Darkness face of the deep/ spirit moved across the water and there/ was light/ 'It was good.'"

––––––––

After Freddie Gray was arrested for possession of a knife, he was put in a tactical hold, chained to the back of a police wagon and given a "rough ride." His spine was severed 80% at the neck. I tried to watch the video in which he tries to walk after his injury. But the brutality of that killing, the way they chose to break him, still causes my body to squirm, sends my hands to my face where I try to press the image out of my head with the palm of my hand.

When I heard about Gray's death, I thought about the way I stretch my neck. I thought of every lynching. Every chokehold. Each act of violence toward this part of the body that connects us to the brain. Out of curiosity, I bent my neck, let the fire travel along the axis of my spine. I wondered exactly what it was that was being released. If it was even mine.

The Western world likes to separate the mind from the body. It likes to say, too, that some people, some races, are more body than thought. This makes it easier to degrade and oppress. Because, after all, who's there? But the collective wisdom of oppressed bodies, the memory of what has been done to the dead, percolates through us, upward into our ideas, our beliefs and our dreams. We know.

––––––––

People like to tell the story of Basquiat's death. His addiction has been confused with his talent, as if drug use explains that torrential flow of exquisitely rendered canvases. Only after reading his biography did I learn how badly Basquiat wanted to be healthy. In his notebooks he wrote over and over again, "Not in praise of poison."

Before he died, Basquiat met a painter from the Ivory Coast named Outarra. They went to a Cy Twombly exhibition together in Paris and walked through the Marais, deep in conversation, eating pastries. Basquiat was starting to think about writing more, and began to make a plan for getting clean. Outarra planned a ritual for Basquiat in his village on the Ivory Coast to cure him of addiction on August 7th. Basquiat died of an overdose on August 12th. They did the ceremony anyway. A ritual for the dead.

Many see Basquiat's paintings and think only of his sad story, his illness. Not ours. And it's been a thing, lately, for white artists to render, simply, the limp black body, or to utter the contents of an autopsy report. But Basquiat whispered "alchemy alchemy alchemy alchemy alchemy" into the fractured diagrams of the body with what feels like sacred intention, dreaming these anatomical elements back to life. He drew disembodied skulls next to torsos and surrounded them with music, good tidings, rhythm, and crowns as if, upon his command, these disparate parts would dance back together again. What is the name of the Adrienne Rich essay? *When We Dead Awaken.*

"Black Girl Going Mad" by Rivers Solomon

Rivers Solomon writes about life in the margins, where they're much at home. They're the author of the novel *An Unkindness of Ghosts*, and their short fiction and essays appear in *Emrys Journal*, *Paste Magazine*, *the New York Times*, *Black Warrior Review*, *North American Review*, *The Rumpus*, and other publications. This essay first appeared in *Guernica*.

I'd been living in Dallas, Texas, for six months when the city began to reject me like a hastily transplanted kidney. The comfort and convenience of being close to family—they were a half hour's drive away in the northern suburbs—no longer eased my various disquiets. I'd abandoned the Gulf of Mexico with its infinite rain to resettle the beige-lawn land of my childhood, but I was as disassembled here as I was in the previous cities I'd lived.

It was a lie I'd invented, that moving past pain was at its heart a locational matter, an issue of trading memory-soaked geography for a pristine place. But the problem lived in me. I awoke regularly at 2 a.m., feverish and sweating, certain my mattress was a conveyor belt. I pictured my limbs arranged in a row on the black rubber, an invisible mechanic carrying them toward a disembodied torso where they clicked into place.

"Traumatized people chronically feel unsafe inside their bodies," Bessel Van der Kolk argues in *The Body Keeps the Score*, his book on trauma and recovery. "The past is alive in the form of gnawing interior discomfort." By sixth grade I'd already collected a small backpack's worth of misfortunes. My mother, baffled, would stare at me as I cried inconsolably and begged her not to make me go to school. By the time I was a teenager, I was already familiar with the numerous ways a body could make itself into a stranger because of pain.

Dallas during the Bush II years was Peak Texas. The sort of Texas that lives in the collective imagination of both its fans and discontents. Sexual harassment, racism, and misogyny were a daily reality at the fundamentalist, Baptist school where I was a student.

In retrospect, it seems strange that at twenty-six I chose to return to this city of Good Christian Bitches, but I'm not the first person to be fooled by the notion of a fresh start. My spouse and I had just had a baby. Born three months early, Little F. brought a level of upheaval into our lives that left us wondering why we stayed in a city we had little to no connection to. In Dallas I had my mother, cousins, and old friends, at least. We hoped a move would undo the crushing loneliness that is new parenthood.

My partner worked from home at a job she despised to support us financially. This was the solid, dependable woman I'd fallen in love with at college eight years earlier. I was an eighteen-year-old, already mercurial, prone to volatile relationships, while she was anchored, a remarkably good student from an intact two-parent family. Her life seemed like a sitcom and I wanted to be her quirky love interest.

I cared for our newborn as lovingly and devotedly as I could. Despite the baby's demands, which were overwhelming and many, mothering was a stabilizing force for me: warm, regurgitated milk running down the skin of my back, pea-sized toes digging into my belly during joint naps.

I should've been content in our little East Dallas bungalow. The tiny three-bedroom was in a family-friendly, working-class neighborhood, home to many Mexican immigrants. The neighbors had a cockerel they hid in their garden shed that woke us up most mornings at dawn, and that seemed like a dream to me, like I'd hit the big time.

That didn't stop me from going crazy. True crazy. While my days spent at home meant few knew about what I was going through, my behavior had passed the lines of what was socially acceptable. Not for the first time, I started seeing a psychiatrist, confessed to him about the things I saw that others didn't see (messages in the stars, in street signs, in numbers on billboards). He prescribed medications whose only saving grace was that they were small and therefore easy to swallow.

Despite this, I still felt a profound wrongness that would not go away. In the middle of one January night, I left my home. I left for a place that did not exist.

I was going to a place called the Facility. It was Nikita's "Division." The *Men in Black* headquarters. I felt certain this underground laboratory contained wondrous things relevant to my redemption. Nanobots to scrape my brain of unpleasant data. Scientists to remove the magnetic chip in my neck that drew ugliness toward me.

Lost in delusion, I fixated on a metallic and silicone baptism. Lasers scrubbing me clean. A mechanical Jesus who, in addition to washing away what I'd done, washed away various things that had been done to me.

Even lost in the depths of hallucination, it didn't occur to my misfiring neurotransmitters to build a fantasy in which I blew up the Man or brought my victimizers to violent ends. Instead, my brain exaggerated a real-life scenario in which I was the one at fault and needed to be cleaned.

I was well versed in how to turn blame inward. I knew that whatever my life was, whatever misfortune came to me, it was of my own making. Is that not the heart of independence? Of bootstraps? I'd been properly indoctrinated into the dog-eat-dog tenets of capitalism, and I constructed my delusions around a myth of self-sufficiency. I was a frontierswoman, and I would shoot my traumas like they were attacking grizzlies or invading marauders.

Tanya Luhrrman, an anthropologist and professor at Stanford University, has devoted a large portion of her career to chronicling and understanding the intersections of mental illness and sociopolitical location. She, along with other scholars, conducted the interview-based study "Differences in voice-hearing experiences of people with psychosis in the USA, India and Ghana" in June 2014, which revealed that local culture shapes the voice-hearing experiences of those with psychotic disorders. Auditory hallucinations in Americans were almost universally persecutory and violent. They perceived their voices as interlopers and violators. Indians and Ghanaians tended to view their voices as more benign. Not only were the hallucinations not experienced as invasive, the study found, but people formed "rich relationships" with them.

My Western upbringing has had its toll, then. My paranoid delusions that late January evening had absorbed a distinctly American message: independence being the greatest virtue, we must suffer trauma and illness alone. There's a reason we call mental disturbances "personal demons" and not "culturally orchestrated demons" or "societal demons." My bad brain designed an appropriately American scenario in which I, by sheer will and gumption, would fix myself.

The night I went to the Facility, I walked an ambling course. I looked skyward, searching for messages, signs, or coordinates in the heavens. The sky was marled gray-black, but I saw a cluster of seven stars in the shape of an arrow.

Dogs barked at me from every backyard. Every family kept a semi-neglected pit bull chained behind the house. "I know," I told them. They sensed it, too. The wrongness of this place.

A woman across the street smoked a cigarette from a beach chair on her porch and I wondered if she was a spy. Her nightgown and house slippers appeared too new.

Stop acting so crazy.
I arrived at an empty playground and walked into the field, madly in love with its openness. The grass was wet and dewy against the bottoms of my bare feet. A single street lamp lit the cul-de-sac at the end of the block. I took off my clothes because they were laced with wires, bugs, threats I couldn't articulate but could feel.

My partner called my name, repeating it again and again, but I could not hear her for the persistent beeping telling me I was close to my destination. There was a portal underground that would transport me to the Facility, where I would be saved.
Soon, there was a blanket about my shoulders, my partner leading me home for the fifth time that week.

———

Madness and I have been companions for some time. Eleven years old, at a summer camp in rural Texas, I swam alone in the lake, fifteen yards from the nearest camper, my head underwater and my hands clasped around my ankles, cannonball-style, for minutes at a time.

One of the camp counselors shouted at me to resurface, then asked, "What are you doing?"

"I'm seeing what it'd be like to be tied up and thrown into the water."

214

But the most exhilarating moment came later that summer. Coun-selors took us to a small cliff where we could jump into the icy river. When I took my turn, the dam opened, and the current changed from light and frolicking to massive and deity-strong. My whole body numb, I let myself be dragged. When a counselor called my name, an arm reached out toward me (they were anchored to a tree on the riverbank with a rope). I swam as hard I could toward them. Once safe in their arms, I imagined them taking me back to a secret cabin and having sex with me. This was my ultimate dream.

So young, and already strange and deviant. I look back on my lit-tle-girl self with fascination. I don't know how she survived.

Black women are mad even when we're not mad. Loud, defiant, expressive, emotional, oversensitive, dumb, hypersexual. The domi-nant cultural image of the Black woman projects deviant traits onto her. This is evident in angry-Black-woman and promiscuous-Jezebel stereotypes, in media portrayals that disproportionately show us as unreasonably outspoken, and in the demonization of our religious expression—whether it be the raucous Holy Ghost–filled Christianity with bodies convulsing in church aisles and shouting praises in angel-ic tongues; women singing so good they must've made a crossroads deal (heels thrown to the side, choir robes abandoned); or veiled heads at the mosque, showing we're repressed, extremist, terrorists.

An article in *The Guardian* recently addressed the struggles Black women in England face with mental health, devoting large attention to the pressure on women of African-Caribbean descent to conceal their natural selves to fit into white work environments. Being careful not to talk too loud, or to gesticulate, or to somehow play into the image of the mad Black woman. Constantly policing your expression has a damaging effect on the psyche. The article notes that Black people are hospitalized for mental health reasons at twice the rate of white people—not surprising, considering the overlap between mental illness and poverty, trauma, neglect, racism, and sexism. For those outside the white Western mold because of their ethnicity or background, life is a constant barrage of stressors. Those stressors have long-lasting impact. How could they not?

For Black women further outside the realm of social acceptability because of their sexuality and/or coercively assigned sex at birth, because of their chronic illness or disability, because of their status as a recent immigrant, because of their accented English, mental illness, or, at least, mental health crises, can seem like an inevitability.

———

Depression, it's true, is considered a White Folk Thing. Search "Black women and mental health" and you'll turn up several results on the stigma surrounding mental illness in Black communities. It's been my experience, however, that mental illness is a rather mundane topic for many Black people. We may not use the same naming conventions, and we may not medicalize or pathologize it in the same ways. While I cannot deny the subset of people in the "pray it away" camp, I would argue that they are greatly influenced by the larger, white, Protestant version of Christianity that considers mental upset a personal failing.

Then there is my bipolar aunt, whose unpredictable moods are shrugged at, and my hot-tempered grandmother, often deeply sad, who saw ghosts. I see ghosts, too. My family would say, *That's because ghosts are real.*

———

When I was fifteen, my mother called the police after I'd been stalked by a sixty-year-old white man. I'd initiated the relationship.

216

I'd been acting out like that since I was young. At the interview with the detective assigned to the case, I sat in a rolling chair, twisting in a semicircle on its axis. Jeans and Chuck Taylors, hair cut short, glasses, I could've just as easily been in the principal's office. It was the same sort of police station you'd see in a movie. Oversized brown desks from a different era. Handcuffed people, mostly Black and brown, here and there. Everyone was drinking black coffee. The detective seemed compassionate—realist but compassionate. I told him about my part in the relationship with this much older man and he understood that confession for what it was: absolutely irrelevant.

"First, you're going to testify to a grand jury," he said, and that's when I shut down. I believed I'd lured a God-fearing Christian man into sin with my wiles. After all, I'd met him in an AOL Christian chatroom. His screen name was Carl4Jesus.

When the stalker in question had approached me earlier that week, I was standing on the sidewalk outside of my apartment building, backpack hoisted over my shoulder, headphones around my neck. I shook with fear as he demanded to come upstairs. I yelled at him to go away, to leave me alone, my mother would be home soon.

Men and women walked by, fastidiously averting their gazes. I was a child, declaring that I was frightened of this man, and no one thought to intervene and say something as simple as, "Hey, is everything alright?"

I probably sounded hysterical. I was hysterical. I was screaming, but no one heard.

Somewhere between 40 to 60 percent of Black girls under the age of eighteen are assaulted in the United States. This is according to research by the Black Women's Health Imperative and Black Women's Blueprint. Black women and Black girls are so intimately familiar with violence, it is no wonder so many of us are crushed under its weight.

There is a long-established history in the United States, in the world at large, of violating the Black woman, but the effects of it are still widely framed around individuals. Single victims. It's not a cultural problem. It's not a collective campaign of abuse. In America, there aren't societal failings, only personal ones.

Trauma and mental illness braid intricately, neatly, and beautifully together to form a noose around my neck. I speak about them as though they're interchangeable because, for me, they are. There is the trauma that led directly to mental illness in the form of stress disorders and maladaptive behavioral traits. There is the trauma I've experienced as a result of being mentally ill.

My schizophrenic aunt, whom I met only once, used to be "perfectly fine." That's how my paternal extended family describes it. Something happened, some catastrophic event, from which she never recovered. Some know. Some don't. All of us can guess.

I hear voices, I see things. I don't know if this would be true about me if I lived in a different world. If I lived in a different world, my relationship to these phenomena, and society's relationship to me as someone who experiences these things, might be vastly different, built on genuine compassion and understanding. In a world where caring and compassion were the default, where we understood mental illness as part of a larger network of relationships and policies, there might not be fewer mad people, but fewer people who felt plagued so violently by it.

218

Recently, during a pregnancy scare, a very close friend of mine told me they were worried by the prospect of another baby for me because postpartum depression could trigger preexisting psychosis. "Does that mean I can never have more children?" I asked them. Their council and friendship had saved my life before, and I wanted to know what they thought. We were talking via Internet messaging, so I'm able to quote their response exactly:

I think you absolutely can have more pregnancies and kids, but I would really hope for you to get a great medical and psych team assembled beforehand even if the psych side was largely non-professional supports. I would want to know you had committed members of a community ready to care for you. And contingency plans. And live in a place where a hospital stay wouldn't mean losing your kids.

The implication is that I lack the community and support to help me get through a mental health crisis safely. My friend is right, of course. I've always counted myself more fortunate than most that so far I've been able to avoid the frequent repercussions of mental illness, especially as a Black, queer person, a category already precarious unto itself. I have never had to make a park bench my bed or sleep in a shelter. I do not have an addiction. I have not killed myself, though I know too many who have, one being my first serious girlfriend. She was a Black, queer woman whom I was certainly not there for enough in the years after our breakup. Anyone who has lost someone in this way has done the math, trying to calculate how much of the cause was the person's own madness, and how much of it was the madness of this world.

I am alive but by the skin of my teeth. I am alive due to the support of people I can count on one hand.

I cannot yet talk about the experiences that made me a preteen obsessed with being destroyed and an adult who talks to ghosts. I was corrupted and I was corrupt. Born this way or made this way, when I cast the cherry pits onto the table in the manner of ancient runes, the universe told me I'd grow up to be a mad Black girl.

"Growing Up With My Brothers"
by Rachel Williams-Smith

Rachel Williams-Smith is an educator, writer, and communicator, and author of *Born Yesterday: The True Story of a Girl Born in the 20th Century but Raised in the 19th*. "Growing Up with My Brothers" is adapted from the book, which tells her story of growing up in a truly isolated childhood due to religious extremism. Dr. Williams-Smith currently serves as academic dean and holds degrees in Educational Leadership and Management (Ed.D.), Communication (Ph.D.), English (MA), and Language Arts Education (BS). She is married and has four grown children and four grandchildren.

My growing up years were anything but typical. One reason was my parents' radical religious beliefs on raising their children; the other reason was my two older brothers who made life dangerously interesting. Paul and Jeff, three and two years my senior, were always up to something, and I often got to be a part of the action, though not in ways that worked well for me.

When I was four, they created an elaborate set up of strings and wires attached to an oversized grinning skeleton complete with movable parts that they hung on their door to scare the life out of me. At five, I had the honor of serving as target for the slingshots they made from branches and rubber bands, and at six, for their carved bows and stone-tipped branches. In both cases, I made a wise, last-minute decision to run like the wind over the privilege of being shot through or impaled alive.

My brothers and I did not realize that our lives were undergoing a major change. Mom and Dad rapidly were becoming disenchanted with our church and becoming more independent—and radical—in their beliefs. Mom got rid of my pants and added swatches of cloth to my dresses in order to lengthen the hemlines. Our diet changed from vegetarian to vegan and later to raw for a while. Then homeschooling started and someone reported us. Faced with an ultimatum to either enroll us in school or have us taken away, my parents decided to remove us from society.

When I was seven, my brothers mounted a bunch of electric wires and parts on a small board and dared me to memorize the names and functions of each. I passed their quiz with a perfect score but failed their next dare–to beat them at building a real transistor radio, one that worked. They experimented endlessly with their resistors, transistors, capacitors, and diodes, and one day Jeff and Paul touched some wires together and a faint sound of static crinkled through the air: "It's working!" they shouted. Nothing could stop them. They moved on from one experiment to another. They rigged a lift from 2x4 boards and a heavy chain and used it to hoist the blown engine from Dad's yellow Volkswagen beetle. When they lowered and fastened it back in place, the engine roared to life on the first try.

Once, my brothers found Mom and Dad's nursing kits, complete with various-sized stainless steel syringe-and-needle sets and immediately initiated a series of "experiments." We filled the syringes with various substances and shot up plants in the garden to see if we could find something that would have an immediate effect. I happened to hit the jackpot when I injected the thick, main stem of a three-foot mustard plant with Clorox: the entire plant instantly wilted and turned black.

By the time I was eight, our family was living in a school-converted-into-a-mobile home camped out on a mountaintop in a state park. Mom and I were wearing bonnets daily by then, but that didn't stop me from competing with my brothers. So when a three-inch snowfall offered the chance for a snowball fight, I was game! The battleground was stick-and-snow fortresses–Paul and Jeff's versus mine–and our weapons, snowballs. At least mine were snowballs.

Paul had said that both sides needed plenty of ammunition, and he warned me to pack my snowballs tight. I took the warning seriously and stockpiled my snowballs on a flat board like I saw my brothers doing so I wouldn't have to slow down to form them once things got started. At last the battle began, and snowballs flew. I managed to dodge enemy fire while scoring some good hits. I felt triumphant—until one of their missiles struck me in the head; I found myself reeling from the blow. I sprang back quickly though, and hurled a snowball right into Paul's left shoulder, feeling satisfied as it exploded on impact into a harmless spray. Paul laughed, pulled back his arm, and hurled a snowball-looking missile at me. Too late. It hit me, full force, just above my right eye. I dropped to the ground screaming while blood trickled down my face.

They rushed to get me patched up and back on my feet, but the battle was over. I just wanted to know how they had packed such hard snowballs. After I promised not to tell on them, Paul shared that they had dipped theirs in a bucket of water they had hidden behind their fort and set them out on the board to freeze first.

———

By the time I was nine, we were living on an isolated, fifty-acre tract of land in Tennessee, miles from the nearest paved road, atop of a range of hills that could only be accessed by a single, steep, very rutted dirt road. We had no electricity, plumbing, telephone, indoor heating, or any other normal conveniences, and so hard work, necessary for survival, cut down on our sibling competitions. Dad and the boys built an outhouse, learned to cut and haul wood, and built a cistern for catching rainwater. Mom and I carried drinking from the stream, used rainwater from the cistern to wash clothes on a scrub board, and learned how to preserve food by canning it. We all worked together to plant a huge vegetable garden plot near the house and prepare and plant the extensive fields on our property with corn and potatoes and other staples.

We lived by strict schedules, had three daily, one-hour worship periods each day, and were homeschooled—when there was time for it. Sometimes we had to forego academics in favor of survival. Food could be scarce; at times, we only had rice and pinto beans to eat. We even ran out of food completely, so my brothers and I searched the woods and empty fields for something to eat, eventually gathering roots and wild greens for Mom to cook. But the lack of food did not curb my brothers' inventiveness.

Even though it was against Dad's rules by then, Jeff made a transistor radio once again as he had done years before. Mom and I had heard about Lady Di and Prince Charles wedding date, and he overheard us daydreaming aloud about watching the event, even though we knew that was impossible. The day before the wedding, Jeff said he wanted to show us something and took us to his room. He lifted his pillow, and there lay a tiny transistor radio, complete with a small speaker and a thin antenna wire that ran inconspicuously up the corner of the wall, along the edge of the ceiling to the window and on outside. Thanks to his creativity, the next day after Dad left for work at dawn, my two brothers, my mother, and I gathered around that tiny, homemade transistor radio and listened as Lady Di became Princess Diana of Wales.

One chilly February day, just after our noon worship hour (we had three one-hour worships a day), my brothers went outside to tinker with a truck motor they were using as a sawmill engine. Time lulled in the warm sunshine and sounds floated lazily through the cool air. Even a sharp bang from the direction of the sawmill seemed to drift into our senses. The next sound that floated in didn't make sense. I looked up. My father stood up, book still in hand, and moved toward the front door. Mom and I simultaneously got up and followed. As we reached it, we all broke into a run.

The instant before we rounded the corner, I recognized that

it was Paul Jr.'s voice making the most horrible sound I had ever heard. I was terrified of what we might see. There was Paul near the sawmill, perfectly fine, bending over a mound of black plastic on the ground. He wasn't hurt—but where was Jeff? And then the awful bellow came again, terrifyingly distinct this time: "Mom! Dad! Help! Help!"

We bolted toward Paul. Just as we reached him, Jeff sat up from out of the black plastic. I gasped, in relief that he was alive and in horror at the sight of his charred and smoking flesh.

The engine Jeff had been working on had backfired and a stream of burning gas had sprayed onto his neck and chest. Instantly engulfed in a billowing tower of flames, he panicked and ran and likely would have burned to death if his brother had not been nearby. Paul tackled him, breaking a rib in the process, and smothered the flames with, of all things, black plastic from a roll that was lying nearby.

I stared at Jeff in horror. His shirt had burned half off of him, and his entire left side and upper chest was exposed. A large flap of still-smoldering skin hung loosely over a charred edge of his shirt. He was covered with deep burns on his neck, chest, and side, to the point where pure muscle was exposed in places. In his neck, a major artery just beneath thin, white tissue was clearly visible, pulsing away. Jeff forced himself to his feet and, amazingly, started walking unassisted toward the house. But his steps faltered and he seemed confused. When he reached the corner, he reeled and let out a short, harsh scream. Dad caught him and Paul quickly grabbed his arm to steady him. He made it to the steps with Dad and Paul's help and sat down uneasily as if he might get right back up. When Mom tried to give him water and some vitamins, he became visibly agitated and began to shake.

"I can't swallow!" he protested, but Mom gently pushed the first vitamin into his mouth and held the cup to his lips. After what I thought was forever, he managed to swallow it. She got two more down him before the pain hit. Jeff began to scream. Somehow Dad and Paul got him inside the house and onto the sofa. I was terrified as I heard his horrible screams and cries for mercy. He went into convulsions, shaking so hard that the house's windows rattled. I couldn't stand it. Jumping up without a word, I ran outside and around the corner to the cistern. It was February and a layer of ice covered it. I quickly chiseled some away, threw the chunks in a basin, and filled it with water. Running back inside, I grabbed a large towel, dipped it in the ice water, and laid it across his burns. Jeff immediately reacted positively to the coolness, so I continued draping him for hours with cold, wet towels until even that no longer brought him relief.

The hour was getting late and Mom and Dad kept discussing what to do for Jeff so that he could make it through the night. They tried spreading aloe Vera gel on him from the plants we grew, but he screamed. Mom suggested wrapping him in honey-dipped cloths as a sealant. That soothed some of his pain, and my parents decided to go to bed. I didn't want to leave Jeff alone and sat with him late into the night, listening to his terrible moans as he begged God for mercy and prayed for death. For the next month, I sat with Jeff as much as possible, reading to him, listening to him, and just being there so that he would not to be alone in his suffering. It took about two months before he could sit up for hours, walk around some, and involve himself in light activities. Within six months he had mostly recovered, except for the scars, which he bears to this day.

———————

A few years later, our tough, atypical life came to an end after my father abruptly picked up and left. Paul, Jeff, and I went in different directions, taking with us differing perspectives on the upbringing which helped shape us. Jeff got as far away from religion as he possibly could, discovering his own language of love. Paul abandoned religion too, but eventually found a new faith to which he could dedicate himself. I took the path of rejecting the extremism of my upbringing without leaving the underlying religion; however, it took years for me to find wholeness. Looking back, thirty years later, one thing stands out to me. Despite the fact that my upbringing was so different from most, my brothers made it interesting to say the least.